LOST AND FOUND

C.P. Surendran is a poet and novelist. His poetry collections include *Gemini II*, *Posthumous Poems*, *Canaries on the Moon*, and *Portraits of the Space We Occupy*. He is also the author of the novel, *An Iron Harvest*.

Surendran is a journalist and columnist as well. His popular columns include 'Low Life', 'Bitch', 'Cat Scan', and 'Brief Grief'. Currently, he is a senior editor with the *Times of India* and is based in Delhi.

LOST AND FOUND

C.P. Surendran

HarperCollins *Publishers* India

First published in India in 2010 by
HarperCollins *Publishers* India

Building 10, Tower A, 4th Floor, DLF Cyber City, Phase II,
Gurugram Haryana – 122002, India
www.harpercollins.co.in

2 4 6 8 10 9 7 5 3

ISBN: 978-93-5029-021-7

Typeset in 9/14 ITC Giovanni Std
Jojy Philip New Delhi 110 015

Printed and bound at
MicroPrints India, New Delhi

To Kittu and Cherumu, more brothers than sons

Contents

BOOK I

ONE

Six Vodkas, Bollywood, and the Return of a Rapist

Lakshmi pushes open the glass doors of the restaurant, watching her face split in two. She is thinking of the man she kidnapped the night before, now lying trussed up in her bathtub.

She takes in the cheap cheerfulness of the place. 'Cold coffee,' she says without conviction to two boys behind the counter spilling a laugh over a newspaper. The place has just opened for business. A third waiter stands next to a window, staring.

Outside, the sea breaks white against the black rocks that erupt like a rash of warts on the face of Land's End, Bombay.

Lakshmi sinks into a sofa, exhausted. At thirty-five, she is ageing faster than a video game. Are all single women like this, Lakshmi wonders, each moment fraught, irresolute? A sense of impending doom informing each minor act that constitutes the day? No, it must be her. If only she could wash off the smell of failure that envelops her like a cheap scent, from dawn to dusk.

'Please be calm,' Mr Iyyer had appealed to her as he unhappily shuffled out of her bedroom last week. Mr Iyyer is in his early sixties. He is her boss and lover. Lakshmi works as a content provider for his online porn firm, whose serial theme centres on the sensory adventures of Kavita, a beautiful, blind girl. Lakshmi doesn't mind the attentions of Mr Iyyer as it affords her job security. It's a career decision.

Mr Iyyer is not a very demanding lover. He comes once a month to her company apartment in Bandra, spends a few hours with her and leaves. They have sex at times, but it is not the kind that sets anybody's loins on fire, least of all theirs.

Last week, it was that time, and Mr Iyyer had turned up in his grey suit, bearing in his hand a gift wrapped in reams of shiny paper. Mr Iyyer always called on Lakshmi with a present.

Lakshmi lay in bed, waiting for the ritual to get over. The whole day, she had felt like a hormonal ball bounced by a machine.

Mr Iyyer placed the heavy parcel carefully on the dressing table, and began taking off his clothes. He was a thin, brown man with a slight paunch: a withered stick with a little knob in the middle. A long nose that flared into a perfect 'm' and a wide mouth that underlined it for emphasis gave him a permanently apologetic air. By the time he came down to folding the legs of his trousers neatly over a chair, Lakshmi was beginning to feel sad. She couldn't tell exactly why, though.

Comfortable at last in his long, loose underwear, a kind of Bermudas for the groin, Mr Iyyer now began to unravel the gift. This one was a four-handed Saraswati—goddess of letters and learning—in white marble. Mr Iyyer had seen it in the shop below his office and was impressed by the details of styling, and the fact that the big eyes and the pretty, round face bore a remarkable resemblance to Lakshmi. Since Lakshmi was a writer of sorts, Mr Iyyer thought she might appreciate the idol as an inspiration.

Mr Iyyer now freed the Saraswati from miles of tinsel paper and padding, lifted it high like a football trophy and turned around so that Lakshmi could see it.

But her response was muted.

Mr Iyyer shrugged and placed the goddess apologetically back on the table. Lakshmi was in one of her moods, he thought. He turned to the absorbing task of gathering and putting the wrapping material away in the bin.

Mr Iyyer did not like litter. He believed that if his countrymen took to the waste basket with a little more zeal, India would be a cleaner and healthier place.

Meanwhile, Lakshmi had cruelly kicked the basket under the cot, where it lay out of sight.

Mr Iyyer walked about the room uncertainly, wearing garlands of tinsel around his neck. There was a lot left over yet. This, he held in both hands over his head, as if looking for a safe place to deposit the toxic entrails of some beast he had slain. Fully festooned, in the dim light of the bedroom lamp, Mr Iyyer cast fearful shadows on the wall. 'Where's the waste basket, Lakshmi?' Mr Iyyer asked at last, after what seemed to him a night of wanderings.

'It's been missing for some time,' Lakshmi said.

'Isn't there one in the kitchen?'

'No, it was in such a bad condition that I threw it away this morning. Are you coming to bed?' Lakshmi asked, knowing full well he would not.

'No, I don't think so.' Mr Iyyer saw no possibility of making love with so much trash all over the place. 'But Lakshmi, why are you shouting? Do you realize you almost screamed at me just now?' Since Mr Iyyer had chosen to make his grief known exactly when his vest was over his face, his words were muffled.

But Lakshmi could make some sense of the plaintive sounds. She felt like bursting into tears. She turned to her side and pulled the loose half of the bed sheet over her and listened to Mr Iyyer reversing himself into his clothes: shirt, trousers, belt, jacket, tie and coat. When the osmosis was complete, he stuffed all his pockets with the gift wrappings. He no longer looked thin.

'Would you like to have a drink?' Lakshmi asked from under her tent in some cut-off mountain shrouded in mist.

'No, thank you. I'd better take this rubbish back home to a proper bin.'

'Yes. Bye, then. Sorry about the basket.'

'Never mind. Please stay calm, please.' Mr Iyyer came over to where Lakshmi was hiding, bent over and kissed the air near her head. He didn't sit on the bed since he was in office clothes. 'Bye. Don't bother to see me out. Get a good night's sleep.'

The Saraswati incident troubles Lakshmi. Why is she being mean and unfair to Mr Iyyer? Not that her conduct was ever overly warm. But, of late, it seemed that she was not capable of normal reactions. She thought she had a clear idea of what 'normal' was: wake up in the morning without that unflagging sense of catastrophe, have coffee, smoke a cigarette, go to work without fear, watch TV, have a drink …

And then, last night, she had complicated her life further by kidnapping Placid Hari Odannur. If normalcy was ever a prospect, it seemed more distant than ever now.

Lakshmi flushes at the thought of Placid. She notices that the two top buttons of her denim jacket and the pink T-shirt have synchronically conspired to slip out of their slots, revealing a bit of her cleavage to migratory eyes. She lifts her hands to set her clothes straight, but, midway drops them to her side. Cleavage be damned.

She wishes now that she hadn't gone to the Sheraton party the night before. It was thrown by the PR firm that her friend Beverly worked for and was the pre-release bash for a movie. Lakshmi thought she'd gawk at the stars, have a couple of drinks and leave. She ended up having six vodkas ... and the evening soon drifted into delirium.

Not for the first time in the evening, Lakshmi marvels at the flowing curves of a Shilpa Shetty, an Aishwarya Rai. Such unearthly bodies! And the nonchalance with which they flaunt their wares!

The stars float about, reducing Lakshmi to a compulsive voyeur. She sees the apples of their breasts ripening under the arc lights; senses the swell of pleasure in their undulating hips; admires their melon-like butts sliced in the middle. She registers helplessly that their long legs are lean as bamboo shoots; their smiles brighter than halogen lamps; their eyes smoulder like blown coal; hair cascades like a Niagara of nights. Ah, they are a kind of porn, Lakshmi decides, but porn with clothes on. The kind of porn meant for family viewing.

Lakshmi is a Hindi-movie buff. She is most relaxed in the dark of a theatre, waiting for a Bollywood film to make its loud beginnings. She takes comfort in the predictability of the tacky situations. Why, everything about a Hindi film exudes a comic reassurance: the plush sets, the unlikely snow (the heroine in a bikini; the hero in a suit, greatcoat, dark glasses and hat), the hero's final triumph over evil, not to mention the lilting songs implausibly sung in impossible places, the group weddings, the happy endings ...

... all in a country, Lakshmi will grant, disintegrating into dust and reeking of waste, and whose wretched poor look up in astonishment as their motherland plays superpower and hurls a billion-dollar rocket into the moon over their kismet-kicked heads.

On the one hand, the moon; on the other, a million emaciated souls straight out of Auschwitz, gathering and dissolving at traffic lights, arms outstretched for alms. On the third hand, the colourful movies full of faith, hope and charity. On the fourth... No wonder Hindu gods and goddesses have four hands, like the Saraswati Mr Iyyer brought. The reality they spawned is too complex for just two.

There are contradictions here, Lakshmi acknowledges, sipping her vodka, but she can't help it. Nobody can. In this country, as in Bollywood, no one resolves contradictions; they just let them exist. Cheek by howl.

Lakshmi's valedictory drink is a glass of beer. A cold beer, she tells herself, to hold all the vodkas down, a drink that will walk her to the door and lead her home, a drink to lean on, to put an arm around, go to bed with.

Lakshmi makes it to the bar, negotiating a floor resting on a geological fault line, to perch elegantly on a tall stool which, without warning, lands her on the floor. She pretends that she was about to tie her laces but realizes too late that she is wearing slip-ons. 'Voh-voh,' she says, mimicking her Tamilian neighbour Githaa, the one with the extra 'a' for luck. She needs help to get back on her feet.

Just as Lakshmi resigns to her station in life, a voice says, 'May I?' and extends a slender hand along which run veins blue as tobacco smoke.

'Oh, thank you,' Lakshmi says without looking up. Who wants to complicate an act of momentary generosity with a look full of further appeals, which she is sure to make at the first opportunity? She is always in need of help, a woman to whom everybody could be of some use.

He holds the stool firmly by its edges so that Lakshmi can sit without incident.

'A drink?' he offers.

'Beer.'

He gets her a mug of cold beer.

Lakshmi takes a sip, turns around. Her heart leaps off its moorings and lifts skywards. Such eyes. 'Ah,' she says. A moment later, all her blood falls to her feet like a fountain switched off; the occult night has revealed its oracle.

Lakshmi is looking into the eyes of the man who raped her sixteen years ago.

TWO

Loving Fatima

Since Maulana Abul Razak wants to bomb Bombay to bits, make love to anyone except his wife and go out for a walk under the trees, all at the same time, he decides to stay put on his mat. The decision is not difficult. The weather allows no other course of action.

This April has been the worst in Sultanpur. Most of Pakistan is having a Saharan summer, but the dust-and-brick village seems to have gravitated to the very centre of the sun, which paints the place a blinding white. Houses, fences and fields vaporize in a haze of heat. Distinctions blur, things merge. Cattle collapse. The trees are nearly bare, the tips of the few remaining leaves curled, burnt black. The air shimmers. Men don't step out of their houses, women boil away behind burkhas. The Chenab barely wets one's toes. All of Sultanpur is like an overexposed film.

Abul Razak, leader of the Lashkar-e-Toiba, Army of the Pure, is not taking the heat well. He has been seeing visions, especially of events related to his childhood, which he thought he had forgotten.

Consider what he experienced this morning: the breeze that wandered in from the past breathed of wet earth. The long, white stone slab next to the well to the side of the house was flowing with soap suds. The big, odd bubble floating between the sodden folds of his one and only pair of khaki shorts was a gossamer city of rainbows.

The sound of a bucket plopping into the well released Abul Razak from the spell and he woke up playing out the rope, his muscles taut and ready to winch up the full load.

He experienced spells of dizziness too. And the latest one happened right in the middle of a motivation session. The Maulana was showing a video clip of a member of the Indian security forces stripping a suspect Kashmiri militant and making him hop on one foot, his hands held high, in front of his three children. The youngest of them, a three-year-old baby on the hip of her mother, has her fist out, clasping and unclasping her fingers in uncertain protest. The clip never failed to work.

'Aaah! A father humiliated right in front of his children!' Abul Razak thundered as he turned to face the silent recruits. 'Tell me. Would you like your father to be stripped and paraded before you?'

But before Abul Razak could work himself and the boys to craggy peaks of righteous rage, he found himself dropping down to the floor on his knees, his hand cupping his ear like a qawwali singer in the middle of a performance. The trainees stared at the spectacle with barely concealed concern. Expect the extraordinary, they had been told on the very first day of the camp. And what could be more extraordinary than the six-foot, fire-spewing Maulana on his knees on the floor with his hand to his ear, his eyes closed, while, in the background, an Indian soldier said, 'We will make you remember your grandmother.'

'Grandmother?' Abul Razak mumbled. He felt a constriction

in the chest but slowly hauled himself back on his flat feet. A couple of boys stepped forward to help. But Abul Razak put up a muscular arm to discourage them. His eyes were uncertain and dull. The bumpy forehead was glazed with sweat. The huge launch pad of a nose quivered as if a sneeze would blast forth any moment.

'I am running a temperature,' Abul said, dimly aware that the boys might have been seeing in his fall the disintegration of a legend. 'It's the heat,' he said, more to console himself than as an explanation to others.

Perhaps it was the heat. But where was this heat blowing in from and what was the nature of the pestilence it propagated? And why did it seem to affect the formidable Maulana Abul Razak the most?

Taking his shoes off and sitting on them, Ajmal, a recent recruit, observes that the Indians were tampering with Pakistan's weather system. They had been setting up giant heat blowers along the border. In fact, only last week, two Indian security men had been caught in the act and executed by the Lashkar-e-Toiba. The video footage of the event was awaited. One of the soldiers had promised to convert to Islam if given reprieve. Apparently, this offer had been met with laughter, at the end of which the soldier's head lay separated from his body.

There were other conspiracy theories circulating about the heat, all equally good. But the bottom line, they all agreed, was that if the Maulana suffered, the jihad for Kashmir suffered. And if Kashmir suffered, Islam suffered.

The Maulana's dire health situation throws up names of mystic masseurs and herbal magicians, who throng Sultanpur, and qualified doctors who leave it alone. But the wise among Abul Razak's well wishers agree that the man to consult is the illustrious Dr Dara Zainuddin, who runs a homeopathy clinic in Faridkot, six hours by road from Sultanpur.

Ajmal, the devout suicide-aspirant, is briefed for the mission. He is entrusted with a letter from Abul Razak.

'Guard it with your life,' one of Razak's aides tells him.

'I will,' Ajmal says, hand on heart.

The next day, Ajmal clambers into the crack-of-the-dawn bus, which is covered all over with praises of God and plies the route with trunks and baskets hanging out of the windows and men riding on top. The journey is memorable only for the black hen—tied upside down to the window-bar—that flies up midway in brief revolt and pecks a dozing Ajmal on the head. Ajmal at first thinks it is a bullet, but soon wakes up to the lower order of reality that seems to attend on him at all times. He shakes his head in disappointment and goes back to sleep.

As soon as Ajmal reaches Faridkot, he makes his way to the clinic of the legendary healer who, in his late silver-haired eighties, still works therapeutic magic with the sugary powders and tiny white pills that he puts away in small, brown envelopes with their little flaps, his long fingers trembling with age and exactitude.

'Hmm … and how is my friend Maulana Abdul Aziz?' asks the doctor, whose face is long, thin and triangular, like the mask of a tribal totem.

'*Itne theek thak nahin hain ji*,' says the boy, taking a kind view of the wrong name.

'Not so good, eh?' the doctor says reflectively.

Ajmal fishes out Abul Razak's letter from the recesses of his vest, blows dry the envelope that is beginning to sag a little with sweat, hands it over to the doctor, three fingers of his left hand mock-supporting the right elbow in respect.

The doctor looks at the letter for a long time as if it is an unexpected gift, before stretching out a frail hand to accept it. On the first attempt, he misses it by a finger. The second time, though, he is on target. The achievement brings a faint smile to his face. He opens the letter and reads it, one hand slowly combing his long, silver beard.

> Dear Doctor Dara Zainuddin,
>
> For nearly ten days now, I am down with fever and chest aches. The fever makes my body heavy and listless. I suspect my heart is not sound either. Why else would I feel as if my chest is being squeezed by giant hands? And to complicate my life, I also see things in my sleep, and they often continue through the day. Quite a lot of it has to do with my childhood, which ought to be of no consequence to me now. One other thing ... I just can't seem to get enough sleep. It could be the heat.
>
> Whatever the reason, my indisposition slows down our work in Kashmir, which I am sure is a cause, as with us in Sultanpur, close to your heart as well. I look for relief from you, and hope to see you in person soon. Inshallah!
>
> Yours truly,
>
> Maulana Abul Razak

'I have to think over Maulana Abdul Aziz's complaint,' Dr Zainuddin says, looking up from the letter and addressing Ajmal, who is wondering if the good doctor has something to offer in order to grow hair on his face. Ajmal is eighteen, but his face is smooth as a baby's. And who doesn't know that an AK-47 looks better propped against a three-day stubble?

The boy notices that Dr Zainuddin, despite the heat, is not sweating. His white shirt and baggy white trousers are yellow with age, but they are clean and without any sweat patches. Maybe when you get very old, you don't sweat.

Dr Zainuddin gets to his feet and sways for a moment. 'You may have to wait for a few minutes,' he tells Ajmal.

The doctor steps into his dispensary but realizes that all he can do is go to sleep. It occurs to him that there is no end to consultation. The more he cures, the more they come back sick, each thinking the worst of his disorder. Each, in fact, thinking this is the end. The doctor sits in his armchair and falls asleep. He snores a little, his mouth open, his eyes open, as if staring at a smoke ring he has just blown.

When Dr Zainuddin wakes up late in the evening, the room is nearly dark. Ah, the boy is waiting outside; Dr Zainuddin recalls the unfinished business with some exasperation. Instead of the lights, he switches on the fan. He approaches the work table, covered with a green cloth, on which are lined several bottles and jars. A slow frenzy of forgetfulness assails him. He transfers medicines prescribed in his lucid moments for Abdul Aziz to an envelope meant for Abul Razak. He takes another envelope and empties some more medicines into it. He can barely see what he is doing. There are small, round pills falling and rolling all over the table and the floor. There are tiny brown envelopes fluttering in the air like sparrows. The doctor breathes in and out noisily. He mixes powders at random, rolls them into paper pellets. He puts them all into a third envelope and writes on it: Abdul Razak. It seems to Dr Zainduddin that he has several hands, not just two, and all of them are at cross purposes. What one hand does, the other undoes. A third adds to the confusion of the first. The fourth reorders the various envelopes.

What is this? Dr Zainuddin asks himself. Aziz? Razak. Abul? Abdul. Razak? Abdul. Abul? Aziz. Razak? AzizAbdulRazakAzizRazak AbulAziz!

The fifth hand throws in the towel. Dr Dara Zainuddin has had enough. He takes a deep breath, transfers the contents of various envelopes into one, and steps out, back into the hall.

Dr Zainuddin hands the medicines to the messenger who is patiently waiting in the room that has grown dim and empty with the falling dusk. A giant ceiling fan slowly churns the air, making a tick-tock noise. 'These are strong medicines; very strong,' he tells Ajmal. 'But everything is there. The dosage is written on top of the envelope.'

'Thank you,' Ajmal says, relieved that the long wait is over. He decides this is not the time to trouble the doctor with his facial hair problem. Perhaps he will come back next week for that. Ajmal hands the doctor a folded, sweat-soaked note of Rs 50, extracted from somewhere deep inside his clothes.

He balances the medicines in his hand as if weighing the fortunes of Kashmir and, feeling satisfied, makes for the door.

Abul Razak's heart flutters like the wings of a fledgling. He is not sure if the medicines that Dr Zainuddin sent are agreeing with him. Sweat pours down his hairy chest; his hand goes to his lips as if impelled by the memory of a dear face. Through the window—set low on the wall and perfectly framing one of the green-tiled mosques that have mushroomed in Sultanpur—the fierce Maulana has just caught sight of Fatima, his childhood love, crossing the narrow street leading to the only high school in the village.

But this is not the Fatima who wore a burkha and whose modesty locked her big, dark eyes to the ground—except once in the second grade, when she glanced at Abul Razak and drew a line of blood from his heart.

Abul Razak had tried all he could after that school incident to let her know that he would like her to be his sooner or later, but his callowness and poverty and her riches had stood in the way—not to mention her beauty. At the end of nearly a decade of furtive, unilateral wooing, he had given up. That was years ago, when Razak was nineteen and liberating Kashmir was not yet on the agenda.

Kashmir entered his life two years later, when he was in Jeddah on a scholarship for Koranic studies. Six months into his term, he had come into contact with people who saw in the Koran a manual of war and Kashmir on the wrong side of the map. Would Abul Razak be interested in redrawing the map of the subcontinent? Yes, he would. And that's how he joined Lashkar-e-Toiba.

The Fatima that Abul Razak is seeing now—in the middle of a day that seems to be blazing in a hard, hot light—is wearing a pair of jeans cut so low, it could create mayhem among the mullahs. These are jeans revealing the day of judgement, and every man in Sultanpur will be found wanting.

Abul Razak gazes at the vision with his mouth open, his strong white teeth shining in the sunlight. How she walks! Isn't she just a kid of ten, or twelve, maybe? Should she be out like this, peddling her wares on the steps of the mosque, shaking the edifice with each dainty step? Isn't this Sultanpur in South Punjab, the town from where Lashkar-e-Toiba runs its writ round the world? Is he man enough?

Fatima looks back over her shoulder. 'I am twenty-seven, and I can do what I want,' she says, laughing, and it sounds like the music of seduction, of bliss and ruination. 'I can vote, bring a government down, I can even go watch a movie.' She smiles and the smile can mean only one thing. 'I can also do what you want,' she says, pursing her lips.

Fatima walks on towards the hot, fallow fields. Abul Razak's eyes follow her. No, of course not; she is neither ten nor twenty-seven. She is *his* age. That makes her forty-eight. And this is how she behaves! Like a slut. Who would have thought? Ya Allah! How she walks, throwing her weight from hip to hip! Abul Razak can't but notice that Fatima has her hair in a long, thick plait, and it swings just above her hips like a pendulum made to measure the beats of his vandalized heart.

Where is she going? And why is she whistling?

The road leads to the school and beyond it, melts and breaks into clods as it descends into the Chenab. Abul Razak tries to gather his voluminous white kurta up about him, but the cloth slips through his fingers like so much cloud. 'Fatima!' He calls out with all his soul to the only woman he has really loved and who, in return, punished him with the pain of a paradise withheld.

Abul Razak had once walked about with his palpitating heart pinned to his pocket. He had waited for Fatima for hours together at emerald by-lanes, soft with moss and grass that the spendthrift rain left behind like leftovers from a night of excess, hoping to catch a glimpse of Fatima; to listen, if nothing else, to her footfalls on fallen leaves; he had got drunk at midnight and sat down at the foot of the white steps that led up to the gates of her house; stared for hours at the moonlight stumbling on the stones, not knowing what to do.

Abul Razak had loved and lost.

Abul Razak runs a dry tongue over his lips. This April had been desiccating. America suffered the death of around five thousand of its men in Iraq, the number that the summer killed in Pakistan annually. The West had no idea; it thought apocalypse was what happened when stores ran out of dog biscuits. Before he was through, though, he would teach them different.

But what if it's more than the heat? What if he is, God forbid, changing? From Maulana to Majnu? Abul Razak feels around the floor with both hands, like the blind looking for a fallen coin, for the jug of water that he always keeps by his side, but finds he can't move his body. He can only see through his closed but open eyes, and so clearly, too, in such fine, textured detail: the red-and-yellow dust swirling around Fatima's rounded ankles like a halo. Is it possible that he is seeing a movie within a dream? No, he is in a movie and he is dreaming.

If Abul Razak were a real man like the Prophet, he would be out there with Fatima in the fields.

Abul Razak recalls the Prophet's affair with his cousin Zaynab bint Jahash, whom he got married to his adopted son, Zayid ibn Haritha. Abul Razak sees the Prophet paying a visit to Zayid's house across the distant dunes and, not finding him home, turning to leave, and then stopping in his tracks as he catches sight of the sensational-looking Zaynab pretending not to be there for the Prophet at all. A hot wind lifts the sands. Time drifts. And Razak hears the Prophet exclaim, 'Praise be to Allah who turns the heart of men as He wills!' Now, whatever does that mean, Abul Razak wonders. The Prophet's accidental meeting with Zaynab took place in August 626. Less than a year later, he had married her. A man of action!

Abul Razak blinks his eyes to adjust to the glare of the day. Fatima has stopped at the far end of the deserted street, just after Rahiman's blue-and-white grocery shop—which now rarely opens because his son has started sending money from Oman—and she turns.

She is waiting.

Is it for him? Who else? Her face is clearly that of a child. Does that make Abul Razak a paedophile? So be it. This is a dream after all. Surely he is not responsible for what he dreams? Come to think of it, can he be held responsible for anything when nothing stirs without Allah's will?

Abul Razak places a hand across his open and shut eyes. But his hands are heavy as if encased in stone. I'm giving up, he tells himself, I'm in Fatima's power. He feels as if he is in a well-orchestrated crash, an inevitable accident engineered by Fatima to her own music. Fatima the conductor, inspiring the Sultanpur orchestra to greater heights. Abul Razak bounces from rock to tree to rock, dazed. He needs to wake up from the wreckage, gather up what is left of himself before it's too late. Already, the long room with its green floor—or is it the mat?—has come loose from its moorings and is about to float out like a magic carpet into the febrile day.

Abul Razak presses himself down on to his mat, fighting an intense need to break wind, a bitter struggle which at long last he loses. The defeat brings him relief. Anytime now, he will be airborne. It is possible after all. Only, it seems to Abul Razak that he doesn't seem to be in control of anything. If only he could ... Oh Fatima, how I love you.

Although Abul Razak is famed as one of the greatest orators of Punjab, he has never been able to say those three words till now. Abul Razak is not sure why. Perhaps he is afraid of intimacy? Yes, very likely, Abul Razak hazards a guess. Intimacy is trust, a lowering of the guard, seeing equals in partners, doing away with masks.

Not to love would perhaps be a way out of all this. A determined retreat from the incarnadine hall of the heart. There is, Abul Razak knows, a reassuring, orderly hierarchy of power in impersonal ties. In any relationship, Abul Razak wears the mask of the Master. The others are, well, others. And because he has decided to be the Master at all times, all his relationships turn out to be the same. His pronouncements are received with the same meekness that he is both contemptuous of and dependent on. When he says something, it gets done. He speaks, others listen; he is naturally superior, his wisdom more encompassing. And by virtue of these traits, he always does the right thing in any given situation. He can't help it. Others can't help it either. Doing the right thing makes him continually more powerful.

At home, within the tight circle circumscribed by power, there is an uncluttered space where his wife Amina exists. A presence, pregnant with silence, in the dim back rooms. What else is possible? Indeed, what else is left? There is peace. There is decorum. There is propriety.

But not sex. Physical intimacy demands emotional involvement, Abul Razak suspects. He is not prepared for that because it is just too much trouble; it alters equations, upsets protocol.

The death of their son Usuf at the hands of the Indian army in Kashmir two years ago had been the last nail in the coffin of their sex life. Usuf had turned seventeen the week before he died. When the news reached them, Amina's eyes had filled and Abul Razak writhed like a worm under the burden of her stony gaze.

Abul Razak knew that even in a hundred years, the question of Kashmir would not be resolved, no matter what the sacrifices he made. India might be an insane democracy, but it would never give up Kashmir. And so, for people like him, Kashmir served as a lasting reason for a certain life lived on the edge. It invested in him a sense of purpose, a whole rationale for war, a state of emergency of the mind, which justified many actions, one, for example, being the suspension of liberties that other people might consider as civil. The very impossibility of the odds translated into a kind of divine dispensation. Nothing short of dire acts and deaths would do to carry out its writ.

Yet, right outside his window, Fatima was undoing all the good work he had done, including the sacrifice of his son. There she was, invoking spring in the stifling heat of summer, conjuring roses out of rosaries, proffering him forgotten aches of the heart as a cool, amber light spread over Sultanpur like the shadow of a giant wing, and the street smelled as if it was flowing with sherbet.

THREE

Such a Long Journey

August 15
12.46 a.m.

Lakshmi is on the last train from Churchgate, Bombay city, to Virar, a distant suburb. She is light-headed from the drinks she has had at the house of Beverly, who had thrown a party to celebrate the final break-up of her parents' marriage ('Bev, tell your dad dinner is served, it's in the trash bin').

Lakshmi knows that the fights between Beverly's parents had been going on for a while; a long while, really. She can see Beverly is happy that her parents have split.

Beverly, on her part, realizes that some people come together only to get separated. Of late, there had been just a little too much shouting happening for a home, and she felt it best that her mother, a social activist and a consultant to Oxfam, move out. Beverly has chosen to stay with her father, who is an engineer with the railways. So she gets to stay in this big, four-bedroom apartment next to Churchgate and the sea, within walking distance from her college, where Lakshmi and she are studying literature.

Beverly calls over a few friends, all girls. They drink and talk about boys and sex and listen to The Doors and Madonna and get tipsy on rum and cola. They agree it is easier to have fun without the boys hanging around with just one thought on their minds. They vote for another round of drinks. By midnight, all of them have left, each making a noisy, flamboyant exit, except Lakshmi, who wants to have just one more drink.

'I just love rum and cola,' she tells Beverly.

'Surprise! So do I! Geniuses drink alike,' Beverly says, turning to her father's bar again. 'My father is going to ask hard questions about his missing rum on his return.'

'When's he back?'

'First thing in the morning.'

Lakshmi glances at her watch. It's past 12.40. 'Oh, my god, no, Bev, I'll miss the last train.' She rises to her feet. 'Keep that rum for another day. I really must run.'

'Stay over.'

'No, I'd better go.'

'Off you go, then. Get laid soon.'

Lakshmi has just enough time to tear around the corner to the station and leap on to the train as it starts to life. The cavernous station is deserted. The red electronic letters and timings are burning like coal on the signboard. The tracks gleam dully. The compartment is empty, except for her.

No, not quite. There is a man, a boy really, thin and bearded, lying on the floor, his face resting on an outstretched hand. He has passed out. Lakshmi notices that he has Jesus-good looks.

I just love this poor baby so full of alcohol, Lakshmi thinks, totally drunk.

The boy at her feet stirs in his sleep, his hand tentatively holding Lakshmi's left toe, as if offering her a gift he is not sure of, just as the power goes off. The fans rattle to a stop and the city, streaming its neon hair on either side of the tracks, runs backwards into the blemishless dark.

The train picks up speed on some errant emergency line and is soon hurtling down the tracks. Has she got into a train bound for the yard? Lakshmi is disoriented. It seems to her that the night itself is a carriage juddering into motion, pulling the dark of the world with it, the furious movement of the train making a primal music of functional collapse and recovery as iron clashes with iron, in and out of sockets.

Lakshmi clings for life to the window bars that stretch between a few stars, dim and distant, like estranged children about to disappear on life-journeys.

She gradually becomes aware that a cool, nimble hand is finding its way up her waxed legs, all the way up to her (just-in-case-perfumed) panties, and pauses in puzzlement at her ruby-cunt: Oh, allow him to cross it or not? Cross, cross, Lakshmi tells herself, overwhelmed by the mixed feelings of the moment.

But she ends up saying, 'What are you doing?' as if she doesn't bloody well know what drives a hand up a skirt, but wanting all the while that he go further than any man has ever ventured, arrive at last at the final frontier to the accompaniment of cymbals and conches, enter like a king the triumphal arch.

'Exkiss me,' says the drunk, who is now on his knees, slurring into Lakshmi's crotch—has he for a devout moment mistaken it for a confessional?—where the wings of her vagina open and close like a butterfly in a bower, and the million and one hairs of the silken, black moss around her blooming bud are standing on end to catch a glimpse of the rousing action.

Go on, is what Lakshmi tries to say to the man who smells of jasmine (Tata hair oil!), hooch and the sea. But her middle-class, matrimonial-column morality—'Convent-educated, attractive nineteen-year-old girl of wheatish complexion, trained in domestic duties, well-settled family, father in service, mother pious, WANTS tall, handsome, middle-class boy with Green Card. No brokers please'—

makes a sudden, if fleeting, appearance in a cassock and a scowl, and Lakshmi coughs weakly as into a muffler: 'What are you doing! Please stop, stop, stop.' It is incredible what women want and what we finally say, she notes in passing. A genetically schizoid gender.

Lakshmi discovers that her molester's fingers can see in the dark. He has eyes for nails. She is digitally mastered. The unbuttoning of her shirt happens with ease, and he draws her hard, tight tits from their sartorial suppression—'These doves I feed, these doves I free. Fly where you will, you will come back to me'—kisses their tips, his beard tickling her skin, sucks them hard, weighs them in his hands as if he is a juggler about to toss his balls, kneads them with care, breathing heavily all the while, 'Please, please, may I' to Lakshmi's tumultuous but silent Victorian negations in French—Non, non, Monsieur—a college fad she slips into when under stress. He pulls her panties down all the way to her ankles where she toes the flimsy thing out of harm's way.

Lakshmi is melting down all over and, a moment later, her clitoris is in thrall to strange sensations. 'Hold my dick,' he suggests thickly to Lakshmi, who however declines the generous offer.

Instead, she spreads her legs. He duly proceeds to ram his oaken oar into what feels like a bush full of bricks, which suddenly gives way after a few punitive attempts to a slushy creek. Oh oh. A moment later, the inlet is opening out to sea. They are to the vastness bound. They clutch at each other, fall to a rhythm. Eddies of endorphins assail them. They sink in a swamp of pheromones. Gaily, they sail the sea of the senses.

Lakshmi's legs go round his waist and she arches her back and climaxes in ahs and ohs and yeses, as if she has come a long way. Which she has, because the train is now nearing Borivali, a few stations this side of Virar.

But in a court of law, Lakshmi may well be represented as resisting at Bandra and surrendering for fear of life at Borivali, where she weeps half a dozen or so sodden sobs in memory of her loss, suffers through a bout of intense nostalgia for the person that she used to be: Eve before she got addicted to the mood-altering apple, the Lakshmi pre-oh oh.

Was it rape? Because she did tell him not to come inside at least, no?—though, to her own ears, it had sounded as if she was reading out from an instruction manual on safe sex. As if the real point of it all was his not coming inside, the consequence of the act, but not the violation itself.

At some point, Lakshmi had tried to push him away from her. But, of course, she was confused in her responses. The body-soup. After all, there was the pleasure of the senses, and the pleasure of the mind that she was desirable, of erotic value to someone else: surely, she was responsible for his arousal?

And then the fear of punishment had washed over her like a wave: the irrevocability of the accident, the utter randomness of the event, the sheer shock of an act so private in its essence taking place in so public a place as a train, the unpredictability of the outcome … the shame of wanting more of the same.

If a journey could be said to have changed a life, this one had changed Lakshmi. She was a new woman, or a very old one, depending on how you looked at this business.

FOUR

The Amulet of the Soul

The back of the Breeze is caving in; the bright day is bursting like a bubblegum. Ajmal comes out of the restroom of the restaurant, flesh smoking, face black, quite the chimney boy fallen into the fireplace. He is not looking well at all, though it appears he is laughing. But that's because part of his chin has been blown off. In fact, he is walking blind with his innards in his hands, as if looking for someone worthy enough to pass on a precious heirloom.

Ajmal had made his way to the washroom—three bottles filled with caustic soda, kerosene and nails strapped to his stomach, ammonium nitrate and diesel fuel in separate compartments, ammunition bag slung over his back—with the assurance of a plumber about to fix a leak no one has noticed yet.

Once inside, he had made a call to his father, a truck driver, on his cellphone. It was a call he had wanted to make since he was ten. A call to get even. But his father did not pick up the phone. Sometimes people knew from the ring alone who the caller was.

'So like him,' Ajmal thought. If his father had answered the call, Ajmal would have told him that he had done the impossible; that he had arrived in Bombay safe; and that, in a moment, he would be waging the good war with guns blazing, grenades going, eyes flashing; a colossus smiling coldly at the stone worshippers and handing out punishment. 'Pick up that phone, you fool,' Ajmal said to his cell. 'For once, you'd be proud of me.'

Ever since Ajmal had taken to hanging around with the Lashkar-e-Toiba leader, Maulana Abul Razak, he and his father had not been on good terms. His father wanted him to run a garage. 'I'll set it all up for you. You just sit behind the table and count the cash,' his father kept telling him.

Whenever Ajmal interacted with his father, he had the feeling that his father was talking to a different person: a stern, disapproving man sitting on a straight-backed chair in a garage, one hand resting across the counter, the other in the table drawer squeezing change, like a pawn broker.

Ajmal's father was in his late fifties and had had enough of the highway life. With the roads in Sultanpur in a state of perpetual disrepair, just like other roads all over Pakistan, the garage would do well, Ajmal's father pointed out to him. He would do all the dirty work; Ajmal just had to man the counter.

Counter, always the counter, Ajmal thought. For Ajmal, the idea of liberating Kashmir had a far more magnetic appeal than a workshop, no matter how state-of-the-art it was. There was no comparison really, as Maulana Abul Razak ('May he live for ever') kept reminding Ajmal all through his training. Kashmir was myth and martyrdom, heavy guns and heroism. Kashmir was garden. The garage was grease.

His father had looked at him and shaken his head. He saw a fair, effeminate boy with red lips and round eyes. Some man would take him as his lover if he took care to keep his teeth clean. With sons like this, you were fated to toil to your last tooth. Placing a concerned hand on his truck-tender tailbone, Ajmal's father thought he could see the prospect of an early retirement receding like a milestone in the rear-view mirror.

Ajmal's calling condemned his father to a life behind the wheel. It was like a death sentence. I'll die driving, the father thought. 'Go get killed, you idiot,' he said at last. 'I am done with you. I thought you would help me in my old age. But that Maulana has got into your head.'

Ajmal listened to the ring tone and lit an absent-minded cigarette. Fathers didn't understand sons; that was how it was. And so, eventually, you could only hate your father, just as you ended up pitying your mother. If he, Ajmal, survived all this and married and had a son, he would try his best to treat him better.

But, for the present, he would rather his father picked up the phone. Now that Ajmal had reached Bombay after four nights on the boat, his father might accord a minimal respect to his mission, if not him. Face-to-face with his father, Ajmal found it hard to communicate. Everything got downsized to a plea, a favour. But perhaps, over the phone, with the distance crystallizing their respective stances, he could talk to his father as an equal.

Ajmal switched off his cellphone and inhaled the first mouthful of smoke. Manfully, he held it inside for a longish moment, thinking his father could be on the road. Where else? His truck plied all over Pakistan. Perhaps he was taking a break at a place where the signal was weak. One of those hamlets with a clutch of mud huts and a ramshackle tea shop with four or five charpoys in the shade of a gritty tree. The drivers would stretch their tired bodies on the coir cots, hands clasped behind their heads, their trucks parked at a distance with their bonnets open, like tamed beasts gone to sleep in the middle of a yawn. He will have to try later, Ajmal thought. He had things to do. Ajmal exhaled. He noticed the smoke billowing, and everything exploded.

Ajmal seems to have blown it, Salim thinks, and now he had better hurry with the operation. Everything is possible for a person who is already dead, and I died quite a while ago, he thinks. When the six of them set sail from Karachi four days ago, the plan was to land at Cuffe Parade, South Bombay, in three inflatable dinghies and fan out from there. On the third day since setting sail from Karachi, they had spotted a fishing trawler lazing off the coast of Gujarat. They had pretended to be students on an adventure and asked the captain, who seemed to be the sole occupant of the trawler, if they could come on board as their boat had developed a leak.

'Hop on,' the captain said and brought the trawler close enough for them to jump across. Within minutes, the captain was in their custody. Salim and team leader Shafi reset the course. The next morning, when they could see the Bombay shoreline, its vertical slums wrapped in a shroud of smog, they slit the captain's throat exactly as had been shown in a video clip at Maulana Abul Razak's house—cut the windpipe clean and quick—and threw the body overboard.

Salim had suggested a bullet to the head. But Shafi said, 'Get tough, wet your hand.' Salim shrugged, he didn't see the point. If they weren't tough, they wouldn't be here. But if that's what Shafi wanted, so be it. They tied the man's hands to the back of the chair. Salim noted that the captain's hands were shiny with a coat of fish scales. Shafi looked around and reached for a sawing knife lying next to the fishing tackle. 'This should do,' Shafi said, picking up the knife.

If he asked me to do it, I would, Salim thought. What had he to lose? It was a knife, and you pressed it against the man's throat and drew it deep across, much as you would slaughter a lamb on Eid. That was it. But, in your mind, you needed to set no value for life, and had to think nothing of another's pain. The training he received was more than adequate for the occasion. Really, Salim told himself, all of it came down to just one thing: your absolute eagerness to die. Your death preceded the murders you committed. The moment you ceased to be afraid of your own death, you were set free.

That freedom was arrived at through faith, and it was not just a piece of knowledge. It was a state of mind in which death became nothing. You vaulted into that zone on the pole of faith. A jihadi ceased to be just another person simply because of the infinite freedom that faith invested in him: the freedom to be more than himself, to overcome the limits that humans set for themselves. To soar above the barriers of logic and reason predicated on the sanctity of life and the fear of death. Faith wrought its own miraculous fate. Crashing a jet into a skyscraper ceased to be a fantasy, it became news. A realized event.

But at the last moment, Shafi surprised Salim. He didn't ask him to kill the captain. 'First casualty of the expedition,' Shafi said. 'I'll take care of it myself.' They watched as Shafi set to work.

It was clear that he was setting an example.

In the morning, a while before the execution, the captain said to Salim, 'Please, could you free my hands? I want to show you something.'

The sun was just a glimmer over the rim of the sea. The water, calm. Salim looked at Shafi, who was standing at a distance behind the captain, gazing in the direction of Bombay.

Shafi nodded. It made no difference what the captain was going to show. He would die, no matter what.

Salim freed the captain's left hand.

The captain took a snap out of his wallet and held it out to Salim, like an invitation. 'My wife and kids,' he said, looking at the photograph intently. The situation he was in was so terminal that he already seemed to find the people in the picture to be in another life. They had no idea what was happening to him, the extremity of his fate.

'I have two daughters,' the captain said to Salim, 'one turned six last week. The other is ten.' The captain raised the photograph high over his eyes, against the purple haze of the sea: the younger girl is holding a bar of chocolate in her hand; the elder one staring hard at her sister as if to say that it isn't fair; the mother is smiling—she doesn't realize the undercurrent of tension between the daughters.

Salim nodded.

The captain held the snap uncertainly for a moment between his trembling thumb and forefinger, tapped it against the wallet and returned it to the fold. His invitation had been rejected. Neither of them said anything. Salim noted that the captain had tufts of hair over his ears, waving in the breeze.

The captain watched Shafi approaching him, the stranger who would steal the sea and fish from him, remove from his possession the sun, the moon and the stars. It really was a lot; he was going to die at the hands of a man who he never knew existed till all this began. He would never hold his kids in his arms again because this man had been born and grew up with another god.

The captain suddenly felt thirsty. He saw no logic to life. Death wins because it respects no reason. The unreasonable always has the upper hand. If only he didn't have to die, he would never regret anything. He would be happy forever if he was spared. He would even help these boys do whatever they had set out to do, though he could see that they were not up to any good. These were people who would kill, no matter what he promised to give in return for his life.

They had said they were going to tear Bombay to pieces, kill as many people as they could and then get killed themselves. They said it matter-of-factly, as if there was no other option. In a way, they were as condemned as he was. In that sense, perhaps, they *were* helpless. And somehow their helplessness translated into the captain's hopelessness. Still, he offered assistance. He knew people in Bombay who could help them. He had useful connections. Such as reliable taxi drivers. Or, places where they could hide. If only they would let him go.

Salim looked on as the man pleaded for mercy. 'I have a wife and two daughters. Please, let me go. Take the trawler. I will swim back, take, take anything …'

They all give reasons for not dying, Salim thought. And none of them is good enough, simply because you really don't need a reason to live.

Shafi took position behind the captain, tilted his head backwards as if he were going to give him a shave, and began to press the knife against the hard column of the throat. Then, he drew it across in a swift, firm movement.

The captain's pleas ended in a scream. The sea and the sky rang with its terror. The captain was trying to say something now. But it was hard to make out as the blood bubbling up from the slit throat drowned his speech, turning words into sounds. The captain fell sideways to the floor with the chair. His body was in throes. Shafi looked at his handiwork without expression, and flung the knife into the sea.

Though it looks as if Shafi and his friends had killed all their lives, their commando training started just six months ago, in Muridke, in the Punjab province of Pakistan. And before that, how strange to think that they didn't know how to dismantle a gun, bite the pin of a grenade, read a map, handle a boat and kill a snake and cook it.

Once inside Bombay waters, they had inflated their dinghies and headed for the shore. But soon after, the outboard motor of Salim's dinghy had gone silent. Salim and Ajmal had drifted to the shallow waters of Bandra, away from the south-bound Shafi and others. Inshallah.

Bombay is cooler than Karachi, Salim notes as he clambers with Ajmal by his side from the water to the rocks, shaking the sea off his body and blinking in the sun, unsure of the land he is stepping on, like the first biped.

Cooler. Different.

Precariously balancing themselves on shifting stones and slippery rocks, the youngsters of Bombay, boys and girls in their teens and twenties by the score are making out the best they can, some of them with one hand out, clutching at the air to keep balance, some with one foot in water. Passion has driven them out of their shared one-room tenements in the clogged slums of Dharavi and Mahim to the sea, whose boundless space sets them free from inhibitions.

On these rocks, between a seething sea and a scorching sun, they stand, a calligraphy of desire; a vast tableau of love antics, of twisted limbs and searching mouths, seeking a moment's release in a rich man's slum-city of little space and lesser time.

'Kafir land,' Ajmal says.

'Bandra,' says Salim, recalling the Google map of Bombay.

'Boys and girls are having a good time.'

'Don't look at them. Just step across the rocks and get to some place. We are on our own. Time to go at it.'

'Just like that?' Ajmal asks, twirling the green ghost of a moustache. He steals a glance at Salim's thickening stubble. He should have consulted Dr Zainuddin, after all ... for that facial hair tonic.

Salim looks around. They need to pick their way through the black rocks and an army of rapt lovers, scale a wall and cross a jogging track to reach the main road. The road seems far away, but the prospect has little to do with distance and a lot to do with the utter unreality of their mission.

The very idea of stepping on an alien shore with the sounds and smells of Karachi still clogging their pores, and shooting into a billion-strong crowd had seemed absurd at one point. And now, here he was, right in the middle of the impossible.

It helped that their target was everywhere. A target so vast that wherever you shot, it was bullseye. You went at it till a bullet burst *your* guts. There would be pain. You looked forward to that pain. You took it head-on. The pain was the door to the other side. You butted it open and stepped over, leaving behind the enemy turned inside out. He was dust. You blew him to the winds. Poof.

The quality of violence itself was a record of your passage. No matter what happened now, you were part of the enemy's history as you were of your own land. The heroism involved in the action was so mythical in its dimensions that you passed into folklore. In these times of mindless distractions, the jihadi would make forgetting difficult. And what made martyrdom possible was faith—the charm that kept Salim from harm—the amulet of the soul.

FIVE

The Heart of India

The roads in Bombay are never quite straight where they do exist. Sunil Shinde knows from his experience as an auto-rickshaw driver that roads are, in fact, a very fluid idea. They may be there one day. And far from being straight, the next day they may be missing altogether. There are reasons for this. The contractor may have cut corners, and so the road he built might have been washed away in a night's rain. Or the local political Opposition may have dug it up out of spite. Or the residents may have shovelled it aside as so much dirt to erect a shamiana for a festival or a wedding reception.

Even when the roads *are* there, Shinde knows only too well that they may play truant. They meander through potholes, fall through ditches to dizzying depths and vanish, rise again from rubble and, shaking and stretching themselves into some sort of ribbon-like shape, stray into bedrooms, come out unreprimanded, slip into bathrooms, exit wet, and join the general catatonia of the city's traffic, only to be brought to a dead halt by a herd of wanton cows.

But Shinde has never lost his way in the labyrinth of his locality. He knows the affluent Bombay suburb of Bandra so well, he can pick his way blindfolded through its mayhem.

In fact, he has actually done so once … on a dare born of a drunken night's vagaries.

And the adventure happened within twenty-four hours of Shinde having become a proud rickshaw owner. 'Don't take it out till the Ganpati worship is done,' his father tells him. 'I have made all the arrangements.' So, then, the day after the rickshaw is delivered, his father conducts the rickshaw puja, early in the morning, at exactly six past six, the auspicious time prescribed by the family astrologer and guru, the saffron-clad Shri Shri Vinayak Kudale.

Shinde's father sprinkles water on the rickshaw to exorcise the gleaming black-and-yellow bug of malevolent spirits and free it from any spells or evil eyes that neighbours may have cast on it. The kicking out of the spirits is followed by the breaking of a coconut for a good beginning. Just to be sure that Shinde breaks the coconut at first throw—it is bad luck in the next six lives if he doesn't, not to mention the present one—his father, in an operation of furtive secrecy, judiciously cracks its shell in the kitchen the night before. Just a hairline fracture. But there is no hiding the sacrilegious act from the ever-vigilant gods of rituals who gently—but instantly—caution Shinde's father by making him trip and fall, causing him to sprain his ankle. A little rap on the knuckles, as it were.

Shinde smashes the coconut on a stone placed in front of the rickshaw. The pieces of broken coconut are distributed among friends and relatives who stand in a ring to bless Shinde. The early morning sun has just begun cutting channels of sweat in their powdered faces.

The coconut distribution is followed by the installation of a cute, red terracotta Ganpati, the portly elephant god, on the tinny dashboard. A bunch of powerful agarbattis are lit and stuck in the various orifices of the Obstacle Eliminator.

Celebratory fire crackers are actively considered and rejected, when an elderly well-wisher, Waghmare, reminds Shinde and company of the death of a neighbour's grandfather just two days ago. Propriety demands lower noise levels.

Guru Kudale asks Shinde to prostrate himself before the rickshaw. 'From today,' Guru Kudale tells Shinde, pointing a holy, multi-ringed finger at the machine, 'this rickshaw is your father and mother.'

Shinde contemplates the rickshaw in a new light and bows his head in acknowledgement.

He touches his guru's feet, the nails of which are painted red. Guru Kudale wishes Shinde well, his hand on Shinde's excessively oiled head. Shinde doesn't stir from under the hand so the full power of the blessing flows into him uninterrupted. After a minute or so, Guru Kudale clears his throat to let Shinde know the energy transaction has been completed. The circuit can be broken.

Shinde turns to his father, who hugs him. He has, Shinde notes with gratification, tears in his eyes. It's all just like in a Hindi movie which, Shinde feels, is the way it should be.

For twenty-three years, Shinde's father has taken care of him. Now Shinde is on his own, although he stays with his father and shares the same cot as well—his mother sleeps on a mat on the floor. But Shinde will be expected to bring in a certain amount of money and hand it over to his father on the first of every month.

The neighbours crowd around Shinde, a hive of bees humming congratulations. Shinde steps into the driver's cabin, right foot first for luck, the left part of the body traditionally being the Untouchable Part. Shinde glues himself to the driver's seat and takes a tentative round of the place. A kind of victory lap.

When he is back and the rickshaw is finally parked, he calls his friends for a party. The celebration starts at the Good Luck Country Liquor Bar and winds its way to Waghmare's asbestos-roofed, carcinogenic tenement in the narrow, crowded gully whose cobbled stones are always wet from water spilled in transit from the public tap to their homes.

The party goes well enough. Songs are sung. Jokes are cracked. Stories told. But towards the end of the evening, the revelry inexplicably deteriorates into a showdown between two groups, one led by Shinde and the other by Waghmare, who has been trying hard to raise a bank loan to buy a rickshaw for his son, but so far in vain.

Fuelled by alcohol, the bitterness builds itself into a challenge, centring on Shinde's manhood, which is somehow connected with the rickshaw.

'If you are a man, then …' Waghmare places his fore and middle finger over his mouth in a V and pauses to spit a gob of red paan through it out of the window. The act is a scathing comment on Shinde and his friends.

'If I *am* a man! Hmph, go on,' Shinde says, getting up from the fake tiger-skin rug on the floor and putting out a hand to steady himself as the room tumbles around him. He registers vaguely that Waghmare is wearing a pair of loose, striped, knee-length shorts which could pass for underwear in extreme situations like this.

'If you are a man, do what I did when I was young. Let's see, eh, let's see, ok?'

'Oh, and what did you do?'

'I'll tell you what I did. Certainly, I will. Will I tell you! I will tell you.' Waghmare pauses to recall his heroics, but nothing of significance comes to mind. He desperately scans the room for help. But everyone, especially those on his side, captained by his rickshaw-denied son, is looking at him in expectation. It occurs to Waghmare that he has always been his son's hero and that a hero's life is not easy. Especially if his memory fails him, as now. Whatever did he do, even faintly extraordinary, when he was young? It seems to him that his youth was a long time ago, ancient Indian history really, and that it was singularly dull.

The truth, he thinks, is that I have drunk too much. But there is no backing out now.

'Ha! When I was your age, maybe younger, I drove my taxi blindfolded from Bandra station to here. That's what I did. Let's see if you have balls enough for that. How people talk!' Waghmare turns his face away in disgust.

'Oh!' Shinde does a double take.

'Yes,' Waghmare says in triumph, 'blindfolded. Nothing visible, let me tell you.' He snorts in derision.

Not fair, there wasn't much traffic those days, Shinde wants to shout. But he knows that as an argument, it will not wash. 'All right, I'll do it tomorrow morning!' Shinde says, regretting each compulsive word as he utters it.

'We'll see,' Waghmare says, tightening the strings of his underwear and retying them as if he were girding his loins for a wrestling match. 'That we'll see, eh?'

The next morning when Shinde comes to hazy consciousness, he finds himself looking into the challenging eyes of Waghmare, who is noisily drinking a cup of tea. Obviously, he is waiting. Oh god, Shinde thinks. It was not a nightmare after all. There is nothing for it but fight for his honour. He steps into the rickshaw. Waghmare's son smiles in pity and places a piece of black cloth over Shinde's eyes and ties it at the back of his head, which doesn't do anything for his hangover.

Waghmare regards the blindfolded Shinde, like an

executioner his victim. The fatal implications of his challenge are beginning to dawn on him. 'One friend from Shinde's side can get in with him as back-seat driver only,' he relents. 'And one from my side to check everything. Ok?'

A volunteer steps up and whispers to Shinde, 'One tap's left turn, two taps right, and one punch means stop. Get it?'

Shinde's mouth is dry. He nods.

Three years on, recalling the event makes Shinde shiver. If memory can function as a freezer clamped to his private parts, this one ride—from Pali Hill village to Bandra station—comes very close. Every inch of the road feels close and rises vertically in the nothing-space between the folded cloth and his eyes; the honking, trundling, morning traffic overtakes him, coming at him from all sides, taking little bites of his crazy-thumping heart like a pack of wild dogs. It's death in random doses.

But he makes it to the station, thanks to the powerful Our Lady of Dolours—Dollar Lady! Dollar Lady!—at whose tear-worn altar he furtively pays homage once a month; and whose Christian credentials he overlooks since the Lady is, for all practical purposes, a Hindu, working out of Bombay, and all thanks to the jolly Lord Ganesha, since no one could set up shop in the city without his blessings.

His friends slap his back in admiration. 'Maan gaye, Ustaad,' they say. 'You are the man.' Shinde has never felt so sick and, a little later, though his body continues to tremble, so good. Waghmare shakes the victor's hand. Shinde is gracious in his triumph. He makes no mention of last night's acrimony. Waghmare treats Shinde and his friends to tea, but maintains the resentful silence of the defeated.

Soon after, Shinde gets into the rickshaw and starts the engine. Time he went home. He picks up speed. The Sunday afternoon traffic is not much. Shinde cuts lanes at will, hurls a greeting in friendly abuse at a paanwala in passing, turns a corner and suddenly, from nowhere, the hallucinogenic Indian cow thrusts her massive, prehistoric face through the crumbling windshield of the rickshaw and kisses Shinde on the mouth with enough force to tear his lips and bruise his chin. Muah. Muah.

The rickshaw comes to a stop. The cow is immovable, but persistent, passionate. Its face fills the cabin completely. The eyes roll in pain and excitement. The snout and forehead are bleeding. The rickshaw's windshield has been reduced to smithereens. Shinde pales to his gums. 'Oh, no,' he says.

The cow ruminates, licks Shinde's stricken face. The tongue is rough on his skin. For some reason, Shinde has always thought a cow's tongue to be soft, a point he had mentioned mistakenly in his ninth-grade composition: 'His tongue is soft as butter, which he puts out in times of need,' he had written. His teacher had not bothered to correct him on that point. Now he knows that is not the case.

Shinde reverses the vehicle from the mouth of that mythic face and the cow slowly zooms out of vision. Shinde feels like crying. In fact, he cries. Tears run down his cheeks. He abuses himself vilely. He curses Waghmare, long in years and short in wisdom, who really is responsible for the whole chain of events. He refrains from cursing the cow because it amounts to disrespecting his religion and, for some reason, his mother, who suffers her existence in silence.

Meanwhile, the cow has uniquely sat down on her hind legs like a kangaroo on the road. She is trying to figure out how she got where she is now. People are gathering round the white, abnormally large animal. With the right kind of injections, this surely is a cow that could have become an albino elephant, except that the beast's face is red with blood.

Shinde is not sure where the sympathies of the crowd lie. If they are with the cow, he is in trouble. And since the cow is divine and he assuredly is not, he doesn't fancy his chances. Shinde takes a tight U-turn and flees the scene, aware of the cow's eyes boring into the back of his head. He can't shake the feeling that he is fated to meet the beast again.

SIX

Prophet of Doom

The Breeze is a clean, sunlit place in red brick and wood with enough potted plants to afford cover for an ambushing unit. Its laid-back urbanity encourages hugs, laughs, kisses. The tiger prawns help to keep the juices flowing. The tandoori pomfret and fried Bombay duck facilitate business, lubricate love talk. The chic ambience eases people into thinking the best of their future. It empowers them to drink more, eat more, and spend more. Today, like any other day, there are a good number of well-muscled B-grade film stars brunching with their eyes peeled on the main chance.

A bunch of tight T-shirts in dark glasses at the bar are laughing over a tray of blue drinks. They turn to look in alarm as Ajmal announces his ostentatiously colourful, spectacularly painful arrival to the accompaniment of exploding grenades. 'Oh my god,' one of them says. The others scatter. The glasses come off, they no longer mean anything.

For a moment, Salim is distracted by the girls—shimmering clothes, summery looks, long hair, dark eyes, nice teeth—who have now begun to scream. There are more blasts happening. The ammunition in Ajmal's backpack is seriously getting into the act. There are tables teetering, chairs falling, trays flying. A bottle pops open and spins, showers the room with champagne. A wig sails through the air like a bat in a trance. Curtains curl away from windows, beautifully on fire, and wave in the air like orange flags of terror. At the back, a wall is suddenly gone, and the sea startles by its sudden proximity. Across the blue, in the distance somewhere, is Karachi; and 700 km south from there is Sultanpur, where mangoes ripen in dark green orchards. There, his mother must be busy in the kitchen, far from where he stood fighting for his faith, turning life into death, carrying out God's good work.

Home is on another planet, really, Salim realizes. The place you cannot go back to. It is not the distance that makes a place far; it is what you do, what you *do* renders a place beyond the possibility of return. An act externs you. A thought exiles you. A word you uttered is a door shut in your face.

Another explosion. Salim sees all of Ajmal leap from his left knee and then go down. Salim slowly draws his AK-47 out of the bag. Irrevocable acts must be done with infinite care. Salim finds the gun in his hand unfamiliarly heavy, though its stock has already been removed for easier handling. He holds it over the table and starts shooting into the crowd that is fleeing towards the sea through the vanished wall. He might start here at this restaurant as well as anywhere else. Terror doesn't need to follow a map. Or a plan. It blazes its own trail. In any case, this is what he has got, thanks to Ajmal, whose resentful father once described him to Salim as someone who struggled to change a light bulb. Salim should have paid heed. But Ajmal did seem to do well at the training camp. To hell with it, he thinks, I have come to a point in the story where corrections are impossible. Here I am. Alone. Alive. Armed. Let's see what you can do now, Salim. Let's see what you do. Let's see what you are about.

Silence descends around Salim. His head has become sound proof. He can see people screaming and running for cover. Some of them are coming down in a heap. All of it is in slow motion and in complete silence. A few are picking themselves up and stumbling forward. They want to live. Why is it so important for them to live? The desire for life distorts their features. Their mouths are open, eyes wide. They must be screaming.

Don't be afraid, Salim wants to tell them, all of us were dead before we were born, remember? This is not between you and death. This is between me and my God. This is what I have chosen, over my mother and my future. Over music and movies and sunsets. Over friends and parks and birds, and trees in the rain. The desert of faith I must journey to reach the rivers of paradise.

Salim can see clearly the painterly beauty of spilled blood and torn limbs, the splattered pornography of pain and death; the neon of the bone shearing off the flesh like a sign of Allah's outrage.

The room is turning red. The floor collects blood in great pools. The walls are dripping with it. The roof is spotted with it. The world is a spreading blob of blood. Salim still can't hear anything. Perhaps great violence has only eyes, no ears, which is why pleas for mercy fall on deaf ears.

Salim has never experienced a silence so complete. It's like being in a bubble, deep under the sea, he thinks. But there are ants crawling all over his skin. His skin had crawled earlier too, when he sat out the last few nights on the boat from Karachi—the vast rumbling drum of the sea under him, the endless calendar of the sky with stars for dates above—and did not know what to make of himself or his mission against such scales of space and time.

A woman is in front of him. On all fours. She has crawled out from under a table, an animal forced out of its hole by the earth's seismic seizures. Her eyes are dilated like a paranoid cat's. What was she doing there? Had he seen her on a street in Karachi, begging? Soliciting? Or perhaps he had met someone like her. Indians bore an uncanny resemblance to their brothers and sisters across the great divide. Besides, people tended to look the same in a shared situation.

Not that it matters who this girl is. She is just a target. Just now, nothing matters to Salim except clarity. The clarity of faith. Of power. Of the end. All purpose, for Salim, has shrunk to this moment. All meaning to this act. All life to this death.

For a flaring moment of white, Salim can feel the presence of the Almighty right there with him, a massive, swaddled form, protecting him, guiding him. And then it is gone. In the great circle of humanity, Salim, firing his gun, stands alone again at the centre, isolated in the utter understanding of his God. A hail of bullets announces his prophetic arrival to the world. Around him spins, like roulette, splintered furniture, whamming into bodies that stretch, break, are no more. There are blasts ripping up the place. There are fires breaking out.

But there is not a scratch on Salim.

It's as if the air around him is his armour, keeping harm out. Salim is amazed at the grand scale of His mercy: the infinitesimal gradations of justice; the relentless evening out of punishment and reward in the infinite cycles of creation.

My time, Salim thinks, is now. My day is come. I am witness to the miracle. Maybe I am the miracle. My mind is God's muscle. He moves it and people drop dead.

Salim surveys the carnage. It could be war, it could be art. It could be both. Whatever it is, it would soon get over. In a short while from now, virginal beauties would smile and open for him the gates of jannat. There would be music. Before the evening was out, he'd pace the golden halls in the high pavilions, stroll through jade gardens in permanent bloom. Drink deep from sweet streams.

The girl is on her knees, pleading. It looks like pleading. He can't hear. He doesn't have to. Her whole body is an act of supplication. Please, the body is saying in every language invented by man, please let me live. Salim stares at her moving lips, his fingers crooked around the trigger.

'I just got a role in a movie,' she stutters.

She is aware that she is talking to a boy with an enormous gun. A dark-complexioned boy stretched tight like a wire, whose quiet, straight features show no expression. His hair is long and a lock of it has fallen across his forehead. He is too occupied to brush it back, too busy killing. His eyes are watchful. A handsome boy who may yet grow taller by a few inches if the gun didn't stand in the way.

'A Salman Khan movie,' she says. 'Please, let me go.' A side of her face has been so close to fire, the skin is peeling, like a film off a sheet of glass. Salim's cellphone rings. He returns to life. 'Hello,' Salim says.

'We are moving into the Taj any time now,' Shafi says.

'Very good. We have landed in Bandra.'

'Inshallah. You guys start and finish the job wherever you are.'

'Theekh,' Salim says, 'we have just begun. Ajmal is dead.'

'What happened?'

'The bombs went off.'

'You are on your own then. Khuda hafiz.'

'Khuda hafiz.'

Salim puts the gun down on the table and walks to the bar.

On the counter, a shot of whiskey sparkles in a glass, totally intact, presiding over the ruins. He drains it, bottoms up. The girl is sitting on her haunches now. Hell's witness. Salim picks up his gun and bag from the table. The table crumbles as if released from a spell. The girl falls to the floor, hands covering her face, her body shaking, forehead to the ground, like a devout Muslim in prayer.

The wind ruffles her hair.

SEVEN

The One-in-a-million Chance

Lakshmi sips her coffee, keeps the cup back on the table. She closes her eyes, wishing away a multitude of her chattering selves. She doesn't find the restaurant sofa comfortable, but exhaustion has turned her indifferent to the surroundings. She needs to speak to someone.

'Bev,' she says into her cellphone.

'Hey, where did you disappear last night?'

'Bev,' Lakshmi says.

'Oy, what's it? Lakshmi?'

'I need to talk to you.'

'Talk. Spill your dil to aunty,' Beverly says, still not quite awake.

'No. In person. Now.'

'Now? I need to go for a client meeting.' Beverly is a senior executive at a public relations firm.

'This is, like, dire, Bev. Suicide or murder.'

'Go for murder. Where are you?'

'Barista, Land's End.'

'Forty minutes.'

'All right.'

Lakshmi puts her hand up and asks for the day's papers. The waiter by the window brings her a whole pile.

She runs a critical eye over people whose fate it is to become a headline. 'SALMA HAYEK AVERTS WARDROBE MALFUNCTION'. No kidding, Lakshmi observes, especially since 'the 42-year-old is on a promotional tour to publicize her campaign to eradicate tetanus'. Indeed. How can one eradicate tetanus without a wardrobe malfunction? What's charity without breasts to the fore? 'HINDU ORPHAN RAPED, MURDERED IN ORISSA: MOB MISTOOK VICTIM FOR CHRISTIAN'. They messed up even that, then. Lakshmi shakes her head.

She looks up from the papers to see Beverly striding out of the sea as it were, glittering like a black sword in the sunlight. And then she is in the restaurant, shapely bones tightly wrapped in gleaming ebony skin, her eyes set off by a mass of black curls through which a streak of peroxide blitzes like lightning.

'Hi.' Beverly smiles with the confidence of a person ready to jump a queue or step over a corpse.

'Seen the papers?' Lakshmi asks. She feels a need to stall.

'Lakshmi, you didn't ask me to come here for that!'

'They are priceless, aren't they? The headlines?'

'I didn't look at the papers. Wasn't that a great party?'

'Terrific. All the stars were there.'

'Don't they look just like they do in the movies?'

'They looked just great.'

Lakshmi thinks of the occupant in her tub, maybe she should just let him go, keep things simple. Leave the past alone. Live well in the present. Surely, life is too short for revenge? 'Do I need a drink!'

'You were high as a kite last night, and I thought I saw you trying to share the same corner as Shah Rukh Khan.'

'I was hoping to catch his eye. Fantasies of a middle-aged mammal. I don't care much for the way he acts, though.'

'Who's talking about acting? Where did you disappear after a while?'

'I made my way to the bar for a last drink.' Lakshmi folds the papers neatly and places them on one side of the table, as if they are laundered linen. 'God, I am still drunk. And lost. I should be in the movies, Beverly. In and as Lakshmi. One hit and retire.' Lakshmi leans over the table, lowers her voice. 'I kidnapped a man. He's in my bathtub.'

Beverly opens her mouth as if to say, Oh my god. They listen to waves crashing. A black ship drifts slowly across their vision as if towed by a lazy whale.

'About time,' Beverly finally says. 'Coffee,' she tells the counter, and turns to Lakshmi. 'So. Tell me about it.'

Lakshmi shakes her head, takes a small, red, misty bottle of vodka out of her jacket pocket, and pouring it into a glass of water under the table, drinks it up in one go as if the day is already over.

'Madam, that's not allowed,' says the waiter who was a moment ago at the window staring at the sea and who has now zoomed into close-up at Lakshmi's elbow.

'What? What's not allowed?' Beverly says.

'What Madam just now did? Alcohol not allowed on the premises.'

'Sorry, thought it was water,' Lakshmi says. A vein ticks at her temple like a timer.

'No issues,' the waiter says. 'It is just that alcohol is not allowed. By order.'

'By order,' Lakshmi repeats, wondering whose order. 'Got it.'

The waiter bows his head, retraces his steps to the window. He is glad he intervened. That's what he's paid for, to keep the house in order. I don't understand women, he thinks.

'Well, then?' Beverly asks Lakshmi.

'This drink here has got me right up where I was last night.' Lakshmi reaches for the vodka again, remembers the waiter's strictures, and anyway finds the bottle empty. 'Excuse, excuse,' she says, quite drunk, to Beverly, and makes for the washroom which is painted blood red, where she throws up. She washes her mouth and face, and starts crying into the sink.

The morning vodka alters her case.

What did that night do to me, she asks herself. That night which no one knows about? Surely, she must stop pretending she was raped? After all these years, she must stop lying to herself. Wasn't she wet by the time he was ready for it? Didn't she like the way he touched her? And after the act, for a long time in the dark, didn't she feel gratified by his musky smell of sweat and sea and cheap alcohol? And don't forget that bloody hair oil. No? No. Of course she took pleasure. She didn't. She did. Didn't. Did. All right, maybe she did then. She can't remember. After all, it was so many years ago. And who can tell apart the nuances of an experience from its aftermath? Memory always altered what it tried to remember.

But one thing is clear: her whole life is an after-effect of that accidental night. Even the fact that she couldn't complete her studies and became, of all things, content manager at a porn firm. One night on that train, and all the days since have been different. Lakshmi sits on the toilet seat, presses her thighs together, remembering her panties later that night, wet, sticky, and slightly bloody between her legs.

'We've got to get a drink,' Beverly says. 'You aren't making this up? This train thing?'

'Am I making this up? Let's move to Olive's, where I can maybe make up some more. They open the bar early.'

They pay up and step out. Lakshmi slips behind her sunglasses and, in the freshly darkened world, glances at the waiter by the window. The breakdown in the washroom has calmed her. The waiter is still staring at the sea, as if a ship may come to his rescue any time. Outside, the day falls around them like foils of steel. Beverly raises her hand and conjures up an auto-rickshaw. 'Olive's,' she says, one foot in the cabin of the three-wheeler.

Sunil Shinde spits out paan juice on the road, wipes the blood-red corner of his mouth with a dirty handkerchief in a gesture of practised finality. He rests a leg over the handlebar of the rickshaw. As proof of his loyalty to the Hindu right-wing party, Shiv Sena, a picture of its leader Bal Thackeray seated on a throne is stuck on his windshield. From behind the photograph, joss sticks fume away furiously. There is a tiger roaring at the leader's white-sandalled feet.

The interior of the rickshaw is laminated in hysterical pink and the cabin roof is a mural of semi-nude Bollywood stars.

Shinde raises the volume of music. 'Olive's is too near,' he says, shaking his head, looking ahead in affected indifference.

'Where will you go?'

'Anywhere but Olive's,' Shinde says. 'Olive's too near.'

'Let's go to my place,' Lakshmi whispers to Beverly. 'Oh my god, I need to deal with the guy at home. He must be up.'

'Well, he is not your husband. Get some food in you first. Looks like it's going to be a long day.'

'We will stop over at Breeze, buy a sandwich and then go home.'

'All right,' Beverly says, and turns to Shinde. 'How about a brief halt at Breeze, and then Anderson Road?'

Shinde nods. He sticks his right leg out in signal, viciously U-turns the rickshaw and fires along the marine drive. His beady eyes meet Lakshmi's in the mirror from which hangs a bunch of black, plastic grapes misted over with a fine patina of dirt.

Something about me, Lakshmi thinks. 'Look where you are going,' she tells him.

'Looking, looking,' Shinde says with a grin, tossing his Shah Rukh Khan hair to the music, which is so loud now that all of Bandra is a deafening roar.

Beverly glances at Lakshmi. She had thought she knew her friend, but clearly she didn't. How do you know whether you know a person well?

'And then, Lakshmi? What happened after Borivali?'

'Are you ok?' he asks, as the lamps in the compartment flicker momentarily along their M-shaped filaments and the iron grips overhead sway, first one way and then the other, as if unable to make up their mind. The compartment with its yellow, empty seats; the small advertisements with their black lettering offering crash courses in accountancy and cheap, safe abortions ('Come in morning, go in evening'); the red emergency brakes above the windows asking her to pull them in case of a dire need; the stranger next to her zipping up his jeans and sitting up, the return of electricity lasting not more than two or three seconds; and the compartment rocking through the rain and the dark as if it is no longer connected to the rest of the train: a detached carriage roller-coasting through the universe smothered in roiling clouds, the wheels laying tracks just as they scorch through space, the rain clattering like knives …

'I was till I met you,' she says.

He laughs uncertainly.

'What will I do now?' she says, looking out of the window at the dark rushing by.

'You are beautiful,' he says, taking her hand in his, as if her beauty is an explanation for all that happened. 'There's nothing to be done. I'll never forget you.'

'I must report you to the police.'

'Whatever for?' He removes his hand from hers. 'You will be inviting a lot of trouble for yourself.'

The train slows down to a halt somewhere between stations, over a creek in spate due to the rains. In the distance, hills loom like massive prehistoric animals. Down below, water clucks in remorse at the pylons. The rain has stopped.

'These things happen. Perhaps we will meet again,' he says. 'It's a one-in-a-million chance that we met. We are the one-in-a-million chance. That is what it's all about.'

This is the secret of his freedom, Lakshmi thinks, this formula of numbers. She stares at him as if in a dream, her eyes open, her body frozen. She sees him as if she is not there, as if she is in another room, sees him in a clear absence of herself. She hears words whose meanings elusively overlap with their sounds. She forgets names of familiar objects, like ticket and telephone. She remembers she can't reverse anything. She knows that the party that Beverly threw was in another life.

He gets up and goes towards the door where, without warning, a full moon is close and blazing. 'What we do really has not much to do with us. Everything is chance. Things happen. That is the way it is.' He nods to himself in agreement. 'Things happen.'

'We don't have to look at it that way,' Lakshmi says, forcing herself to be rational. 'We could build on what chance gave us.'

'Not me, that's not me. I can't plan anything. If I did, I wouldn't

have met you. I am that rare thing, a man without a future. Or one with very many. And in all of them, I will remember you.' He blows her a kiss.

Lakshmi reaches out to him with one hand, her heart in her mouth. Neither his ideas of life nor his kind memories of her are an adequate recompense for the night that has fallen on her, sharp and final as a guillotine. She can't figure out the meaning of his seemingly simple words. What is he saying? As if his remembrance of her will nourish her soul. 'Surely, you can't leave me like this?'

But it is too late. He has already turned and is diving out of the door.

That's the last Lakshmi sees of him, a man with his back to her, flying in the black-and-silver zebra air.

'Oh, don't, take me with you, then.' Lakshmi starts to her feet, rushes to the door. 'Tell me your name. Give me a number. Come back.'

Nothing. Just the ghost train, the water and the hills. And the big moon baring the world white.

EIGHT

The Hand that Killed the English Language

A gust of onions announces Amina's arrival to Abul Razak. Onions and mutton, the perfume of the servants. And, most unusually for her, Amina lies down next to him without permission.

So the lamb lies down with the lion, huh?

Brazen, Abul Razak thinks, brazen. Between the morning and noon, the world has changed and women have turned equal to men.

'And why is the Maulana not up? Time for prayers,' Amina says, clearly affecting a brittle cheer, just as the muezzin comes alive and his lonely voice climbs, like a staircase of sad, beautiful, winding sounds, to heaven.

Why, Abul Razak thinks, is calling out to God so sombre an exercise? Where's the joy of talking to one's Creator? Besides, is it prayer time yet?

'Isn't that Fatima out alone on the road?' Amina asks. 'Why, she is almost a child!'

'So was Ayesha,' Abul Razak says, 'and she was only nine when the Prophet married her.'

'You must find me old, then,' Amina says, lifting her veil.

Amina's eyes are dry, like drained pools. Has she been crying again? Hmm, Abul Razak thinks, if Amina weren't so maudlin, she'd be attractive in a gentle, motherly fashion. Abul Razak grunts. 'You shouldn't be here,' he says, more as an instruction than a prohibition.

'Where should I be? In the kitchen?'

Equality laced with back talk? Clearly, a new, outspoken Amina! How is he going to get this under control? 'It's time for me to pray.' Abul Razak invokes piety.

'You were looking at Fatima,' Amina says, retracting into the veil, like a rabbit sensing danger and nipping back into its burrow.

Abul Razak says nothing. Sometimes it is not easy to explain. Each word behaves as if it were a labyrinth all by itself.

'You don't like me any more,' Amina says, snuggling up to him.

Abul Razak thinks of the wart shaped like a nipple near Amina's left armpit. 'I've been busy. Besides, it's daytime.'

'Busy. So busy. Maulana Abul Razak is always busy.'

'It's been one thing after another. And so much washing to be done too, and then all those guns.' Abul Razak hears himself speak, but he is aware that his words are a little disconnected, though deliberately spoken, like a careful drunk's.

'I do all the washing here,' Amina says.

'But the guns? Buying them, hiding them, handing them out? And training the boys. It has been really tough.'

'You have conjugal duties to perform,' Abul Razak hears Amina say as if a lawyer has coached her.

He imagines a unique circus artiste who specializes only in conjugal duties. 'That's over,' Abu Razak says. 'The time for conjugal duties is over.'

'Ooh! Over. Everything is over for the Maulana.'

Is this really Amina? Her voice is hoarse. How people change and become strangers!

'Small things are over.'

'Only big things for the Maulana. Feelings are not small things, though; and you don't get over them so easily.'

'You haven't asked my permission.'

'Feelings are feelings. They don't wait for permissions.'

'Just get the required permission and all shall be well. Remember it is Friday today.'

'Feelings ko chhutti? Don't you have feelings on Friday?'

'Not without permission. Besides, I really must go.'

'You were staring at Fatima just now,' Amina says. 'Whose permission did you ask?'

'This is a dream. I don't think I am well. I must remind you, women are not supposed to speak their mind.'

'Not even in a dream? I want Usuf back,' Amina says between a whisper and a sob, a broken voice without a face. 'Usuf is the name of a feeling, not a dream, and I want him.'

'He is with Allah.'

'Everyone is with Allah. Usuf should be with me.'

'He did his duty and is gone.'

'Let's all be with Allah, then.'

Abul Razak stares at the day outside. It's all getting mixed up. He feels as if he is attending the wrong funeral. What lies between him and Amina? Silence. Their son's death. Obligations. Orders and obedience. A few nights of grunts and exertions. But not love. No overwhelming need to be with the other for a sense of completion of the self. Now, Fatima on the other hand ...

Fatima, Razak notes, is waiting, leaning seductively against a russet block of light which, on scrutiny, is a rock outcrop.

Fatima makes the landscape exotic, no question. No, that is not the thing either. It is as if she is the soul of things made visible. It appears to Abul Razak that Fatima is at once near and far. Though her features are clear, she seems to be stationed at a planetary distance; far, as ever, beyond reach.

'There's nothing between us, is there?' Amina says almost to herself. 'Nothing here? What to do? Where should we go?'

Her mouth is so close to Razak's ear that her breath tickles him. Abul Razak smiles. He is smiling at the smile which is spreading inside. The smile of love. He should be out there with Fatima. That's it. 'Everything is out there,' he says. He is through with all this. It is time to end and begin anew. A time to go away. A time to be free. 'Talaq,' he says to Amina, his mouth sour from Dr Zainuddin's medicines.

'You said something?' Amina asks, pulling the veil aside.

Abul Razak laughs all of a sudden. He is all right with this, now, and with everything, really. There is but one God and He is on his side. The whole world awaits him, as if it is his first day. 'Talaq, talaq,' he says again, with relish, with relief, as if it is his personal freedom chant.

The talaqs reverberate through the mosque's loudspeakers.

All of Sultanpur, Faridkot and Punjab must hear it. This is not called for, Abul Razak makes a mental note. This loudspeaker business is a bit too much. This is a personal matter, nothing to make a din out of. I don't mean Amina harm, she has been a dutiful wife, but unfortunately this has little to do with duty. This is something else, something to do with what I did not grow up to become, and in any case, it's not in my hands any more.

'No,' Amina says, stricken, 'this is a mistake.'

'All correct. Every answer correct,' Abul Razak says. 'I passed the exam with full marks. Ask the master.'

'You are dreaming,' Amina says. 'You make mistakes in dreams. No talaqs in sleep, please. You are not well, remember?'

'This is not in my hands. Not in my hands at all. Not this, not the guns. I am free and flying,' Abul Razak says with a light laugh which he hopes will make it clear to Amina that he means no ill.

Amina sits up and leans against the wall with a sob. She feels like a parcel coming apart. She raises one onion-smelling hand in defence of her marriage, and thinks of her father with whom she was great friends till the age of ten. Soon after, the burkha had intervened. 'You are a big woman now,' her father would say with a sad smile when Amina approached him to be cuddled, and Amina would feel small and confused because between father and daughter had dropped the curtain of serpents. He was not to touch her any more. He was, after all, man, and she, woman.

And then it was time for him to die, maybe from eating too much mutton.

One morning, her father had got up and, as was usually the first thing with him, had gone to the kitchen to get a glass of water. As he dipped the tall bronze glass into the earthen pot lodged in a pile of sand, he had fallen to the floor, dead. Gone. End of the man who loved Amina and mutton burra.

Everyone who is close to me will vanish fast, Amina thinks; I am here only to see people go. But she can only bring herself to say, 'Biryani is ready.' As if biryani would make things all right; restore order to her life.

Her husband smiles and shakes his head. He is in another world; one with gardens and streams and a full moon.

Amina lets her hand fall heavily, like a stone in a scum pond. I am finished, she thinks, I have no way of making sense of what is happening to me, except in terms of food and work and memories of loss; if someone had told me the story of my life when I was a child, I would have told him, that this is not me, it's someone else.

Amina lies on the floor, her face close to the wall. She runs a finger along the cracks racing on it like fault lines. She can't remember seeing them before.

Maulana Abul Razak's mat takes off with him on it, hovering over the small terrace for a moment, and is then afloat in the air, heading in Fatima's direction. The hour sways in the breeze, comes unstuck and is awash with lyrical possibilities. Abul Razak hears himself giggling, and the loudspeaker relays the giggle all over Sultanpur, Faridkot, Lahore, London, Mecca and Medina.

'So there you are, finally!' Fatima laughs.

Indeed, there he is. Maulana Abul Razak, supine on a mat, looking up at the only woman in his life.

Fatima offers a slim, smooth hand. 'Get up, then,' she says, all the scents of Arabia in her one breath.

Abul Razak touches the offered hand tentatively, like a flame, and then lets it go. 'I just divorced Amina.'

'Umm, we need to talk, maybe?'

'But how? You are married already.'

'Stupid man. What has marriage got to do with anything? Besides, my husband has been missing all these years.'

'Everything is possible, then?'

'Like life after death? We are living it, Maulana Abul Razak.'

'Your clothes reveal a lot.'

'Only what you want to see. And then, again, children can wear anything; especially in the afterlife.'

'It's against Islam.'

'Nothing in the Koran against Jordache jeans.'

'Not specifically, but—'

'Nothing is against Islam. Want to go watch a movie? We will have to go all the way to Faridkot, though, if you want to see anything new.'

'Fatima, you are the one for me. Will you marry me?'

'Divorce in the morning, nikaah in the afternoon?' Fatima smiles. 'I don't mind, except that you sent my favourite nephew to his death. Would I marry my nephew's killer?'

'Careful. The loudspeaker picks up everything.'

'Ashraf became a mujahideen after listening to you. He was sitting in the market square eating dates when you said Allah was waiting for the martyrs on the other side. "Oh, then only these dates separate me from Him," Ashraf said, and volunteered for the suicide squad for Kashmir. Your people gave him the usual six-month training. On the third day of the mission, he was killed in an encounter. Foolish boy. He was eighteen.'

'That's the way these things happen. I lost my son to Kashmir, too.'

'Hmm, men watch children die for Islam.'

'I just sent another batch of boys to Bombay. None of them will return.'

'Poor Maulana! Always fighting for something.'

'Kashmir is a cause.'

'Kashmir is an invention, Abul Razak. But we need to talk about the second batch you sent. My son, Salim, is a member of the team. I want him back.'

'They are on their way to Bombay by boat. Must have reached by now. Have you been on a ship ever? The nights are really strange on the sea.'

'Actually, Amina and I are even. We are even as far as feelings are concerned.'

'Feelings?'

'Movements of the heart.'

'I can't call off a suicide mission! The boys must have reached Bombay already.'

'It's getting dark. But the clouds are alive and there is colour everywhere. The world is brighter than we think. Why did you say the nights on the sea are strange?'

Abul Razak looks around. How true Fatima is! The day is getting over. Wasn't it noon just a moment ago? The sky is melting into a rare winter-line, shades of orange, blue, mauve and yellow spread out and merge in the west, a flowing emulsion of colours. A crescent moon is rising from an unlikely corner of the evening. A cool breeze tugs at the corners of Abul Razak's mat. 'You make everything different,' Abul Razak smiles at Fatima.

'It's the weather,' Fatima says. 'Let's take a walk around the school. I love the school. It's such a ruin in the twilight.'

Abul Razak rolls up the mat and tucks it under his arm. They walk up the street, counting the lamp posts—wrapped in garish movie posters peeling in the wind—from which the bulbs have all been stolen, or broken. All except the last one, which glimmers briefly just as they pass under it. 'Both of us did our second grade here, remember?' Abul Razak says.

'I remember the smell of urine in the backyard very well.'

'Ah, that. And the river used to flow closer under the gulmohars there.'

They go up the eighteen steps to the first terrace where a barrack of classrooms once stood. But now the roof has caved in and the walls are crumbling. The school is in ruins because everyone in Sultanpur prefers to send their children to madrassas, which give two meals a day along with education.

Abul Razak points to the fourth room in the row and says,

'Ah, there, my second grade.' He looks through a hole in the boarded-up window. 'They are all there!' he says aloud, surprised.

'You have to show the master your slate with all the English letters,' Fatima says. 'From A to Z.'

'Hussain just scrawled something and showed it to the master, and he didn't even look up. He just said, "Good, now you go out and play."'

'You don't do that. The master will catch you out.'

Abul Razak shakes his head. 'And Hussain doesn't know one thing!'

Abul Razak takes his slate out from his bag and writes 'A' like an arch caving in under its own weight. He sees neither meaning nor future in the letter. He wills himself to write 'B', and it comes out like a hastily strung bow.

Abul Razak puts his chalk down on the broken desk which bears a hundred scars from children's endless struggles with wisdom. He finds the idea of twenty-four more letters outlandish. They all sound so strange in his mouth. To prove just how strange, he says 'A' to himself. To his ears, it comes out like the scream of a lamb being slaughtered. Imagine a letter like that! No, he will take a gamble. Abul Razak makes dubious excoriations on the slate with his chalk and takes his offering to the master, all the time looking out of the door at Hussain throwing a small red ball high up in the blue air, and what's the bet he won't catch it on its way down?

The master looks up from his work. Both sides of Abul Razak's slate are covered with doodles. The master's spectacles are miraculously balanced on the small wart—a dark pebble—teetering at the very tip of his cliff of a nose. 'What's this?'

'Nothing,' Abul Razak says, genuinely shocked at what he has done.

'Is this English?' The master's face is red with rage. His mouth is working, but for what seems a long time, no sounds issue from the mastication.

'No,' Abul Razak says truthfully. 'This is not English.' What has he gone and done?

'I asked you to write A to Z of the greatest language in the world and you make a mockery of it?' the master says, drawing out a long cane wedged under his table. The tip of the cane is wrapped in rubber bands. He holds it high in the air like the sword of Tipu Sultan.

Yellow and green rubber, Abul Razak notes. He hopes Fatima will not mind his shame, though there is nothing between them.

'Go, show your beautiful work to each and every one,' the master screams. 'Everyone.' He swishes the cane hard in the petrified air.

Where the cane strikes, Abul Razak sees the air rise in red welts.

'And everyone spit at him,' the master roars. 'Spit, you all hear? I want spit.'

Abul Razak's legs are trembling. His calf muscles jump about.

There are twenty-three children in the class. There ought to be forty. But today there are only twenty-three. And so the master has written 23/40 on the top-left-hand corner of the blackboard. At the centre of the board is written ENGLISH in red chalk. The red indicates the importance that the master attaches to the subject.

'Take the slate around. Show the world what you have done to the English language,' the master shouts, pointing the cane at the class like a fencer about to cut and thrust. Fury has made the master theatrical.

Maulana Abul Razak walks to the first desk on the right and holds up the slate. Hanif Mohammed, his arch enemy—and a crook, to Razak's mind—looks at the slate, shows exaggerated surprise at the infamy by rolling his eyes, and spits at Abul Razak. A gob of sticky vengeance lands on his chest.

Razak moves to the next, holds up the slate for inspection. This time it is Hamid Quraishi, who takes a look at the slate and shakes his head, although he himself can't tell A from Z. To get his projectile right, he leans back on his hips like a contortionist and comes up with enough force to drill a hole in Razak's forehead, as the class breaks out in applause. And to think he had actually shared his lunch with him!

Soon, Abul Razak is dripping with spit, top to toe. He thinks of his mother, the seamstress of the village. Her uncomplaining ways, her desperate dignity, a pride shorn of all frills, and for the first time since the ordeal began, he feels a lump in his throat, hard as stone and as unforgiving.

I will not let my mother down. I will not cry. Watch me, you bastards, he thinks.

There is perfect silence in the class now, except for the noises of glottal exertions—a smelly beast perpetually clearing its throat.

Abul Razak walks around in a daze towards the girls' section, holding up his slate like a banner. There are four girls. The last one, next to the door, is Fatima. The three girls go through the motion of spitting at him, but they are too shy to do any real damage. Razak gets through them quickly.

He approaches Fatima, the twenty-third person—and, to his mind, the only real one—in the class. He has never been so close to her. So close, he can inhale the fragrance of her presence. It's like standing dazed right in the middle of a garden, Abul Razak thinks.

Through gummed-up lids, through taunts, through stink, through all the gibberish letters of the English language, through the veils of the world, through the various masks of himself, Abul Razak looks at Fatima, and he could faint.

Everything he will ever need is here. His eyes store her light for all time to come. He waits for her to do the honours and closes his eyes. But nothing happens. No wet blob lands on him. He opens his eyes, a little disappointed. She turns her head, meets his gaze with a sideways glance—whose revelation quickens Razak's heart—and winks at him. For some reason, the master doesn't force her to obey his instruction. Maybe she is too beautiful for coercion. Or perhaps her father, a glad-eyed sand contractor who single-handedly killed the Chenab, is too rich and famous in all of Sultanpur for spoiling Fatima silly with his affection.

Abul Razak makes his way back to the master. He doesn't look so angry now. 'Show me your right hand,' he says to Abul Razak, 'the hand that killed the English language.'

Abul Razak transfers the slate from his right hand to the left, and stretches his palm as if about to shake hands with the master over a difficult truce.

'Palm up,' the master says.

Abul Razak puts his palm up.

The cane comes down hard on it, thrice.

'Now get out,' the master shouts. The caning has somehow stoked his fury again. He is foaming at the mouth.

Abul Razak goes to his desk, picks up his bag, crosses the room and walks towards the door. Once there, he turns: a dark, heavy-set, thick-browed little boy who is unable to cry, and keeps his slate on the floor. You shouldn't hit a child, he wants to tell the master, each blow to the body is a word deleted from the dictionary. But it sounds too complicated; the idea is not clear in his battered mind. Instead, he says, 'I am not coming back.'

'Get out,' the master screams again.

'Allah doesn't speak English,' Abul Razak says quietly, addressing the whole class.

He walks out of the door, through a dark corridor, past the babel of other classrooms, down the steps, towards the river that is spread out like an endless carpet of light streaming out of Allah's merciful eyes.

NINE

The Tale of the Tub

'Once upon a place where it was always noon, a blade of grass found shade under a stone which was beaten red and yellow by the sun. It was neither willing nor wanting to grow beyond … '

Placid Hari Odannur hears a voice: slow, raspy and desperate, as if plugged into the voice box of a nightmare. It is his own, and it is inside his head.

Placid is still alive, but unable to move. Mother is to blame, he thinks in panic. All your suppressed instincts for thoughtless fun, dear Amma, will live after you in your son—if he survives *this*.

Why else would he drink the way he did last night and walk out with a tripping woman who looked like she suffered from PMS every day? A woman he hadn't met before, whose name he still did not know.

Placid spits out the soft stuffing in his mouth. His mouth is dry. He forces himself to be calm. He is not meant for crises. Not meant for extreme situations. Not meant to face his killer blindfolded. He wants to break into a scream. A scream so powerful that it will free him from his own stupidities. How on earth did he land in this mess? Surely this is the end?

He knows only too well that he is not the stuff of immortal fame; not the kind of talent that history will swear by during a crisis a thousand years from now; not the kind of writer whose lines people will recall in an emergency; not a turner of phrases that free fraught souls. But, surely, he still considered it his right to do enough to justify his presence on this precious planet? In any case, he has not foreseen death happening any time too soon. But clearly he is wrong—yet again.

When he had gone home to Kerala the fortnight before, he should have stayed on, given private English tuitions to students, and made good with the little money he made. But his mother, Ammini, had been insufferable with her fits of melancholy and her eternal anxiety that there was a way to live other than the one she knew—the alternative presumably marked by ceaseless celebrations, laughter and camaraderie. And, of course, there were her periodic attempts to end it all. ('Please, I have a right NOT to exist.' Yes, Placid thought, yes, but you exercise it too often, Amma.)

Placid would try to play down his mother's moods by not reacting to them, or—and this was less taxing—by staying in his room.

But when he did step out, Ammini would be waiting outside the door, ready to assail him with long spells of accusatory silence, her unique sideways glances—the whites crowding to one end, the eyeballs to the other, like a dog eating food guiltily—full of longing for his attention. Her genius for victimhood informed almost everything she did—even in the desperate embraces she was hourly addicted to, and which invariably upset his balance.

And. Worst of all, perhaps, she never failed him in her life-enterprise of making him self-conscious. He was her son! The boyfriend she never had! The man who should protect her!

Home was awful.

A week into his vacation, Placid couldn't take it any more. Each time he went home—saturated to sickness with Bombay's garish glitter, fly-ridden filth, the endless commuting, the milling crowd, the gut-wrenching abuse of the street children, the brown clouds that wafted with the winds of traffic and massed together at lights—he had thought he was through with Bombay. But three days at home was all it took to change his mind.

And so, once again, he had gone, seen for himself that nothing had changed. Neither he, nor his mother. And once again had he cut short his stay and caught that godawful train, the Kanyakumari Express; clambered into a compartment packed, like sand in a bag, with people, hens, mangoes, fish pickle, and the metal smell of urine in the aisle—a damp, yellowing, amoebic pool, collecting here and there on the floor, from which toxic fumes rose and spread in the steady heat of the incredibly high-resolution Indian sun.

His name—which he prefixed, to the disgust of his fastidious girlfriend Susan, with 'Placid' so that people remembered his by-line for its oddity, if not for the quality of his contributions—was on the reservation chart stuck on the rectangular black plate next to the door of the compartment.

It afforded him a twinge of pleasure to see his name featured on that faded printout. Only, it was misspelt. He had been rechristened Harry. But in full, the tag was still recognizably his own.

There were other names, too, on the chart—the train was, after all, a mode of public transport—but he found them without a face or a future; of no consequence in contrast to his name, which seemed to exude a potential that the ghetto-democracy of the train failed to suppress. He was unique; more than his circumstances.

Placid put his finger on his name and emphatically ran it across in a line to the extreme right, where his berth number was listed.

The flattering logic of the reservation chart, though, was deceptive. Despite the crowd, there was a semblance of order for the duration of the day. But once the train crossed the Kerala state border and the night gathered, the reservation list had quickly turned into a tattered collection of hieroglyphs. Ticket-less hordes had torn the list to pieces. The bits that survived flapped in the wind like little white wings pinned to the wall. Too much demand, too little supply; too many people, too few seats.

Soon, Placid's berth was taken over by a group of smelly mendicants in red robes and dreadlocks. He got up from his seat and moved in contempt to the vestibule, hoping his magisterial action would put the usurpers to shame, but they didn't so much as look in his direction.

He hung around the toilet area for some time, but found the smell radiating from it overpowering. Placid's utter contempt for—even fear of—Indian toilet habits was reinforced. His countrymen did not believe in flushing the tank. They hoarded their waste. Perhaps they were conserving water from a congenital habit of thrift? In any case, he had always thought the idea of passengers crapping through a hole in the floor strange in these times of vacuum and chemical toilets. Imagine, he thought as he turned away from the toilet enclosure to his seemingly expropriated berth, a million passengers defecating up and down the country at hundred kilometres an hour!

The train chugged on. Its repetitive rhythm dulled Placid's

senses. Entangled in a forest of limbs, inhaling the acid fumes of alien body secretions, his self slowly dissolved. He became just another commuter. One among a throng of desperadoes who would die for a different life, a quality-refugee who had fled Kerala, the Cartoon Land of Communism.

Fully grown Keralites, Placid knew, talked of Marx and Mao, Lenin and Stalin as if the august personalities had just got up and left their favourite parlour chairs for a walk and, fantastically enough, the imprint of their posterior was hot and clear on the cushions for the believers to see and marvel at, and perhaps to inhale—as part of an exercise in nostalgia—the vinegar vapours of the Revolution.

To flee from the fictive place, Placid rode that train like a rodeo for fifty-one hours, a detour in universal chaos: sped by stations limned by lanterns; past the phantasmagoria of stark backlit landscapes; round a barren river bed where an old man put his hand between the legs of a young girl squatting to pee; raced with cratered ravines lowered directly from the loft of Mars; past the mirage of one-horse towns suspended in dust and sunlight; shot by carcasses of cows hanging upside down from windows; past giant, bald trees clutching at the air as the train sped by; through emerald paddy fields kissing the straw feet of crucified scarecrows; skirted mustard fields that flamed as if out of Van Gogh's brush; trundled past a procession of naked ascetics over a bridge in the gloaming. Visibly aged, Placid got off the time-travelling machine at the massive obduracy in stone, Victoria Terminus, which the British had built with that false sense of permanency so typical of urbane conquerors.

Placid took in the fetid, humid air of Bombay like a bullet in the face: the smell of freshly caught fish in ice-packed wicker baskets that dripped all over the platform, the unmistakable vapours of sulphur from burnt tyres, shit and spit. He made his way through the vaporous haze and waved down an old Fiat cab with a battered black body and yellow top.

He told the cabbie where to go, and rolled the window glass down. The narrow street leading to his quarters had taken on a dull grey sheen in the sad, beaten blue light before the day broke through telephone wires. He noted six crows on a pole, tight as a cross-stitch, three showing their beaks, three their backs. When he reached home, he found it a dusty mess, but he successfully resisted the urge to clean it up. A cold shower and a coffee later, Placid was right back in the life of the city, the open prison which he had fought so hard to flee.

When it was past ten, he called up Shantanu Roy, editor of the tabloid *Bombay Express* ('Make the Most of Where You Live'), who won everyone over by repeatedly taking out and replacing his dentures in his mouth. One minute they were in his mouth and sitting on the table the next, laughing at a joke. Placid apologized for returning earlier than scheduled and asked, without much hope, for work though half a dozen of his articles were pending with Roy. Or maybe the oily haired Mrs Kulkarni—Roy's mistress and deputy, the one whose gaze made him feel like an old sofa—was sitting on them.

'Sure. Meet Arun Kanetkar and do a profile. His latest book is about to be released. Need it by six in the evening. Around 1,000 words.'

'Today?'

'Everything today. There is no tomorrow.'

Click. The dentures had remembered a joke and were coming out to appreciate it. Six was a close call. Though the feature was probably meant for Sunday. But Placid, like a good freelancer, didn't argue. 'Sure, will do,' he said.

As soon as he put the phone down, he went into hyperactivity. Made calls, did the research and met with the reclusive poet whose voice sounded like he had grown tired of the world that he was translating into poetry.

Later in the evening he went to a cyber café and keyed in his copy, which turned out to be more than 1,000 words, but what the hell. As was his habit, he punched the keys for a printout. Then he selected matter, control+A, and pressed his finger hard on Delete. He couldn't explain it. He watched the screen go blank. No, his mouth said. But no voice came. In panic, Placid pressed control+Z, to bring it all back from nothingness, but somehow he knew it wouldn't work. And it didn't.

Damn, he thought, damn. This was the story of his life. Always, some final careless gesture that undermined all the hours that he had put in. Some slight stupid thing that he did which forced him to begin again from scratch. He was his own worst enemy. He couldn't remember one word of what he had written. I suffer from dementia, he thought. But printouts? Surely, he had asked the computer for printouts?

He rushed to the printer, and there lay in the tray three neatly typed sheets. All his! He ran his eyes quickly down the sheets. Yes, it was all there! He could have wept. He folded the sheets; thrust them into his hip pocket. He patted the stuffed pocket and was reassured: the sheets were there, tight and snug. He called up Roy. Could he bring the matter tomorrow, please? Placid braced, but Roy said, 'Yes, but before three p.m.' Placid thanked him and, humming, made his way to the Sheraton.

And woke up in a bathtub that didn't belong to him.

TEN

One Foot in Heaven's Door

Salim steps out of the restaurant. Tropical sunlight and industrial sounds fall around him like shutters, caging him in. There is no escape from anything now. He is exhilarated at the finality of the prospect. His nostrils tickle. The salt in the air mixed with fish and silt and the fecund smell of earth characteristic of reclaimed areas suspire from the surroundings. Salim sneezes in acknowledgement.

It is a new city for Salim, but he has done enough in it already to feel as if he has been around for a long time. A very long time. His toes itch, his body is bathed in sweat, his eyes smart from salts. The humidity in the air stirs against his senses like a curtain soaked in hot water. The world he has come to die in is a moist place, seeping away inexorably. A world in which everything, sooner or later, turned to water.

It is not just the heavy, sodden air. Right beneath where he stands, if he puts his gun down and digs with his hands, soon enough, he will see the sea, shorn of its blue beauty, exacting its due. Dark water rising, frothing faintly at the mouth, sucking at the foundations of the tall buildings. A gentle to and fro movement of the waters that will eventually take back everything wrested from it. The certain wetness that seeps out of the city—from humans, buildings, roads, giant hoardings of movie stars and TV serials—could be mistaken for the usual coastal humidity of Karachi. But there is a rank finality about it in Bombay, like a corpse sweating its last salts: the saline signature of mortification.

Suddenly, Bombay's rumble—a farrago of machine and man-made sounds, a cacophony of barely salvaged catastrophes—takes life in Salim's ears, as if a drop of water clogging his ears for hours had rolled out on its own.

Salim can hear again, and with clarity. Each sound clear and separate, like words on a page. The screech of a car, the cawing of crows, a rickshaw backfiring, a window behind him coughing out glass and collapsing in the wreckage of the restaurant, and an invisible boy shouting himself hoarse for alms: 'Ya Allah, Ya Allah.' Good to hear God's name so far from home, Salim thinks.

A silent crowd gathers around the gate of the private drive leading to Breeze, watching him, forming an eddying circle. Salim's gun has turned him into a spectacle in a country perpetually hungry for distractions, just like Pakistan. The subcontinental time-pass gene that morphed quotidian events into blockbuster shows is at work. Potentially, anything—murder, rape, accident, even chit-chat that is at a distance convenient enough to be overheard—is spectator sport.

Often has Salim seen that gene at work in his own home terrain: a truck breaks down in the middle of nowhere. The news, like a virus, radiates through the very air. People drop what they are doing and trudge towards the event.

There they stand in the heat, in rain and in snow: a ring of ragged people taking in the event of a mere man challenging his lot by changing a tyre; the onlookers shuffling on their feet, watching how the jack is cranked into place, how the spare tyre is rolled and fitted in, how someone stands on the spanner and tightens the nuts, how the calf muscles strain and stretch. Will he succeed? Doubtful. Will the hub hold? Equally doubtful.

The outcome of all enterprise is, like their existence, doubtful. A condition of anxiety and despair defines each moment of their lives. A racial software adapted to eternal poverty and compatible with all the grim implications of hopelessness: a survival mechanism in a land that allows for neither relief nor promise, and vengefully accommodates a certain subsistence.

But behold! The truck moves again! The fault has been fixed. Destiny relents inexplicably. The spectators shake their heads at the mysterious ways of Providence. They are almost disappointed. If the man had failed, it would have proved how pointless it is to even attempt to fix a tyre. Or set off on a journey in the first place. But the show is over. And, incredibly, against all odds, the crowd has lost. The majority has been arsed. Democracy in danger! The circle breaks up in confusion. For a long moment, they were loosely one, united by a broken-down truck and the prospect of witnessing failure. Alas, the truck is back on its feet, raising dust and lurching forward, fleeing the land of the lost. One man's triumph has driven a wedge into the heart of their team spirit.

The villagers slowly walk back to their trades: earthen pots, terracotta idols, oracular parrots, magic oils. Back to digging wells, chipping stones, butchering sheep, selling herbs, pushing peacock oil; back to prayers, drunken bouts. The kind of things they have been doing since the Harappa civilization, for close to 3,500 years.

Salim holds his gun down, pointing it at the ground, and walks towards the crowd, which parts for him. An exodus of one.

'Are you a commando?' someone asks him.

'No, he looks too young,' says another.

'Of course he is a commando. Maybe a Black Cat. Look at the gun.'

Salim reaches the road and waits, one hand on his hip, the other holding the AK-47, guarding his faith. One foot in heaven's door, the other in an alien city in an enemy country.

ELEVEN

A Man Who Might Die before He Knew How to be Happy

Placid feels himself with his elbows, which seem to him the only parts of his body he can move without dire consequences. He is naked. Naked. And soon he will be dead. Naked and dead. And he doesn't even know why.

His throat is parched. He tries to move and finds himself in knots. Naked, dead and trussed up. He recalls his mother's parting words: 'It's not that you are going away. It's that you are going away to Bombay, leaving me in this dump.' As if Bombay were New York or something. As if this city is fun at all. Look at the fun he is having just now. One whale of a time, waiting for his executioner.

In his mind, Placid replays all the murder scenes he has seen in movies. But nothing matches the terror of the tub and the silence broken by the traffic down below. Where is his kidnapper? And what does she want? Why him?

Placid squirms into a half-sitting position and knocks his head against a tap. He presses his head against it till a trickle of water issues out of it. Placid drinks some, and lets it run over his head. He feels a little better.

He thinks of her: the way she undressed while he foolishly accepted the drink she offered at around four in the morning; the way she took her long, grey-streaked hair down, all the while looking at him with her great worry-worn eyes, as if they had met before, and undid her buttons. She had a nice, slim body all right. Nice body! Slim body! Please, she was beautiful.

Placid becomes aware of a stirring down below. He is beginning to have an absurd, unstoppable erection. He is a moment or two away from certain death, but his body doesn't buy it. Oh hell, Eros in the face of Thanatos!

Placid tries to think of dire things like the holocaust, Osama bin Laden, bombs on a Bombay train, George Bush in military uniform, all of which only stoke his fires. He has a massive erection, no question.

Shame on you, Placid, he tells himself, mortified. With any luck, the tumescence will be tamed before his kidnapper arrived. Surely, God will not subject him to the dreaded experience of his execution even as he fights the humiliation of an erection? He feels like Job fingered all over again by a bored god.

Placid hears voices in the room. Actually, a single female voice talking to itself and expecting compliance. A south Indian voice. Brahmin, Tamil Nadu. Tam Bram. She doesn't sound like the one who honey-trapped him last night. Rescue? Or, relapse? Who knows if it is not a whole team of perverts arriving to have fun at his expense? A bunch of female Hannibal Lecters?

Really, he should have stuck to that clean, green land after all. What is it to him if people cultivate the myth of Marxism and march to the music of the '*Internationale*'? Everybody has to have a belief, a faith to forge a kinship, the ennobling sense of selflessness that supporting a cause releases, a frame of reference to handle the mysteries of life. Marx or Mohammad does not matter. There may be nothing at the end of it all, just as there was nothing in the beginning. Meanwhile, there are sixty or seventy years to live, depending on which country you are born in. And you try to be extra careful in a city like Bombay where you get shot if you live on the wrong side of the street. You live those years the best you can. And if your fellowmen have found a lifeline in an ideology that sounds superbly righteous over a drink in a bar, or under a razor in a barbershop, why not? You don't have to take it seriously.

And what if his mother rehearses her tragic acts before him as if he were a select audience? As if he is to blame for her lot? That is what women in general and mothers in particular do. Every Indian mother he knows abuses her children out of love. She screams. She pinches. She punches. She blackmails. Why? Because I llow them too much. Because it's for *their* goood. Llow justifies everything.

Placid considers himself a victim of maternal neuroses. But there is no need to take his mother to heart. Or Susan, with whom he bitterly quarrelled and parted ways. People are the way they are. They are their own burden.

He could have sold the little property that he has and rented a house up in the hills or maybe down in the backwaters. Lived his life in splendid isolation, watching the light shift on grass, the bananas swelling in silence, the congregation of fish in prayer under water; he could have lived away from the heartless ironies of urban India.

It has taken billions of years to forge him in the fire of the stars, and he doesn't have to live as a mere complex of responses to synthetic social stimuli. All he needs to do is to overcome his niggling need to be a famous journalist. Fame, social acceptance on a grand scale ... surely that is the name of his defining problem?

He had thought that affirmation and acceptance were possible only in terms of others. But it now struck him that the truth was that questions and answers are all within one's own power. Each to his own, as the Buddha said. Own or disown each to each. If only he knew how to look within!

Instead, he tried to play ball with the world like a coward and where has that got him? In a bathtub shaped, remember, like a coffin. And soon he would adorn it with his own corpse. One, nevertheless, with a now reinforced, rigor-mortified erection.

Smart of him, yes?

Except, he would be hacked to pieces and packed into a suitcase and Our Lady of the Dark would lug it around until she found a place to dump it, and the worms would throw a party. End of the short, unhappy life of PH Odannur. A man who died before he knew how to be happy. Wonderful, Placid recalls the characteristic expression of an overly appreciative TV anchor, very wonderful. Everything is wonderful to the anchor.

'Lakshmeee!' A high-pitched, invitational voice meant to break down all conventional distances between two people makes its presence felt. Placid can sense tendrils and creepers with little phonemic roses climbing all over the air. 'Lakshmeee,' trills the voice again, 'eet ees mee, yuvar diyar friend Githaa!'

Fear freezes Placid's heart. What if this is one of the vampire spirits who suddenly seem to have taken over the city? Only last week, he had read in the newspapers of a doctor who, tired of the demands made on her by her lover, had administered him sedatives, cut him up, and packed the body into a suitcase. Afterwards, she hired a car and went around for two whole days, looking for a place to lose her love. On the third day, the exhausted driver alerted a passing cop, and then sat under a low, grey sky and wept. All the while, the lady in the car stared ahead, one hand protectively laid across her reeking burden.

Placid foresees sharing a similar fate. Rest in Pieces. Wonderful. Very wonderful. If the suitcase option doesn't by some chance materialize, Placid can still see the sinister face of fate following him with a sneer even after death. In the blindfolded dark, he can make out with startling clarity the headlines rolling hot off the press: 'DEAD MAN FOUND IN TUB WITH DICK UP', 'COCKY JOURNO DROWNS IN TUB'. Finally, he is going to be a headline. Just his luck that he won't be around to enjoy it.

'There ees no one 'ere?' Githaa says to herself in disbelief. 'See, how careless Lakshmee ees, the milk ees lying autside, the fan ees awn …'

Placid decides it's safe to make his presence known. The soliloquies sound harmless. He tries to pinch his penis, the perpetual source of his shame, into submission, but it's an organ with a mind of its own and stands up to its tormentor. Never mind, better to be embarrassed than to end up dead. 'Help,' he shouts, 'please help.'

'Ai ayyo!' exclaims Githaa equally loudly, after a shocked pause. 'Woo ees thees?'

'Placid,' says Placid, aware of the inadequacy of the explanation.

'Whaat eet ees? You are een thee baathroomm?'

'Yes. Please help me out of this place.'

'Wot you aar doing een thee baathroomm?'

'Somebody brought me here. I am all in knots.'

'Howw ai know you aar a good man?'

'I promise.'

'Whai Lakshmee put you een thee baathrooomm?'

'Honestly, I don't know.'

'Ai'll come een?'

'Please, but I am naked.'

'Howw ai'll come een, thenn?'

'It doesn't matter. Just come in, please.'

'You aar reallee naked? Joking, noo?'

'Yes. No!'

'If ai help you, Lakshmee weel be angry, noo?'

'She will kill me for sure ... once she is back. Is she crazy or something?'

'Ai'll come een and see. Wokay? Don't vorry, ai'll keep mhai eyes closed. Wokay? Ai need to see if you aar a wokay person. Wokay?'

'I swear I am an okay person. Just free me, and I'll never come back anywhere near here. I won't press charges against your friend either.'

'You close your ice alsoh, wokay?'

'Wokay.' Placid finds himself imitating Githaa. 'I am blindfolded anyway.'

'You cannot see mee then.'

'Could you take this blindfold away?' Placid says, beginning to feel lucky.

'Ai yyam verry pretty, you knowh.'

'Of course. But I'd like to see for myself.'

'But whai Lakshmee has done thiss?'

Placid resigns himself to further humiliation. He feels helpless. There is the sound of the bathroom door opening, the swish of a sari, a whiff of Mysore sandalwood soap and talcum powder.

'Woh, mhai god,' says Githaa.

'Sorry.'

'Woh, mhai god, wot ees thees?'

'I am really sorry. I'll explain everything if you just free me and give me my clothes.'

'Ai cannot do that, you knowh. Lakshmee weel bee angry. Ai yyam herr best friend, you knowh. Ai haw a key to herr house, you knowh. She ees a creeyativ purrson, verry careless, so ai take cayr of thee house. Ai yyam herr neighburr, you knowh.'

'Yes. I just want to get out from here. I am afraid.'

'Then whai you aar getting erectionn?'

Placid doesn't know.

'Thinking of Lakshmee? She ees beauttiful, you knowh. But this ees very bad of herr.'

'I know.'

'Wot you doing in Bombay?'

'I am a freelance journalist.'

'Not a robarr?'

'No, no, not a robber. Now if you will let me go ...' Placid doesn't quite know how to complete the sentence. All he knows is that this is, as they would say in a Hollywood movie, a situation.

'Ai yyam married, you knowh?' Githaa says.

'Please let me go, please.'

'Howw ai'll knowh you aar not a robarr and that you aar a jarnalisst?'

Placid thinks furiously. He never carries a card. His mind skids and slips all over the place, like a desperate axe looking for purchase on a sheer wall of ice. Kanetkar!

'I have in the hip pockets of my jeans a copy of what I wrote for *Bombay Express*. You could read it, talk to the paper's editor for reference.'

'Hmm,' Githaa says, 'ai read a lot, you knowh. Ai like Tamil short stories verry much. You write stories alsoh?'

'No, no stories.'

'Where yuvar pants aar?'

'Um, I don't know. Lakshmi must have kept them somewhere.'

'Let mee see.'

A few tense moments later, Placid hears the rush of sari sailing through the air again. Githaa is back. He hears her drop his jeans on the floor.

'Three pages?'

'Yes, yes, yes.'

'You wrote eet?'

'Yes, yesterday.' Yesterday seems to Placid very far back in the past. He has met so many strange women since. Or so it seems to him.

'Wokay. Ai'll read eet, wokay?'

'Yes. But if you could …'

'Sailaynce,' Githaa says, and starts reading Placid's copy aloud:

HEADLINE: OUT OF THIS WORLD

INTRO: *The reclusive poet Arun Kanetkar has just finished his master work,* Tear Lines. *Placid Hari Odannur meets the writer to figure out the man behind the mystery of his words.*

The Military Café and Beer Bar is a rather run-down Irani restaurant on the crowded Ash Lane off Flora Fountain in downtown Mumbai. The café's small tables are covered with yellow plastic sheets with Canada Ice logos. It is one of the very few places in this wide world where you could meet the poet, Arun Kanetkar. There was a time when he used to sit out Thursday evenings with his friends at Wayside Inn, a quiet place across the road from the National Gallery of Modern Art. Widely perceived to be a recluse, Kanetkar is a warm

> person who has done away with contemporary lifelines such as telephones, wristwatches and TVs …

Despite the crisis, the sound of his words soothes Placid. Yes, he had written them. And they were good words. He would be happy to own up to them any time. All too briefly, a sense of well-being washes over him: he is probably the best writer Roy has ever had, even if he doesn't admit it.

'Hmm,' Githaa says, raising her eyes from the loose sheets of paper.

'You see? I wrote it.'

'Ai yyam not underrsttandinng yeverything.'

'Please …'

'Whai Kanetkar ees not wearing a woch?'

'Some people are like that.'

'Poyets aar crranky, you aar telling?'

'I don't know if I am saying that.'

Githaa flips to the last page and begins reading again:

> Kanetkar and I part at the entrance of the Military Café. I take a few steps and turn to watch the poet leave in his round-necked maroon T-shirt, grey pants and well-worn brown shoes tied around the ankles. He walks somehow separated from his surroundings: loose-limbed, keen-eyed, a little hunched. It is almost as if he is hiding himself from the world, protecting the flame within from the mean winds of change. Protecting the Word. It's more than a man can do. But Kanetkar is more. He is a poet.

'You didn't read the whole thing!' Placid feels betrayed.

'You wrote eet forr *Bombay Yexpress*?'

'Yes.'

'It's a good papper?'

'Just another paper. But they pay well.'

'Howw much they pay?'

'Depends.'

'You aar stayying alone?'

'Yes. Look, Mrs Githaa, please, please let me go before Lakshmi turns up.'

'Hmm, ai still don't know you wrote eet, you knowh?'

'Ask the editor, Shantanu Roy.'

'But, how ai know hee ees thee yedittar? Yenybudy can pickkup thee phone! See, thees vill tayke taime. And Lakshmee weel bee yangry if ai let you go. Ai vill talk to Lakshmee in the yevening. Now ai reely have werk to do, wokay? Nuthingg will happen to you, wokay? Ai promise, you knowh?' Githaa caresses Placid's face in a gesture of reassurance.

Placid listens to the rustling of Githaa's sari as she gets up to go. The fragrance of Cuticura powder fades from the surroundings, and Placid's penis, like a barometer of suffering, shrinks in acknowledgement of his helplessness.

TWELVE

Cows and Other Wild Animals

Something closely related to the Indian cow is advancing towards Sunil Shinde.

'This is going to be trouble,' he tells Lakshmi in the mirror.

Through the windshield, Shinde can see a procession waving saffron flags and cutouts of a cow and a calf, singing Vedic chants and shouting anti-Muslim slogans. At the very front of the procession is a massive, decked-out cow. The cow is a holy animal for the Hindus but, for reasons Shinde can never figure out, not the goat or the hen, though both come across as equally ancient, useful creatures.

Shinde is not one to pick arguments with given wisdoms, though. Better people than he had settled on the cow as an animal of heroic proportions, and he is content to go along with it.

The Cow Sena is not directly affiliated to the Shiv Sena. But with the elections coming up, there could very well be an alliance between the two. Certainly, both Hindu right-wing parties considered the cow holy, and located her at the centre of Hindu history. Still, what exactly made the cow right-wing politically (as was, inexplicably, its foe the tiger, Shiv Sena's heraldic animal) was an abiding mystery to Shinde.

And now, a visibly excited Cow Sena, shaking its horns and raising its tail, is staging a procession, right up the road, demanding a ban on cow slaughter, pressing for the declaration of the cow as an endangered animal, affirmative action for Brahmins, and promotion of Cow Cola, a soft drink based on the therapeutic cow urine—which the Cow Sena will market aggressively to the detriment of Coke and Pepsi, whose toxic properties are slowly enervating the Indian youth. COW NOW, says one of the leading banners. Shinde has no opinion on the matter. He knows the cow to be a dangerous dog. A beast that follows no rules. Right now, though, his priority is to beat an alarmed retreat from the cow—its forehead emblazoned with a plate of gold, saffron powder and flowers—leading the procession.

'You believe in cow?' Shinde asks Lakshmi in the driver's mirror. Lakshmi, he thinks, is more his type. The other one is beautiful, but in a curls-loose, claws-out sort of way which he finds just too intimidating.

'What?' Beverly asks.

Shinde shakes his head. No, he'd rather avoid this one.

'What's that crowd?' Lakshmi asks.

'The Cow Sena. You ever drink Gau Ark?'

'Gau Ark?'

'Cow's holy urine. Good for health.'

'No, not had holy urine yet. Actually, we prefer coffee. The road is blocked ahead,' Beverly says.

'Good for fever and joint pains,' Shinde can't resist.

'You must take it next time you run a temperature. I think you should take a turn now,' Lakshmi says.

'Never go to a doctor again,' Beverly puts in. 'When sick, look for a cow with its tail up.'

'No,' says Shinde, 'it's not like that. They are going to put it in a bottle and sell it. Cow Cola. CC. They will add sugar and colour. It's all in the packaging, let me tell you.'

'Sure. You really need to turn back. Looks like a big procession to me,' Beverly says.

'I know another way,' Shinde says, turning the three-wheeler around. 'Do you think the cow should be our national animal?'

'I don't know if the cow is that important,' Lakshmi says.

'The cow is important. There is no doubt about that. It is a symbol of prosperity.'

'And now medical care.'

'Are you Hindu?'

'She is Hindu. I am Christian,' Beverly intervenes.

'Christians are all right. But Muslims—' Shinde says.

'Which route are you going to take now?' Lakshmi asks to divert Shinde's attention.

'Up Pali Hill and around to Breej.'

'What have you got against Muslims?' Beverly says.

'They eat beef.'

'So do Christians and a lot of Hindus that I know.'

'Not the same.'

'How do you mean?'

Shinde shakes his head. He is not sure why *Muslims* eating beef is different from *Hindus* and *Christians* eating beef. There is a reason, he is certain. 'Muslims eat beef compulsorily. It is in the Koran,' Shinde says vaguely and tries to drown his words in a storm of honking.

'You are going too fast,' Beverly says.

'Time is money.' Shinde grins, looking at Lakshmi in the mirror, and narrowly missing a motorcyclist. He screeches to a halt at the feet of a young, bearded man with a gun. A crowd hangs around the place. The restaurant itself is in ruins. Shinde is puzzled that the landscape seems altered. Undaunted, he announces to his passengers with characteristic cheer: 'Breej.'

THIRTEEN

The Great Indissoluble Indian Marriage

Githaa knocks on Rajgopal's door. Why does her husband lock it from within? Always locking-locking. It occurs to Githaa that her husband is constantly shutting her out. It is as if, after all these years, he still has a world of his own, one full of secrets. This she considers an insult to her sacrifices for him, acts ranging from kitchen services to counselling him during crises. How he takes her for granted! She's like a smile unappreciated in the dark.

'Do you knowh wot's going on 'ere?' Githaa shouts from this side of the door to Rajgopal, who is clawing at the computer, which seems to have hung.

'Hell,' Rajgopal says, looking at the screen, sick. The screen shows a 'big boobed Latino giving head to her friend's lover'. Rajgopal has been spending time on online porn sites since his retirement last year from a charity firm WISH, where he had put in close to twenty years as coordinator. 'Coming,' he says, his eyes stuck to the unknown Latino adulteress whose mouth is clamped on an equally unknown cock. He wonders if he would recognize any of the porn stars on the road if they walked past him. Would anyone? Rajgopal gets up from his chair with some discomfort as his left knee is arthritic. Age, he thinks, there is no walking away from it. He tries closing the tab again, in vain. 'Oh oh,' he says.

'Appa,' Githaa says, beating on the door now with open palms in rising frenzy. 'Please wopen thee door. So much ees happening 'ere and you haw disappeared from the arth. Wot you aar doing there, ai'd like to knowh. And you aren't evan gaynfully yemployed.'

'Nothing,' Rajgopal says, pulling at the plug which threatens to come out along with the socket. It has always been a faulty power point, and Rajgopal has been planning to change it for long. 'Coming,' he shouts. He leaves the plug alone, grabs a towel from the rack and drapes it over the computer. He pats down his shock of spiky, iron-grey hair, adjusts his Bermudas up over his paunch and opens the door. He stands, hands spread out, clutching the door frame, blocking Githaa's entry. 'Yes, yes, what's it now?' he says, affecting impatience. He holds his butt back so that his half-erection is not conspicuous.

Githaa stares at her husband in confusion. Rajgopal's forehead is glistening with sweat; his wide-set lotus-eyes are glazed. His lips are dry, and his goatee appears to have been freshly dyed. I could have married better, Githaa thinks, two-and-a-half decades too late into her great, indissoluble Indian marriage. Married someone who read a little and who sweated less, perhaps. Someone who discussed with her the news headlines in the morning over a cup of coffee, someone who made love at least on festive occasions like Diwali or New Year.

'Whai you standing thair laik Christ without thee cross? Thee world ees von fire.'

'What happened?'

'Thair ees sumvon in Lakshmee's house.'

'Someone in Lakshmi's house! Who? Why?'

'Hee says hee ees a jarnalisst.'

'Must be to interview Lakshmi.'

'Appa, he ees in the bathtub, wokay?'

'Oh. Not a journalist then. But why?'

'He ees a jarnalisst and he ees all tied up.'

'My god.'

'And he ees naked, Appa.'

'Can't be! You saw?'

'Wot you mean, can't be?'

'Can't be.'

'You just close that door of yuvars, sit thair and say can't be.'

'I was doing some work.'

'Wot werk, ai'd laik to knowh, wokay? Werk! Wot you doing in yuvar room anyway, Appa?'

'Some insurance policy work. Paperwork.'

'That ees a brand-new towwel you have hung on thee computer. Let me puttit back in the cupbird.'

'Oh, I forgot, the towel is a mistake. I'll put it back myself.'

'Ai didn't know we aar inshuvard.'

'We are insured. Don't worry.'

'Laik eef something happens to us …'

'What can happen to you? Things happen to men.'

'Verry bad attitude, Appa, verry bad.'

'You are getting influenced by Lakshmi, I'm noticing.'

'Lakshmee ees good, wokay?'

'Then why is she working for some sex company?'

'That ees her bisiness. People haw to do things to get by.'

'Have you seen what she writes?'

'Never mind what shee writes.'

'If I wrote what she writes, you wouldn't like it, let me tell you.'

'Lakshmi ees different, Appa.'

'Sure, that's why she's got a naked man in her tub?'

'Thair hass to be a reason.'

'If you are very different, you don't need a reason maybe. Why has she tied him up?'

'Ai don't know, Appa. How would ai knowh? Should ai let him go?'

'Maybe they are playing a game or something? Just don't get involved.'

'You come then with mee and talk to him right away. Ai haven't locked the door.'

'Talk what? I don't know him.'

'Hee says hee was kidnapped laast night, Appa.'

'Don't believe it. Kidnapped! By a woman! Is he her boyfriend? No? Must be a thief, then.'

'Lakshmi doesn't haw a boyfriend. And hee doesn't look laik a theef. Just come with mee and see if hee can go.'

'What does a thief look like? Really, Githaa, this is none of my business.'

'Look, the man ees in danger, you knowh?'

'I know and I know. At least now you know your friend is mental? I am glad.'

'You coming orr not?'

'You go on. I'll be with you in a minute.'

'Poot that towwel back, please. It eess a new towwel and whai you haw poot eet over that computer ai don't knowh. Sometimes you act strange, Appa.'

'Don't worry about the towel,' Rajgopal says, thinking of the Latino girl. He waits for Githaa to go before closing the door to his room again. He must somehow shut down the computer before joining Githaa in the foyer and trying to figure out the mystery of the stranger in his neighbour's bathtub.

FOURTEEN

A Passenger Who Won't Pay

Salim sees the rickshaw as a sign. It had come at him at full tilt and stopped at his feet as if the driver had suddenly remembered something important. Salim wondered what mad man might be driving it. Perhaps he was drunk. Salim raises his gun. The driver smiles at him. Salim notices that the driver's lips are blood-red and that there are two women at the back. It is clear to Salim that the rickshaw was sent to him by Allah. And god knows he needs time to think; go somewhere safe, plan his next move. Salim points the gun at Beverly and Lakshmi. 'Move over.'

Beverly turns pale, then recovers. 'What do you think you are doing? Who do you think you are? This is our rickshaw.'

'If you talk again, you won't talk again,' Salim says without raising his voice.

'Come closer, Bev,' Lakshmi says, laying a restraining hand over Beverly's.

Salim gets in, bag over one shoulder, gun across his lap.

'Where do you live?' Salim asks Lakshmi.

'Zircon, Anderson Road.'

'Anyone staying with you?'

'Nobody,' Lakshmi stutters, and recalls too late the naked

and captive man in the bathtub. But she is too scared to correct herself. She doesn't want to provoke a man—a boy, actually—with a gun.

'Zircon, Anderson Road,' Salim tells Shinde. At Zircon, he will hold the two women and the rickshaw driver hostage and strategize. Shinde nods. He is nervous. He turns on the music.

'No music,' Salim says.

'No music?' Shinde switches the system off. 'Is that a real gun?'

'Just drive,' Salim says.

Is this guy a terrorist, that rare and mythical being? Shinde wonders. Is this guy a terrorist! Of course he is. Mr Sunil Shinde, Shinde addresses himself respectfully, you and your rickshaw are in trouble again. He shakes his head, half proud and half mystified by the hazards of his occupation.

BOOK II

ONE

Noises of the Night Opening

A SEASON IN HELL

Recently, the government banned Mujra, a courtesan dance form that had deteriorated into an excuse for soliciting. But, legal or not, Mujra is still very much in business, as Placid Hari Odannur finds out.

The October night is close upon me, like the hot breath of a sick animal. I hang around the crumbling, four-storey Old Congress House, behind Pakeeza Market, Central Bombay, waiting for Aseem to show up.

Mujra—a dance form that was originally all fast turns and rhythmic footwork—has dumbed itself down to a tease-art down the centuries. Here at Old Congress House, it has been reduced to women dancing, or singing Hindi film songs of longing and desire, most of it off-key ... and all of this in six or seven small rooms,. Old men with new hair pieces shake a leg to the songs and drink till they are senseless. The young strut in at irregular intervals. The girls finally go with the guys who throw the most money at them. If in the process things get nasty, the Mujra girls call in Aseem, who is my escort tonight. Aseem is a quiet, tough man with an impenetrable stare and a pleasant smile.

Outside, at the mouth of the narrow reptilian gully, Rashid runs his kebab place. The smell of masala-flavoured meat on coal-fire wafts through the night air. Next to the ovens, in the searing heat, children clang and wash heavy barbecue irons and frying pans. And all around, you can hear the noises of the night opening.

There are customers like Nilesh Bhatia, body builder and stock broker, who splurge up to a hundred grand a night in one of those stifling rooms. The Mujra girls fight over him with feline ferocity. But, usually, it is Chanda who gets to sleep with him.

Chanda's room is tiny, with a blue fridge and two ceiling fans. She is in her late forties and her fleshy attractiveness is slowly fading like an old, exotic flag. She has great masses of thick black hair, all the way down to her generous hips.

Chanda sits directly under the fan and, in an ostentatious display of wealth, pours down her hair on either side of her head and smiles. She is sweating profusely. As soon as she sits, her two musicians, generally referred to as ustads, materialize from behind a curtain. From behind the fridge appears Zainub, a subdued eighteen-year-old ghost of a girl, thin, dark, luminous eyed, with a make-up box in hand.

Chanda is a Mujrawali from Rajasthan. She makes around Rs 1000 a night from the dead art.

'I used to make Rs 10,000,' Chanda says. Her face falls at the memory of the days when she was the big draw.

I think she is going to cry. Instead, she sings an old Hindi film song in a strong, high-pitched, unpleasant voice.

After a while, the cockroaches start nibbling at our toes. We get up to go. It's five a.m.

'Ruk jao, raat to jawan hai,' Chanda says. Don't go yet, the night is still young.

'I'll be back,' I say. I pay Aseem for his trouble, but, strangely, he refuses to accept the cash. I catch a cab and go home. I have no intention of coming back.

TWO

Bombay Blues

Nirmal sits on a bench facing the road, half blowing, half killing an A.R. Rahman song on his red and silver harmonica, a gift from Robert Davis, the film-maker. A pitch-black crow struts close to his feet, its pink mouth open. Behind him is the sea. Across the road, in front of him, rise two tall apartment blocks, Zircon and Sea Star. Both buildings seem new and not fully occupied. The sun's rays are sharp off their polished glass facades.

Nirmal zips open a pocket of his backpack, finds the pair of large dark glasses he wore in a shot in Davis's movie, and slides his face behind them, instantly managing to look older than his sixteen years. In his bright yellow Polo shirt, blue jeans, red sneakers and dark glasses, he is overdressed—like a construction worker returning home from an overseas assignment.

When Nirmal met Robert Davis, the award-winning film-maker, for the first time over a month ago, he just had a plastic bag with one change in it and no underwear. Now he had new clothes and money in his wallet. He knew that the last few days at the Taj had softened him. He loved everything about the Taj: the fragrance of cleanliness; the cold bed linen; the trapped stillness of the room. This was the life.

Ah, and the bathroom.

The bathroom was where he belonged, he would tell himself as he lay down on the neat white tiles, a pillow under his head. He would cross his feet and wiggle his toes, smirking to himself. It was as if he had cheated destiny, got himself a deal which was not there in the original plan.

The first time Nirmal filled the tub with hot water, he had had a frantic time with the levers, taps and receivers. When he finally slid into the water in the tub, all of him had gone out in a sigh; he watched the room fill with vapour and turn mysterious like a museum of rare art, and read in the silent servitude of the fixtures and the pregnant blue vases next to the misted-over mirror the reason why people killed and loved and lied to make money.

Earlier in the day, after checking out, he had made his way to the exit, taken a full circle with the revolving door and come right back in. He sat in the lobby for long, staring at the day outside, psyching himself to return to familiar scenes of grime.

Outside, where he came from, the streets burned. The tar on the road lay half melting. When he walked on it, he sank a little and his footprints were clear on it. The sunlight was hard, yellow, unwavering. It was on him all the time, like a great torch held to his face, a whole sun burning just for him. Sweat seeped out of his body in a slow, steady tide. His soiled clothes stuck to his skin while, within, his heart shrivelled black.

Cease now, his heart rasped. But there was no ceasing. It went on. Permanent exposure. He could take nothing for granted. Everything he wanted for a normal life was a reminder of everything he lacked. So much of nothing. So much of it at daybreak, and so much of it at dusk. The nothing dawn. The nothing noon. The nothing night. He was the emperor of nothing. He did not know what to do with so much nothing. Or, how he came to inherit it. But it was all his. He trained himself to take each day's nothing as it came. One nothing at a time.

There were occasions when he stopped in his tracks, aghast at the grinding pointlessness of it. All of his life just came down to food. He *lived* hunger. His body trembled. His head spun. Hunger was an animal growing in his stomach, it growled, it snarled, and attacked from inside. He couldn't keep fighting it. He was weak. He was just a boy. He needed someone to take care of him. He sat on the road; he sat anywhere, it didn't matter. It was the end, and it was all he could do to wait for the beast to claw through his stomach and come out, so he could meet hunger in the flesh; shake hands with his enemy in person before dying.

Then, incredibly, his eyes lit on a slice of stale cake lying on the sidewalk, a grudged gift from heaven, a tattered message of hope from a relenting god. Chal, bachhu, enjoy.

Or, a foreigner walked up to him.

'Here,' she said, offering a can of Coke.

Nirmal stared at her, rolling the cold, condensing can over his burning forehead. A young girl with golden hair and blue, trusting eyes, who didn't know the first thing about the hellhole called Bombay, or that she could be raped by a cabbie before the night got over. A tourist from paradise, who paid to see misery first hand.

'Have it.' She smiled. 'Are you all right?'

She meant good. She probably thought this was a lean

patch Nirmal was going through. Only Nirmal knew that the lean patch was the only patch. There was no other.

Nirmal reached for the Coke, drank it up, closing his eyes. He didn't see her taking a snap of his, translating him into a postcard: a boy drinking Coke on an Indian road.

He got on his feet. He walked.

And with him walked, in step, a million good men and women. People with homes and food and quarrels and children and dogs. And, Nirmal thought, one of them was his father. One, his mother. There they went, in disguise as themselves. And though he could see them all marching by, he couldn't touch them. The good people were enclosed in a bubble. All of them, and all of it—their homes, restaurants, malls, movies, footballs and dogs—living happily inside the bubble. Nirmal pressed his face against the bubble till his nose flattened and he looked like someone else, but no matter how hard he tried, he couldn't break in.

So he went around it, walking about, stopping by, sitting down, scratching his head, always looking in, trying to find a way into the bubble, looking for a means of breaking it, perhaps with a knife, an axe, a gun, or with his bare hands. But it was impossible. The bubble barred entry like a fort.

Resigned, he looked away, and slowly turned his gaze to himself and was surprised that he too was unmistakably human despite where he stood, which was on the narrow ledge that went around the bubble, for he too had a face, a nose, two eyes, ears and a mouth.

He could, incredibly, even laugh; laugh at a fat man getting off a bike and landing on his butt on the road; laugh at a pair of slippers chained to a tree so they wouldn't be stolen; or at a performing monkey bowing in elaborate farewell to an abusive master before it took off into the trees.

Hope returned to Nirmal. Before the world blacked out and he collapsed, again, into a ragged puddle of barely breathing secretions plummeting through the dark spaces, he had to work his charms and make total strangers part with change so that he could buy vada pav. He had to stay in the game.

He looked around for the blue-eyed girl. A foreigner was more generous than an inured native, he knew. And, like a miracle, there she was, right behind him, following him, looking at him with concern.

He turned around and said softly, so as not to upset her: 'I need money. Just a little, for food.'

'What do you want to eat?'

'Vada pav, please?'

Vada pav was the core of Bombay's street life. It explained everything—the nature of Nirmal's life, the essence of his existence. It sought no information from Nirmal. It asked nothing of his antecedents, his name or religion. It was impersonal. All it asked for was five rupees.

'Yes, of course,' the girl said. She knew about vada pav from the Google homework she had done before landing in Bombay—a cake of spiced, mashed potato wedged inside a sliced bun. She was a traveller, not just a tourist like most fellow Americans. Tourists killed the places they visited, she believed.

She gave him a twenty-rupee note. It was nothing, she knew; it was less than half a dollar. But it was not clear to her what more she was expected to do. 'Take care,' she said, waving a taxi down.

Nirmal pressed the vada carefully between the slices which might have been buttered if he paid extra, and ate it hot. As his teeth sank into the bun and the mashed potato spread its life juice around his mouth, he watched the Bubble City move in its big, tinted-window cars, the rich kids blowing a cool grand with every cocaine breath they took, the boys looking like girls, the girls looking like boys, and some who were neither; the black-glassed limousines that trailed painted women, their tiny purses stuffed into their bras, past the dark, decrepit textile mills of Lower Parel; the red double-deckers with their ads on the back in which father, mother and two kids laughed around a tube of toothpaste; the dope-docks of Ballard Pier over which cranes, feathered with multicoloured hazard-beacons reared their heads like large birds; the lit-up hotels on Marine Drive looking like palaces about to drift out into the sea in the buffeting breeze; and the fluorescent Ferris wheels on Juhu Beach picking up speed over ships hulking out in the far dark.

And, suddenly, none of it registered. Neither the brittle, distant, planetary glitz of it all, nor its mindless, meticulous cruelty. What mattered was the sensation of some hot food going down the gullet and the stomach muscles relaxing, and the light winging back into his eyes. The world was suddenly brighter, like a lamp had been switched on in the dark. Vada pav had rescued Nirmal from total disintegration.

Nirmal had realized early on that begging in Bombay was big business, done by cartels, especially in areas around traffic lights. Nirmal avoided them. He focussed on Marine Drive, where young couples sat hand in hand on the parapet. Lovers always parted with money faster. Nirmal knew all begging was a kind of blackmail. You just had to make it sound like an appeal, so that egos were not hurt.

Nirmal presented himself as a caricature, an extreme version of penury and pathos. When he passed by a potential donor, he would slap his stomach hard—so it made a noise like a cracker going off—to show it was empty, and contrive to make a bleating noise between two slaps: one slap, one bleat, one slap. This was to show that he couldn't speak either. He was ugly, hungry and mute. To a halfway charitable Indian with a wallet, it was an irresistible combination of misfortunes that only small change could compensate.

During his begging days, before the movie and his career as a kebabwala's assistant, Nirmal would be up early. He would have his morning fix of vada pav and catch the 9.20 ladies' special from Churchgate to Grant Road. He always took care to hit the ground running. He would race up the steps of the over-bridge before ticket inspectors got into position at the Grant Road station.

Once out and safe, he would walk briskly to Alfred Cinema, behind which Aseem ran a beauty salon. The central feature of the salon was a red dentist's chair, which looked like some kind of a throne to Nirmal. Aseem ran a flourishing pimping and bodyguard business from the salon.

If a girl had to go to a stranger's house, and she was not sure of what to expect there, she would take Aseem along. He would hang around the joint for as long as it took. If there was trouble, he would get a missed call on his cell and he would be at the door with his knuckle duster. Aseem would get a cut out of the girl's pay for his services. And when he beat up an unreasonable customer, it was a professional job. He was never angry with the victim. In fact, there were occasions when he had escorted the broken and bleeding spirits to the doctor, bought them a drink and, a few days later, beat them up again.

Aseem kept pretty much to himself, Nirmal noticed. It was as if he was ashamed of the particular ape he descended from. But he was kind and often jovial to Nirmal. Perhaps Nirmal reminded him of his own childhood. Nirmal didn't know for sure, of course. On the streets, no one went around asking about a person's past. Or his future. One barely had a present.

Occasionally, Aseem allowed Nirmal to sit on the dentist's chair—an honour usually reserved for his more important clients—while he read the Urdu newspaper *Inquilab* aloud as if he had an audience. 'Sit on the throne, O king,' Aseem would say on a good day, looking up from the paper for a moment as Nirmal made a hesitant entry, ready to fade at Aseem's first frown.

Aseem would read his paper end to end. Then he folded it neatly and placed it over the window sill, where a growing stack of yesterdays' newspapers stood silent and self-conscious, their screaming all done.

'Go get me a smoke, will you?' Aseem said to Nirmal one day.

Nirmal rushed out and got back in no time.

Aseem smoked the cigarette, staring at the papers as if his life story was buried deep in one of them, and which he had somehow missed. All the seven minutes that Aseem took to smoke his mid-morning cigarette, he stared at the newspapers. When the cigarette was over, he stubbed it out on the sole of his left sandal and then ordered bun masca and tea for both of them. They ate the buttered buns, listening to the noisy fan overhead. 'All well?' Aseem asked Nirmal.

'Yes.'

'Good. Let's get to work,' Aseem said.

Nirmal sat still, his eyes shut tight, waiting for the brush to wet his skin. When he opened them at the end of twenty minutes, he was head-turningly ugly.

The make-up idea was Aseem's.

'People feel like they owe you something if you are deformed,' Aseem said. 'The paint is a bit uncomfortable, but you will make more money.'

For Aseem's pains, Nirmal paid him Rs 200 a month. It was not much, but the Indian economy was doing well, and as it grew, so did the number of beggars thronging his door. And they all seemed only too willing to pay.

Soon, Aseem hung up a sign asking them to maintain a queue system. Those who jumped the line were denied paint for the day. But these punitive steps did not diminish the crowd.

'The paint will take you only this far,' a tired Aseem would finally mutter, dipping his brush in water. 'What will get you ahead is discipline.'

'Get on with your job, Aseem,' one of the senior beggars had said once. 'We need to hurry.'

'Why do you all want to beg, huh? Why not do some real work, like construction or something? Begging is a tough talent and not all of you have it,' Aseem said, squinting at the face at hand.

'We'll manage, Aseem the Artist,' the senior beggar said, 'bring on the paint. See us as your beautiful creations, we beg you.'

A funny beggar, Nirmal thought.

Paint job done, Nirmal caught the train to Marine Lines and did his crescent-beat from Chowpatty Beach to Cuffe Parade and back, a sixteen-kilometre seaside walk—a little too long for a stroll, he thought wryly—which he covered by late evening. 'I'm in a movie,' he told himself, 'a full-length feature film.' He was enacting a role and getting paid for it; one of those slow, depressing movies no one paid to watch. 'Call it Bombay Blues,' he thought.

When the sun set, he caught a bus back to the Asiatic Library. He sat next to the window, the sea breeze warm on his theatrical face, and watched people turn black against the setting sun, like charcoal lines on an orange canvas.

He lay down on one of the library steps, listening to the city's traffic thinning as the night took over. At Congress House, Aseem must have started on his other shift, Nirmal thought. It must be tough to be a pimp *and* be in love with his favourite prostitute. Everyone knew there was something going on between Aseem and Chanda. Nirmal knew that the only person from whom Aseem took nothing for his escort service was Chanda. Aseem thought money would taint his love. 'My love for Chanda is pure,' he told Nirmal, 'one hundred per cent pure, like bottled water.'

THREE

Making the Most of Where They Stay

The city is under siege and Shantanu Roy is not quite clear how to go about covering the event, which is too ghastly to lend itself to any kind of upbeat treatment. Over the years, Roy has come to see news as something that enables business transactions. Crusaders could say what they wanted, but he knew that bad news made for poor advertising ecology.

Unfortunately, there is so much of it happening today that Roy finds himself stumped. Perhaps he could explore the angle of human interest, the grit that saw the survivors through the ordeal. The 'Spirit of Bombay' could be stressed, its resilience recalled, its indefatigable character invoked.

As usual, matutinal fumes announce Shantanu Roy's entrance. If you lit a match in the air that he displaced with his breath, it would go up in flames, chief reporter John Lobo notes surreptitiously as Roy walks past his desk.

John doesn't look up for fear of detection. He holds a newspaper over his fat frame and pretends to be engrossed in a bank heist in which the robber had forgotten his car key on the counter and was held when he returned to retrieve it. Though John has been working at *Bombay Express* for long, he can never bring himself to feel a sense of ownership with the product.

As ever, Roy's rear is brought up by the dusky and sickly Mrs Kulkarni of the long hair and dark eyes, who smiles at everyone with her small, even, yellow teeth, a mere dental exercise from which eyes and heart have long ago flown.

Roy is married and has a sixteen-year-old daughter. It is not a happy marriage, and the daughter does not much care for him. His daughter's coldness hurts Roy more than his wife's disenchantment with him. But he hangs in there out of a sense of solemn duty as father and husband, and also because he is from a family that honours conventions. His parents considered conventions a reasonable substitute for happiness and so does he.

Mrs Kulkarni has been long separated from her husband, but is not yet a divorcee. Neither her husband nor she has the will to take themselves to the family court. Besides, Mrs Kulkarni's much propertied mother is against divorce. 'It's a matter of principle,' she shouted at her daughter when she broached the topic, 'a matter of ethics and family reputation. Please understand.'

To Roy, Mrs Kulkarni's presence promises sexual fulfilment any moment now; but, as he knows from these past nine years, somehow the promise never quite translates into performance, no matter how propitious the circumstances. Mrs Kulkarni is like a festival that cannot be celebrated, Roy is beginning to believe. She does allow him to touch her, hold her hand in the dark of the movie house, caress her hair pungent with herbal oil—whose formula he can only marvel at as pure cosmetic witchery—and brush his heavy and trembling fingers against her slight breasts.

The closest Roy had come to having sex with Mrs Kulkarni was on a cold night in Mcleodganj above Dharamsala up in the Himalayas, where the seniors in office had been taken for an off-site meeting.

As the night progressed, Roy and Mrs Kulkarni had sat apart and got drunk. The cold white moonlight and the silent peaks towering over them, the sense of Shangri-la-like isolation that the place radiated, had added to their bonding.

Past midnight, as happens at these heights, the weather changed within the space of a breath, and a dark, serpentine cloud swallowed up the moon whole. A steady rain began beating down, and with it the cold grew tooth and claw. They got up from the veranda, just as the lights went out. It was so dark, they couldn't see each other. 'Hey, are you there?' Roy said lightly, happy they were together at last.

'Oh, hell, where's my room key?' Mrs Kulkarni said.

'You brought it with you. I saw it in your hand. And then you went for a walk on the lawns.'

'I know that,' Mrs Kulkani said in exasperation. She had to take care of everything, she thought, even on a holiday. 'But, where's it now? How do I get into my room?' she said in panic.

'Well, there's always my room,' Roy observed with gentle irony, perhaps reminding her of an old pact that was yet to be honoured.

'Please, Shantanu, first let's sort *this* out.'

There's hope then, Roy thought, of a night together in the Himalayas, of a peak to be scaled. 'Let's ask the reception.' He prayed that the key stayed missing.

They went up the creaking staircase of the old villa to the first floor. Over the reception desk, a battery-run, zero-watt bulb burned blue. Below it, a boy in uniform slept, with his head lolling back and his mouth open. It was very cold in the reception area.

You could drink a great deal up here, Roy thought, and the cold would sober you up in no time. 'We need a key to Madam's room,' he said, shaking the boy roughly by the shoulder. The boy had no business sleeping during his work hours.

'Key,' the boy said, waking up and not waking up. He could barely make out two human forms awash in a ghostly sheen. A tall, slightly hunched man, and a short, thin woman, standing close, but not touching. He had noticed the woman in the afternoon, when the group checked in: a bunch of middle-aged people excited like kids on an excursion. 'The Madam was given the key in the afternoon.'

'Of course I had the key, but I lost it. Is that so difficult to understand?' Mrs Kulkarni snapped as the rain hardened against the walls of the villa and the wind roared.

All her things were in the room. Clothes, hair oil, perfumes, cold cream. Without these, she would look odd and old the next morning. Her face secreted too much oil during sleep, her eyes too much goo. She knew she looked like a crime till she touched up. And well, if she *was* a crime, she wanted the accessories within her reach first thing in the morning. She considered cosmetics as a cover-up operation. It was really a matter of knowing her body, she thought. She just looked different in the morning. And she knew that, in an unforgiving world, appearance was all.

'Madam has lost her key,' Roy found himself repeating, 'and she needs to go into her room. It's getting late.'

'Where did you lose it?' the boy asked, fully awake now.

'If I knew where I lost it, I would have found it,' Mrs Kulkarni said sharply, though she was conscious that she was breaking her vow to be gentle and kind to menials.

'We have a master key,' the boy said, turning around and rummaging through a drawer in the back of the cubicle. 'But I am not permitted to give it to anyone.'

'Give it to Madam,' Roy said. He was surprised that the boy didn't find them respectable enough to be trusted with the master key. It is not as if they were going to run away with it.

'Can't give master key to anybody,' the boy repeated. He had decided he didn't like either of them.

'You will give me that key, or you will lose your job,' Mrs Kulkarni said. She had had enough of the boy and his cussedness.

'*You* lose your key and *I* lose my job?' the boy said, not quite grasping the logic of the transaction. It seemed unjust.

'Just give Madam the key, boy,' Roy said. 'Be done with it.'

The boy took a folded blanket kept at one end of the desk and wrapped it around him. The cold had suddenly got to him. He took an aluminium-alloy, three-cell torch from another drawer, shook it to energize the cells and pressed the switch. It emitted a glow of yellow light, just enough to bare the nails on his toes.

'Can't give the master key to anybody,' the boy said, coming out from behind the desk.

'What a nut! Shantanu, I can't believe I am locked out of my own room in the Himalayas!' Mrs Kulkarni wailed. 'In the Himalayas! My toothbrush is in there, for god's sake. It's *my* room. *My* key!'

'Madam's toothbrush is in the room. Give the key now and we will look for the other one in the morning,' Roy said quietly. But I'd love you, Roy thought, even if you didn't brush your teeth. 'She wants the key to her room. Why can't you understand that?' Roy was surprised at his own reasonableness even in a crisis.

'I will come down and open the room myself,' the boy said.

'Give me that key.' Mrs Kulkarni lunged at the boy.

He stepped sideways with the agility of a boxer. Mrs Kulkarni stumbled, swayed drunkenly for a moment on her feet, fell to the floor and found her legs locked under her in her favourite lotus position.

'My god, she is hurt,' Roy said with concern. Clumsily, he crouched by her side, as if he was on the starting block, participating in a 100-metre race. 'Are you ok?'

'This moron hit me, and you just stood there watching?'

'I'll take care of that. Now get up slowly. Here, take my hand.'

'I did not hit her,' the boy said, scared now.

'You hit her and pushed her?' Roy said in slow-dawning disbelief. What did the boy take himself to be? They were journalists! They knew everybody.

'Hold him for me. He deserves to be slapped,' Mrs Kulkarni hissed. 'How dare he hit me? Me? Is he out of his bloody mind?'

'If you don't slap him, I will,' Roy said. I'm truly angry now, he thought. The boy had no business getting physical with Mrs Kulkarni. All they wanted was to take a break from their work in the city. It was up to the guest house to ensure that they went away refreshed. Instead, there was this cheeky boy telling them off in the middle of the night. Well, he would show him who the boss was. Roy turned and attempted to push the boy down the stairs.

But the boy stood his ground.

'Oh, you think you are that tough, do you?' Roy said, grabbing the boy's hand and twisting it. He panted with the effort and the excitement.

The boy half turned to ease the pain.

Roy took hold of the boy's other hand as well, and pinned both to his back. 'Madam asked for a key and you should have given it. Why is that so difficult to understand? I'll teach you to be polite to your guests.'

'If I give you the master key, I'll lose my job,' the boy said through clenched teeth.

'I'll see to it that you lose it anyway,' Mrs Kulkarni said, swinging her body like a clumsy dancer and slapping the boy with all her strength.

'Pass the key to Madam now,' Roy said, releasing the boy with a push.

The boy shook his head. Roy raised his hand in threat.

'Here,' the boy said, ducking. He handed the key to Mrs Kulkarni. 'Please bring it back,' he said, passing a comforting hand over his smarting cheek. His left eye watered from the slap.

'Give me that torch,' Mrs Kulkarni said. 'I can't believe I have to go through this.'

The boy was about to refuse, but then thought the better of it. He handed the torch over to Roy.

'It's nothing, baby,' Roy said to Mrs Kulkarni. 'You'll be just fine in the morning.'

Roy and Mrs Kulkarni went down the staircase. The torch was not of much help, but at least they could see the steps one at a time.

When they reached the landing, Roy put his arm around Mrs Kulkarni, who did not resist. Her body was shaking. 'Don't cry,' Roy said, though she was not crying. 'It's all right.'

Her proximity, the alcohol, and the physical violence in the intimate dark aroused him. It's all fated, he thought. This was to be. Thank god she lost the key.

He held the torch while she slipped the key into the hole and flung the door open with a sigh. The fragrance of her oils and clothes wafted out from the unpacked bags, welcoming her home to her assurances.

'Ah,' she said, and sat heavily on the bed. The night had taken a toll on her sensitivities.

Roy sat close to her. The closest ever, in spirit and body. He put an arm around her. She leaned her head on his bony shoulder. She could smell his sweat. How he sweats in this cold, she thought. Must be the alcohol and the fight. They sat without talking for a few minutes. The night was very quiet. They could hear their own breathing. Mrs Kulkarni thought about her husband, a high-strung chartered accountant. If she had just been a little more tactful with him, the marriage might have held out. She might have had grown-up children by now. The children would have been something, not just an appearance. They might even have meant a full life, definitely more than this half life. She was not sure where she was going with it. She was not even a great journalist.

Mrs Kulkarni felt like crying. But only her body shook. Her eyes remained dry. She was aware of Roy's hand cupping her breast. She let him play with her nipple, but she felt nothing.

'I want to sleep,' she said after a while, her head still on his shoulder.

'You want to sleep now?' Roy asked. He couldn't believe it. He had arranged the trip so this moment would happen. He had thought that a different setting, free from the pressures of office and family, would help Mrs Kulkarni shed her inhibitions. That opportunity was here. And she wanted to sleep it off? 'Would you like me to share your bed,' he said carefully, not letting his desire for her take over the occasion and ruin the relationship, which he set much store by, more than anyone could imagine. 'Or, would you rather be alone?'

'I'm fine. Just tired, I guess. This trip has been too much for me. Something always happens to me in the mountains.'

'All right then, some other time, maybe,' Roy said. He was disappointed. But he respected her privacy. He was a civilized human being, a well-known journalist. He had travelled with the prime minister thrice on his foreign jaunts. 'You keep the torch with you. You might need it. Good night. I am in the next room.'

'Good night.'

Roy closed the door after him. The rain had slackened, but the wind was still strong. He stood on the edge of the steps leading from the veranda and looked up at the dark mountain rising over him in cold contempt, its pine trees stacked thick and black and climbing in ranks. They swayed in a body in the wind. Roy looked on for some time, till he thought the whole mountain was moving from side to side.

Roy lit a cigarette, blew the smoke into the night. He noted with sadness that there was nothing in his head except sex and boredom. Sex with Mrs Kulkarni, boredom with life. He waited the length of the cigarette for Mrs Kulkarni to change her mind, come out, call him. But she didn't. He flung the stub out on to the lawn, turned, and went inside his room, leaving the door ajar. He lay on the cold bed, his eyes open in the dark.

FOUR

Tandoori Nights: Fowl Means and Fare

One day, as Aseem was applying make-up on Nirmal, he said, 'Rashid needs a boy for the kebab irons. He pays hundred a night and has got a room where the boy can stay. Are you interested?'

Nirmal was beginning to tire of the ugly beggar's role. This sounded like a job. At least you didn't have to fake a life more miserable than the one you actually led. You worked, you got paid. 'Yes,' he said, running a hand over his shaven head. With money like that, he could afford to grow hair, and buy clothes and toothpaste. He didn't have to look like a monkey on ration all the time.

'Good. I'll fix it for you.'

At Rashid's, there were six tandoor ovens. They started burning like hellfires at nine in the night and were put out at around five in the morning. Each pit took ten heavy skewering irons. Nirmal had to string the cured chicken and mutton pieces along the length of the irons, and then place them over the oven. Each load took around ten minutes to cook and Nirmal's flesh turned tender as well with the heat.

In the first few months of the job, the heat of the pit and the reek from the red, rubbery mountains of meat overpowered

Nirmal's senses. For a while, he had recurring nightmares in which Rashid skewered him and turned him over the pit, his eyes on a clock. Or the garland of whole, dressed chickens, hanging from hooks, legs up and belly down, slowly throbbed back to life and imperceptibly changed into decapitated babies. Get me out of here, Nirmal thought, waking up; he would go back to begging. He didn't think he would last at the tandoor.

There was something about the tandoor, Nirmal thought, something about that glow. He tried his best not to look for too long at the burning red coals. They hurt his eyes, of course. But the blood-light of his workplace reached deeper. He saw the pit ever encroaching, a volcanic sea of burning coals. It spread, melting everything in its way, from horizon to horizon. The world smouldered. Nirmal tried sitting far from the pit; as far as was possible in a job like this. But the embers rolled out in ones and twos and soon piled around, breathing, burning, encircling him. He felt as if his head had melted away and that burning coals blazed out of the eye sockets of the skull that replaced it.

It took months to get used to the new life before the nightmares faded, replaced by other visions. On hormonally charged nights, as the fat from the meat dripped and the embers spluttered in glee, Nirmal saw, lying on the bed of burning rubies, a naked Chanda. She smiled at him in the lurid red glow. Come, she said, come, don't be afraid, keep the kebabs on the table, sit here next to me.

On a Monday night when business was normally slow, there was an order for kebabs from Chanda's room. The boy who looked after home deliveries was not around.

'I'll take it,' Nirmal said, without looking up from the oven.

Was he too quick to volunteer? He hoped Rashid wouldn't see through him, laugh at his favourite sin.

'All right. Get back fast.'

Nirmal took the packed kebabs, put in some extra mint chutney as a favour in the takeaway bag, and walked fast to Chanda's room on the second floor of the Congress House. He raced up the stairs and, on the second landing, paused to recover his breath. When he thought his heart was under control, he knocked on Chanda's door.

He could hear the TV, so maybe no one heard his knocks. After a minute or so, Nirmal pushed the door open and paused, one hand on the handle. Chanda was sitting naked on a white mattress. Her hair was gathered up in a big bun, and she mouthed little moans of pain as Zainub pricked her with needles.

Chanda's whole body was covered with needles, top of the head, neck, nipples, arms, palms, fingertips, knees, toes. Nirmal stood transfixed. The kebabs breathed warm into his hand, and sweat poured down his back. Chanda looked up, smiling—in invitation or appeal? Zainub did not turn around. Spooky girl, Nirmal thought.

'Come on in,' Chanda said.

Nirmal closed the door behind him.

'Put off the TV,' Chanda said, still smiling. 'Remote on the table.'

Nirmal switched off the TV. Suddenly, it was very quiet in the room.

'These needles hurt. Would you like to take them off one by one?'

Would he? He would. Nirmal wet his lips.

'Keep the kebabs on the table.'

Nirmal kept the kebabs on the table stacked with face creams and powders and variously coloured bottles of scents.

'Come, sit next to me.'

'No, I'm fine,' Nirmal said, wiping the sweat off his forehead with the back of his hand. His heart beat faster.

'You don't want to come closer to Chanda? I suppose I am getting old. You can stand right where you are and watch me if you want to. Only if you want to.'

'I have got work to do.' He was surprised he had found his voice.

'Important work?' Chanda raised an eyebrow.

Was she mocking him? Of course she was. 'No, not very important.'

'Take these pins off then. They hurt,' Chanda said softly. 'Zainub says I need to wait at least an hour. She thinks she is a great acupuncturist. You could help me if you like.'

'Can I come some other time?' Nirmal blurted out. I am an idiot, he thought.

Chanda laughed. 'Zainub, little Nirmal wants to go. Maybe he is scared of Aseem.' She turned to Nirmal. 'Go then, and close the door as you do.' She laughed again.

Blood rushed to Nirmal's face. He let himself out and ran to his room, tears of shame and anger streaming down his face. Once inside, he bolted the door and masturbated, like a man who hated himself. He came before the tears dried on his face.

Nirmal never told Aseem about the incident, though on the face of it he had done nothing wrong, except maybe the masturbation part. Which he felt like doing every time he thought of Chanda's full breasts and their big, dark nipples.

'Are you ok?' Rashid asked him one night as he took a moment's break from slicing meat along a long butchering knife gripped between his toes.

'I'm all right,' Nirmal said. He had got used to the heat and the meat.

'We're doing well,' Rashid said. 'We'll be hiring more boys.' There were unceasing orders from Congress House. The thieves, artists and gangsters who frequented the place seemed to have an appetite, no matter what the kind of crime they committed between orders. 'You might get a little more time off.'

'I'd like that.'

'If you want to, you could go for the free weekend classes at Bombay Central luggage room,' Rashid said. 'English and Maths.'

'During the day?'

'No, early evening.'

'That sounds good,' Nirmal said.

The classes were conducted by WISH, a charity organization. Nirmal went, and found the studies incidental. He and his friends had fun checking their collective weight on the large weighing machine and fighting each other off the platform, Sumo style. The last boy standing won money worth his weight.

Occasionally, when circumstances were right, they also stole small parcels, one of which memorably turned out to be a dildo. It was a parcel from Kanpur; small leather works in the dusty northern city exported sex toys primarily to bedrooms in New York and London, making a living from the million kinks in the foreign amour.

Nirmal and his friends presented the dildo to their retiring English teacher, a tough Parsi spinster in her early seventies. 'Ah, a parting gift,' she said in her gruff voice. She opened the envelope and made a show of examining the curious object, holding it close to her face, and finally said, 'At last, my nights turn wild again.'

The class broke into catcalls and applause.

FIVE

Spirits Vacating

Placid Hari's report on the Mujra laid Congress House low. The police raid that followed the report was like a scene out of a movie. They came in blue vans with sirens blowing and lights spinning. They blew whistles and used batons. They fired into the air. And when they thought they had cleared the area of people, they brought in huge yellow bulldozers.

The sight of the bulldozers spurred the scattering inmates to action. They had lived here for decades and were not giving it up without a fair fight. They recouped to pelt the police with stones and threw tins and bottles at them. Some slung stone-packed condoms from instantly improvised catapults. Others flung bags of steaming shit. These were their weapons of mass destruction, but despite their deployment, the police won the day, as they always did.

In a way, Aseem was responsible for the disaster, Nirmal realized. Placid Hari could not have gained entry into the building without Aseem, who was his escort that night. Clearly, Aseem wanted to take revenge on Chanda, who had stopped availing of his services. Of late, Chanda had a regular customer, Nilesh Bhatia, who came in a white BMW and took her out for the night. Nirmal made it a point to wipe his kebab-stained hands on the car whenever the chance presented itself.

When Placid Hari asked for his help, perhaps Aseem saw in it an opportunity to show Chanda and Bhatia what he felt: murder. Nirmal noticed that as Chanda distanced herself from Aseem, his spells of silence became longer and deeper. Aseem now took more time to drink his tea and stared longer at the stack of newspapers. And he was unnecessarily hard on the cigarette stub too.

Congress House lay in ruins. The women sat around in twos and threes in the demolished courtyard and roofless rooms, wailing. They tried to take comfort in shared memories of the good old days. They recalled movies in which similar scenes of destruction had been enacted, scenes where the hero made a last-minute appearance and drove the policemen on the payroll of the corrupt away with his fists. Then he drank and sang with the people he had saved. It was the fate of the Congress House women that they had no such saviour. Oh, for a hero, they wept. They reminded each other of the number of times they had provided the constables and inspectors gratification free of cost. Never again, they said, not even if they were paid money. They abused the sisterfucking police. They were tired of the city. They said to each other that they wanted to go back to their quiet villages. Enough was sisterfucking enough.

But reality got to them soon enough: there was no future in the ruins around them. They had to move to another place, set up camp again, and find beds that patiently bore through the tired noises of pleasure. Their profession was their life, Congress House or no. Within the next couple of days, in small groups, wearing loud clothes, they stepped out and vanished—like spirits who had done their time in the haunted house—into the yellow evening.

The morning after the demolition, a heavily made-up Chanda got into the BMW along with her personal ghost, Zainub. All her belongings were packed into six large suitcases and carried to the car by her weeping ustads. When the car roared to life, Chanda smiled and waved at the small crowd on the steps as if she were a film star: she was leaving after a night's shooting, and was thanking everybody for their cooperation. No one waved back. But all stared at the BMW till it turned the corner. Except her ustads, who ran after the car, beating their chests and pulling their hair in hysterical grief. They, like the other musicians at Congress House, had nowhere to go now but the streets.

On the third morning, as if they had taken a collective resolve, the musicians assembled on the battered steps leading to the road: a bunch of dark, ragged men, drunk to their eyeballs and swaying on their feet. For a while, they played on their harmoniums and tablas in a discordant dirge of dispossession, and then, one by one, wandered into the city's traffic, false notes of music following them like mutilated orphans. They would now play their instruments by the wayside and, on the black piece of cloth that they spread on the ground, coins would occasionally fall, like the last of the leftovers from a tardy heaven.

The pimps hung around, though. They were waiting for the right night to fall. A few days later, a little after the late show at the nearby Alfred Cinema had started, they cornered Aseem in the pit of one of the narrow backstreets running off Congress House.

Nirmal counted ten of them, all with hockey sticks. Aseem knew each one of them by name, but no sound, no plea, escaped his lips. Indeed, the strange thing was the silence of the violence. Neither the attackers nor the victim made any noise. Aseem did not fight. He took the blows in silence. And he went down in silence. The men stopped after about five minutes. At the end of it, one of them put his foot on Aseem's battered head and said, 'You busted our business. You are breathing still because of the good times we had with you.' They threw their hockey sticks down and left the scene.

Nirmal quickly got Aseem into a cab and took him to a nearby hospital run by the Jain community. Aseem had to be operated on his knee, needed several stitches on his head, and his ribs had to be put in a cast.

Nirmal stayed with him in the general ward, and found his spirits sinking like water in a bucket full of holes. The hospital walls were done in a dull olive green and white. On the green part was written, in large black letters, instructions to patients to avoid meat, whose negative points were listed in an unsteady hand. There were ninety-nine points. The white part of the walls was covered with explicit but primitive charcoal drawings of corpses of birds and animals, and humans—all men—their entrails out in the open. The whole hospital was a fearful advertisement against non-vegetarianism.

The nurses, who seemed to be running the place, kept joking to each other in a strange language. While administering painful injections to patients, they looked away and broke needles. Nirmal watched the nurses laugh while patients died. It was as though they were all in on an interminable house-joke the whole time.

When they finally got out, Aseem had changed. He had grown a beard, which rather suited him, Nirmal thought. Perhaps he was trying to hide the scars. More drastically, the hospital had turned him into a vegetarian. 'Why kill to eat?' he said, when Nirmal asked him. Strange! You go for a cure, Nirmal thought, and come back converted. Aseem the Brahmin.

Aseem shifted quarters to the vast Dharavi slums, where he switched full time to providing designer make-up to beggars. On the day before he brought the shutters down for the last time on his salon in Pakeeza Market, Aseem said to Nirmal: 'What about you? If you need a place to stay, you could come with me.'

Rashid's shop had been levelled to the ground, ending Nirmal's nightly baptism by fire, water and iron. 'I'll set up shop again,' Rashid had told him. 'Give me a couple of months.' Nirmal thought it would take more than that. Much more.

'Thanks,' Nirmal told Aseem. 'Maybe I will.'

'Try not to go back to the streets or you might finally end up doing the kind of things I am doing.'

'You are right,' Nirmal replied.

'You are bright. You should be going to a proper school.'

'Hmm,' Nirmal responded. He was not interested in studies. He looked around the street over which towered hoardings with giant film posters. 'I want to act.' Nirmal didn't see how, but he knew that nothing excited him as much as the movies.

'Do well in studies and you could get a proper job.'

'I do go for my weekend classes.'

'Not quite the same.'

'I know. I'm hoping something will happen,' he said vaguely.

'Sure. Let me know.'

Aseem turned to go. His brushes and paints were packed and waiting. The dentist's chair had already gone.

'And thanks, Aseem. For everything,' Nirmal said.

'No, we are same to same,' Aseem said, thinking of the hospital. He put his arm around Nirmal, held him close for a moment. 'We'll stay in touch.'

SIX

Scene 1, Take 9

Robert Davis is doing a true-grit movie, *Wind Surfer*. It is based on the real-life story of Tulsi. 'Here's the story,' Davis tells Nirmal, picking at a tomato omelette with his fork.

Tulsi is a child prodigy who, by the age of ten, can run over forty kilometres at a stretch. His mother, a domestic help, can't afford him. Neither can his father, an alcoholic who has dedicated his life to Ginger, a fire-water spiked with dead battery secretions.

The mother sells Tulsi to a bangle vendor for Rs 800. Exit Tulsi, atop the crossbar of a bicycle, waving farewell to his expressionless mother.

Months later, Tulsi visits his mother in a new shirt, several sizes too big for him. Mother is shocked at the boy's emaciated condition. 'My son,' she shrieks. Mother rushes to Bose, a burly Judo champ and a local don. Bose agrees to take Tulsi under his wing.

Bose buys Tulsi back from the bangle vendor. He puts Tulsi on a diet, trains him. In no time, Tulsi is running huge distances.

Bose holds a solo run of 65km for Tulsi. The temperature is 40°C. Tulsi collapses 7km short of target, but prompt medical care brings him to back to life.

By now, Tulsi is famous. Money pours into the trust set up in his name. His mother wants Tulsi back in the family.

Meanwhile, Vicky, a hoodlum, falls in love with a starlet, Elsa, who approaches Bose for protection. Bose warns Vicky off Elsa in public.

The next day, Vicky shoots Bose, but he survives.

The government intervenes and Tulsi is awarded a scholarship which takes him to the National Sports School.

While Bose is in hospital, Vicky kidnaps Elsa, forces her into a relationship with him.

Bose rescues Tulsi from the sports school, where he is tormented by the gang led by the reigning track champion and chief bully, Sagar Sahu.

Together, Bose and Tulsi race to the hideout in the hills where Elsa is held hostage. Vicky naturally gets to know their plans. He sets up a time bomb under Elsa's bed to which she is bound, and challenges Bose and Tulsi to run the distance of 100km from the city to the hills against an impossible deadline over a rough terrain.

If they do, Elsa lives. This is the race of their life. In the event, only Tulsi survives the ordeal. Bose is murdered halfway through. But not before he kills Vicky.

Tulsi scorches the earth, tears streaming down his face (his mentor and friend is no more, but the show must run), beats the clock, saves Elsa. The credits come up as they slowly walk hand in hand down the hillside in the rain.

'You are Sagar Sahu, the school hero made insecure by little Tulsi's entry.' Davis smiles at Nirmal and puts the fork back on the plate, the omelette uneaten.

Nirmal's first shot is in a cavernous hall set up as the school gym. At the far end of the room, Tulsi is lying on a mat where the last light still holds. He is resting after his stretches.

Nirmal is doing push-ups this side of the hall, which is really dark. He keeps staring at Tulsi all the while. Then he stands up, slowly walks up to Tulsi and sits next to him. He must bring his face very close to him. When Tulsi opens his eyes, he will be looking straight into Sagar's eyes an inch or so away.

'When you are walking towards Tulsi, think of playful cruelty,' Davis tells Nirmal

Nirmal nods, uncertainly. 'What's playful cruelty?'

'Is there anyone whom you detest?' Davis asks. 'Someone who is inferior to you but whose existence is agonizing to you?'

Nirmal ransacks the shelves of his memory, and is surprised that he feels no great personal hatred for anyone. Then he surprises himself even more. 'Yes,' he replies.

Davis looks at him expectantly.

'My father.'

'Where's your father now?' Davis asks.

'I don't know.'

'Right,' Davis says. 'You want to be playfully cruel to him?'

'I don't mind.'

'You have never met him?'

'No.'

'No, that won't do. This is about someone who is a threat to you. Someone real. An intruder in your paradise, out to steal your glory. Everything he does is to please the instructor who, so far, has been *your* mentor. You have no option but bust this guy. But you will bust him with a smile, with a certain light cruelty. Like holding someone's hand down in increasingly hot water. All right?'

'Yes.'

'When I say "action", you just walk slowly towards Tulsi's mat, thinking about the lesson you are going to teach this little pretender. He is in your control. There is no hurry in your movements, ok?'

Davis looks around for his cameraman, who appears at his elbow on cue. 'Lighting good?'

'Perfect,' the cameraman says, looking around the hall, the outer edges of which have dissolved into the dark because of the spotlights.

There are shadows lengthening on the floor. The fitness equipment in the hall takes on the dimensions of torture instruments.

'Action,' Davis says.

Nirmal walks. And walks.

He walks nine times before he gets it right.

Davis is happy with the shot. 'Cut,' he says.

'The script is with you,' Davis says. 'Practise your part in your room.'

'I will. I've got the hang of it,' Nirmal tells him. 'It won't be this bad tomorrow.'

'No, you are good. You will do better tomorrow.'

Nirmal heads back to the hotel.

SEVEN

Blood Is Thicker than Water

Next to the narrow bathroom window, Placid has been jumping clumsily up and down for a while. His blindfold has come undone and hangs loose around his neck like a noose, and the unprofessional knots have slackened from his exertions.

From where he sits, Nirmal sees him, but ignores the sight. Odd things happen in tall buildings. Maybe the man is exercising. Nirmal puts his harmonica away. He notices that the man is shouting something. It is hard to make out the words over the din of the traffic. Curious, Nirmal gets up and crosses the road. He counts the floors and goes up in the lift. If someone asks him, he will tell the truth. But no one stops him. There aren't too many people around, perhaps because the building is new. There are three apartments to each floor. He makes for the one that faces the sea. The door is ajar. A TV mounted on the far wall shows images without sound. Light pours in from the large French window on one side. The place is done in white. Walls, roof, cupboards, sofas, chairs, tables, curtains, all in white. Very clean, too. Someone must be scrubbing the house all the time.

A narrow corridor leads off from the hall, leading to a

bedroom. There are sounds from the attached bathroom. It is bolted from outside. Nirmal opens the door.

'Oh, someone at last! I had given up on rescue. Quick. Get a knife from the kitchen and cut me free,' Placid says.

Nirmal finds a knife and cuts the ropes.

'Placid Hari Odannur,' the man says, extending his hand.

Nirmal shakes it. 'The journalist?'

'Yes,' he says, rubbing circulation back into his wrists, and rotating his hands in the air at the shoulder.

'You wrote that piece on the Mujra.'

'Oh, you read that? Good,' Placid Hari says.

'No, I didn't read it. But a lot of people I know were affected by it. There was a police raid, as you know.'

'Ah, yes,' Placid says with what he thinks is appropriate helplessness. He hadn't intended harm. But writing hurt, that was an occupational hazard.

'It's a miracle you came, a miracle,' Placid says, shaking Nirmal by the shoulder. 'It is just that when I move my head, it aches. Maybe it's the hangover. Or stress. I don't think I will ever drink again. Not for some time anyway.'

Nirmal is silent. It seems to him that he has saved a mad man.

Placid stretches back and raises his arms. 'Aah,' he says. He picks up his jeans from the floor, airs them loudly and gets into them. He splashes water on his head and face.

'I feel like a shower. But every moment is tempting death. Let's go.'

'All right. But what happened to you? Why are you here, all in knots?'

'I'll tell you as soon as we get out of this place. This is a slaughter house, you understand? A slaughter house. Come.' Placid puts a hand around Nirmal's shoulder. He takes a last look in the mirror and shakes his head. He is not happy with what he sees, neither the receding hairline, nor the furrowed forehead with its vertical frown between the eyebrows, nor the tight-set mouth: a grim, strained face. He adjusts his shirt, pulls the collar down to its proper setting and squares his shoulders. 'Let's go.'

They step out of the bathroom and hurry towards the main door.

'My wallet!' Placid says.

They go back to the bathroom. It is not there. They search for it everywhere in the house, but no wallet.

'Forget it. Maybe I lost it sometime last night,' Placid says unhappily. 'We are wasting time.'

They return to the hall. But it is too late. They can hear people right outside the door.

The boy with the beard kicks the door shut. He is pointing his gun at his petrified companions and saying something to them. He seems surprised at the presence of Nirmal and Placid. Nirmal's stomach churns. He feels like screaming. The boy with the gun is his splitting image. There is a pit in Nirmal's stomach and all his innards are falling into it. He feels like coughing. Instead, he sits down. He's about to cry. Nirmal gropes for the harmonica in his pocket. Should he play on it? Some sad tune that might vaguely express everything?

Could it be just chance that the boy with the gun looks like him? It occurs to Nirmal that he might just be in a Bollywood movie. One of those brothers-separated-at-birth movies where the siblings are brought together by destiny in the form of a grief-stricken, nearly crazed mother who remembers the mole in the left ear of the twins; which having been spotted, they all break into a song, the title song of the movie. More often than not, the brothers are separated because they are born out of wedlock; the poor and chaste mother abandons one at a rich man's doorstep and floats the other in a wicker basket down a river. The mother does so because she has to appear as a virgin in society. Or the pre-teen brothers are chased after in opposite directions by killer gangs, whose leader wears custom-made shoes of different sizes, which is how the rebel brother identifies him twenty years later, so he can extract vengeance from him.

Nirmal waits behind his dark glasses for Salim to recognize him.

EIGHT

The Ambush of the Other Sex

A fantastic, 70-mm sky stretches close over Maulana Abul Razak. He raises his hand to feel if it is something held before his eyes, a fold of soft and brilliant cloth, a ribbon of liquescent colours, perhaps? He waves his hands over his eyes. No, it's no cloth. It's the sky. How close he is to it today. Gravity continues to be a matter of laughing lightness for Abul Razak.

The bestiary of the blue transfixes him with wonder. There are bears and lions, wolves and crocodiles, and demons in reds and oranges and greens shedding forms and merging with one another to assume tantalizing shapes, both familiar and phantom-like. It is as if the wind holds in its hands strings and, attached to these, the cumulous beasts rush at each other and back in a mock-epic battle on a screen that stretches from horizon to horizon.

It's cool, too. The breeze after a sudden spell of rain fans Abul Razak's burning body. His feet are wet, the toenails washed clean by the downpour. His drenched clothes slap against his sides when he moves. Around him, brown pools of water drip and gather. The puddles are lit grey from inside, and maddened red ants hurry about their edges.

For the first time in a long while, Maulana Abul Razak feels he may get well yet. He looks around for Fatima, who sits on top of the steps leading to the river, now ignited by the red flames falling from the gulmohar trees.

The river has filled out due to the downpour.

'And how does the Maulana fare after the rains?' Fatima asks, without looking at him.

'Ah, well. But we did visit a few places before the rain, didn't we? It feels so long ago.'

'Yes, but I'd rather stay put. Travel upsets me.'

'We learn a lot from long journeys, new places.'

'But not English, for sure?' Fatima laughs.

'There is not much time now, is there?'

'Only if you want to get somewhere. I have got this new book of south Indian recipes. I thought I should tell you, since you are interested in food. This one is on coastal cookery.'

'South India.'

'Actually, Kerala. A place in south India. Coconuts grow there.'

'I remember. There is a mosque there where women are allowed to go in and pray.'

'Something to be said for coconuts after all,' Fatima says.

'Mangoes are good, too,' Abul Razak can't help remarking. He feels calm saying it.

'I have a hunch that in some of those recipes, mangoes could be substituted for coconuts.'

'But, you realize fruits are very different from each other? Like humans.'

'Coconut palms need a lot of water. That's why they don't grow here. One day I will go to Kerala,' Fatima says, looking across the river. 'They have whole villages floating on water there.'

'Is coconut a fruit or a vegetable?'

'Is the mosquito a bird?'

'I don't know. Have you thought of our marriage?'

'Is it important? I always feel sad when I look at you.'

'What must I do?'

Fatima picks a flat stone and feigns flinging it at Abul Razak, who throws a hand over his face to protect it from the punishment. 'Adulterer,' she says, laughing.

She throws the stone into the river and makes it skim twice before turning to Abul Razak. 'Salim could make a stone skim five or six times.'

'I didn't know that. I have been busy with other things.'

'Terror is a career for you, Abul Razak. I understand that. How does it matter to Allah?'

Abul Razak looks all round him, at the school, the trees, the river. The secret meetings on white cushions on the floor, stones soaked red in blood, the bullet drilling through Usuf's heart for ever, and the earth spinning through space. 'It doesn't matter to Allah,' Abul Razak says; so softly, Fatima can barely make out what he is saying.

'You said something?'

'Are we going out, then? To Faridkot?' Abul Razak asks.

Fatima doesn't respond. She is busy marking the ground with a stick. A hopscotch court. Fatima pauses to take a look at her handiwork. It'll do. She looks for a small flat stone, tosses it into the first square.

She completes the game, balancing herself perfectly on one leg. 'I always win with the girls,' she tells Abul Razak. 'I tire of it fast because I am so good at it,' she says, hands on hips. 'You don't look well. Would you like some water?'

She reaches into her bag, takes out a bottle of water and offers it to Abul Razak.

'Yes, please.' Abul Razak reaches for the bottle.

'Finish it. There is plenty more where that came from.' She smiles at him, pointing to the river.

'Now for the last act,' she says, 'before I go home.' She reaches into the bag again and pulls out a thick roll of black silken cloth with great deliberation. She holds it to one side of her face and throws it high, unfurling its endless darkness. Abul Razak hears the burkha opening out like thunder. The sky is shut out from Abul Razak's eyes.

'Watch me,' Fatima says.

Abul Razak stares at her, hypnotized.

In a slow, sensuous move, Fatima slips the cloth over her head. She could be stripping, but she is not. Hiding a body has never been so revealing.

Fatima is in a flowing burkha. It hugs her body, like a tailor-made gown, except that it trails all over the earth in serpentine folds. 'I am the burkha,' she says. Has her voice changed?

For Abul Razak, life drains of its colour. 'No,' he says, not quite sure what he means.

'The world we made for each other?' Fatima says, only her eyes visible.

'Why do you want to wear that?'

'Call off the mission?'

'You want Salim back?' Abul Razak says weakly. It occurs to him that everybody wants somebody back. Amina wants Usuf, Fatima wants Salim, he wants Fatima …

'A movie is likely at the end of it all. A comedy, or a romantic one, whichever is your preference. And afterwards, we could have ice cream.'

'I don't know about ice cream, though. My throat is still sore,' Abul Razak says, clutching at his Adam's apple.

'That's your nose, not your throat that you are holding.'

Fatima giggles. The giggles soon develop into full-blown laughter. It shakes her body; she throws her head back and claps her hands in liberation. She laughs as if she would bring the sky down. Her nose trembles with the strain of the laughter and her eyes run with helpless tears. 'Oh, Abul Razak,' she says, but it is not clear if she is saying it in mock reprimand or fond disapproval.

And each time she tries saying it, she breaks into fresh peals of laughter. She waves her hand in front of her as if to say enough, but then doubles up holding her tummy. Her stomach hurts from laughing, but there is no stopping it. The more she tries to suppress it, the more forceful is the laughter.

'Someone will hear,' Abul Razak says helplessly.

He doesn't want Fatima to wear a burkha or be laughing like this. It is enough to make my heart stop, he thinks. Since her wearing it a moment ago, Abul Razak feels as if something has been wrested from him; something as precious as Usuf. But he finds the laughter too much. The place rings with it. It is as if the laughter is coming out of a million speakers. No one person could laugh in such a deafening volume.

Abul Razak blinks his eyes in sudden recognition and looks around. His hand goes to his chest: in the new dark world that Fatima has invented for him, the wet steps leading to the river have been taken over by a hundred women in black burkhas.

He is surrounded by veiled women rhythmically bowing to him from the waist and straightening. From their hidden throats issues riotous laughter. The women bear down on him. Abul Razak is trapped in a pit of exhalations of merry women in black. It would make a difference to see their faces in full, he thinks.

'I'll call off the mission,' Abul Razak says.

And though even he can't hear what he is saying, the

promise is met with more laughter. The steps shake as if they rest on a pillow. The puddles shake. The school in the puddles shakes. The beasts of the sky run amok in panic.

But Abul Razak is not daunted. He will make good his word. He reaches into his pocket and fumbles for his cellphone. He will call off the Bombay mission. Enough. He punches Shafi's number, but can't get through to him. He tries Salim's number. He listens to the dial tone, then Salim comes on the line. But Razak can't make his words carry amidst the derisive din around him. 'I am calling off the mission,' Abul Razak says.

'What?' Salim asks.

'Mission. Off. Come back.'

'All's well,' Salim says.

'Come back.'

'We will fight to the last bullet. We'll do you proud. Khuda hafiz.'

'Where's Shafi?'

'Pray for us, Master.'

'Your mother and I …' Abul Razak says and stops, because of a massive ache in his chest. The cellphone slips from his fingers. He puts his right hand out as if to stop something from coming to him. But there is not much he can do because what is approaching is unstoppable. Abul Razak needs to breathe. He needs fresh air.

But the crowd of laughing terrorists in burkha is smothering him with the shimmering, soft, black folds; a sea of susurrant darkness drags him down to depths where no one is in control of anything. A maelstrom of chaos. Is it possible that there is nothing left now? He never thought his end would be at the hands of women. Not that he is afraid. Only, he thinks, the Master is unfair. He shouldn't have done it. Of course, he, Maulana Abul Razak, shouldn't have cheated either. But it is over now. There is no going back. Or forward. The end is in the middle.

Abul Razak sinks to his knees, a hand on his chest, his mouth open, baring his teeth in an agony of want, a need to float out into fresh air and light, to a place without masks and veils, to see Fatima naked and beautiful in the light. To see her and be free. Eat ice cream.

In a prodigious effort, he wills himself to rise to his feet for the last time, hands raised and grabbing at nothingness as if pulling himself up from a deep well by means of a rope. As he reaches his full height, he lets go and begins his long, solo descent to the distant earth he had left behind, the dense layers of black burkha clouds massed against him parting effortlessly to facilitate his free fall. Around him, space empties of objects, the women dissolve into air, and their laughter fades to silence. And a step away from where he lies, one hand in the water, the river bears the flowers to the sea.

NINE

The Great Divide

'We met at the wrong time,' Salim says, sitting down on the floor, his back to the door, the gun placed across his knees. 'I am from Pakistan.'

They are alone in the hall.

'Bombay,' Nirmal says. 'And your father and mother?' Nirmal could have said parents, but somehow father and mother seemed more realistic units.

'Mother is Fatima.'

'We must have the same mother for sure? That's a real gun you have there.'

'AK-47.'

'And father?'

'He was a merchant of mangoes and guns. Went to North Waziristan on some business before I was born and never returned.' Salim places his gun on the floor next to him. 'I need a glass of water.'

'I will get it for you.' Nirmal gets up and makes his way to the kitchen.

Salim makes no effort to stop him.

Nirmal holds a glass to the tap. When it's full, he puts it aside and washes his face: is he wearing a mask? No, it's his face, given to him by his parents; their gift. He resists an impulse to snap his fingers under the tap. Nirmal had ventured to kill his father-in-absentia years ago when a means was presented to him unwittingly by the buck-toothed Kamala Mausi, resident peanut vendor of Congress House, and repository of dark wisdom.

'Nirmal, never snap your fingers in water,' Mausi had said, watching him bathe under a public tap. The city traffic went around his lathered body as if he was an eccentric traffic cop.

'Why?'

'Misfortunes will rain on your parents, Nirmal, they could get killed.'

'Remind me next time I take a bath, Mausi, the tap is about to run out.'

'Don't laugh, Nirmal, you don't want to kill your parents.'

'As if I have parents,' Nirmal said. 'As if I have anything. Bring on the water, Kamala Mausi, and I will snap my fingers till I kill all my parents.'

'No, you don't want to do that. You are just sad.'

'I do, I swear I do, Kamala Mausi, you have no idea how much I'd like to do it.'

'No, you don't, you are just working yourself up into a rage and I don't think I should share my wisdom with you; wisdom I gathered from a life of losses. Wisdom is for adults only; you can't take it when you are this young, and you are very young. God, how young you look with soap on your body, and look at me! Old, old Kamala Mausi. Listen, next time I talk to you, please bring me your age certificate, because you really are young; and now show me your hand, right hand please, and wipe it clean, will you, of soap? And here are some nice, salted peanuts; go and eat and be calm, forget about snapping, ok? You shouldn't snap your fingers in water, or for that matter cut your nails at night because that's bad luck in the morning for the next ten weeks, because you have ten fingers; and one more thing, no bad-mouthing your parents, ok?'

Nirmal didn't know if he should laugh or cry because of this power granted to him over his parents. He threw the peanuts down and turned to the tap to snap his fingers. But it had run dry.

Nirmal carefully picks up the glass from the counter, and walks past the bedroom from where raised voices can be heard. Towards Salim. Towards himself.

'My mother is in Sultanpur,' Salim says, reaching for the water.

Nirmal notes that Salim drinks holding the bottom of the glass with his fingertips, as if he is going to turn a knob.

'You could talk to her, if that would help.'

'If she's my mother, too, what am I doing here?'

'You are right. It's complicated.'

'You have a photograph of hers?'

'No. We are not allowed to carry photographs of anybody.'

On the first day at the training camp, the commander had checked Salim's bag and wallet. He had found a photograph of Salim's mother—sitting on the porch, leaning against a pillar—in the inside pocket of the bag and asked, holding the snap up by a corner: 'Your mother?' Salim nodded. 'Sorry,' the commander said and tore it up. 'When you step into this camp, there's only God.'

'How does a photograph go against God?' Nirmal asks.

'When you are close to your God, you don't think about small things. Listen, you won't understand it unless you are part of it. What are you called?'

'Nirmal. And you?'

'Salim.'

'I am an actor,' Nirmal says. 'I have some money. Maybe you don't have to die? I can take care of you.'

'No, I came here to die. There is no other way now.'

'But we have just met,' Nirmal says.

'I am a jihadi. I'm fighting God's war,' Salim mutters as if remembering a lesson he is in danger of forgetting.

'We are brothers.'

'I don't know.'

'How many did you kill?'

'I didn't keep count. Listen, if you are a Hindu, how am I a Muslim?'

'Who said you are Muslim? And I don't know for sure if I am Hindu either.'

'Where's your mother?'

'She's been missing,' Nirmal says. Not that she was ever found in the first place. He feels the conversation is all wrong. This is not what should happen between twins who were separated at birth and have met just before the death of at least one of them. 'I am acting in a movie.'

'Movie?'

'Yes. A real movie. Camera, lights and all.'

'Made money?'

'Some. I am just starting out. Stayed in a super hotel. The movie is in Hindi and English.'

'What's it about?'

'About a boy who can't stop running. I am one of the villains.'

It occurs to Salim that he himself has come a long way, from the mango orchards of South Punjab. 'We have a nice, big house in Sultanpur.'

Let's go there then, Nirmal wants to tell him; his brother has a mother who could be his as well, and a nice, big house. 'I wish you hadn't killed, though. It gets difficult afterwards.'

'I'm not looking at afterwards.'

'You don't mind giving up your house and your mother?'

'It's what you've got to do. What you've got to do is what you believe in.'

'Maybe your mother is mine as well,' Nirmal says, hope flecking his eyes.

'I don't know,' Salim says.

'It has to be.'

'Well, I'm not sure I can get into all this. I'm going to Heaven.' Salim stretches his legs. 'Jannat,' he says, as if it is the name of a nearby railway station.

'You just met your brother, and off you go to jannat.'

'Well, I didn't know I was going to meet you. And really. I don't know if you are my brother.' Salim smiles for the first time after getting on that boat to Bombay.

'You are a very blind brother.'

'I could ask my mother. But I don't know if I have the time.'

'I think they are showing what you did on TV,' Nirmal says, looking at the screen.

Salim gets up from where he is sitting in the hall and walks towards the TV. Yes, that's me in the picture, he tells himself. And, of course, the scene of carnage is familiar to him. It's Breeze. There is a girl on the floor, clutching at his feet. And below her runs a strip advertisement of Fair and Lovely Cream, urging you to bring out the best in you.

Salim stares at his handiwork for a long moment and walks back. 'I was told.'

'Told what?'

'By someone back in Sultanpur ... to go to India and wage jihad.'

'So you can go to heaven?'

'Yes.'

'You kill people who may not believe in your God and go straight to heaven?'

'You make it sound stupid,' Salim says, 'but it is not.'

'It *is* stupid. You shouldn't have got into it.'

'I have come to do what I promised to do, and I am not afraid to die.'

'You came here so that we would meet.'

'That's also true.'

'What are you going to do?'

'I came with a few others and my boat drifted out. I could talk to them and find out what they have been up to. But whatever I do, I can't leave this place alive.'

'Are you going to kill me?'

'I don't know. I need to think this out. What were you doing before acting?'

'Living off the streets. It's a full-time job. How did you land here in this room?'

'I got out of the restaurant and caught this rickshaw. It had the ladies in it. I wanted to go somewhere and think. When we got out of the lift, that couple from next door was at the door. So I rounded them all up and marched them in, just as you and your friend were coming out.'

'Placid is not my friend. But he is responsible for my movie career. My photograph in an article of his helped my director find me. He is responsible for making me run into you. So I suppose you could call him a friend.'

'It must have been tough on the streets.'

'It is. How did your mother let you go?'

'You don't ask permission for this sort of thing. You are lucky if you have been chosen for the mission. You just go along and work hard to become God's good soldier.'

'I really can't make out the connection between killing and pleasing your God.'

'You need to see some of those videos that we were shown. You watch those videos and if you are a Muslim yourself, you will take to guns and bombs. But you are not a Muslim. So you won't understand.'

'Muslim, Hindu, none of it makes any difference to me. I don't even like this country, though I was born here. If you shoot me, I'll be just an unclaimed corpse.'

Nirmal recalls the other unclaimed corpse he had seen at close quarters. Early one grey, July morning, a livid blue-and-black corpse had washed up on the Chowpatty sands, close to where he lived in one of those big pipes. Death had made the body hard and rigid. The fish had made a meal of its eyes. The lone, hawk-eyed constable on the beat took one look at the sight and covered his nose and mouth with a dirty handkerchief. He looked around, and his eyes swooped down to where Nirmal pretended to be asleep. He poked Nirmal in the groin with his baton. 'Up,' he said. 'Drag that body over to the road.'

It was hard labour and Nirmal did most of it with his eyes closed. But the smell of decay was all around. When he had finished, the policeman handed him a newspaper. Nirmal spread the sheets over the body and placed stones on them so the wind wouldn't blow the loose sheets away. When the task was over, the policeman handed Nirmal some change. 'Go, get a cup of tea for yourself.'

You bastard, Nirmal silently muttered to himself, you wouldn't do this to your son. Nirmal had accepted the money, thanked the policeman, and crawled back into his pipe.

'It's not just me,' Nirmal tells Salim. 'There are millions like me in this city.'

'You need to be a Muslim to understand me. There is no other way.'

'What we have to figure out is how you are going to get out of this.'

'You are wasting your breath,' Salim says, staring at the TV, where a woman in a burkha is climbing down a ladder placed against a first-floor window of the Taj.

'You don't want to give up?' Nirmal asks.

'There is nothing to give up.'

Of course he is my brother, Salim thinks. You'd be blind not to see the likeness. Where has he turned up from in the middle of this mayhem? Is this a test of Allah?

'Listen,' Nirmal says, 'if I am a Hindu, then you are not a Muslim. Then why are you doing this?'

Salim points the gun at Nirmal. 'If you were not my brother, you'd be dead by now.'

'Just ask your mother, will you?'

'I am allowed to make only absolutely necessary calls from my cell.'

'This is absolutely necessary.'

Salim walks up to the bedroom door and listens to the voices emanating from within. He can make out loud arguments. He returns to the hall. 'We need to line up these people.'

'And shoot them?'

'And shoot them.'

'Is that absolutely necessary?'

'I don't know.'

'Call up your mother first. That is necessary.'

'My mother has nothing to do with this.'

'Just make that call.'

'No.'

'Call.'

'No.'

'Pick up the mobile and make that call,' Nirmal says, his face hardening.

'No.'

'Yes.'

'No.'

'Yes.'

'No.'

'What are you afraid of?'

'I am not afraid of anything. If I was afraid, I wouldn't have crossed the sea on a boat and come here to die. And you know it.'

'Here in this city, courage is in the living.'

'All right then, you are a hero. A film star.'

'Just make that call, will you? I'd like to talk to her, too. She is my mother as well, remember?'

'Not yet. In any case, she doesn't look like you.'

'Does she look like you?'

For a moment, Salim looks truly uncomfortable. 'I'll make that call and be damned.'

Salim fishes out his cellphone from one of his eight pockets, presses the keys. He waits for his mother's voice. He can see in his mind the old-fashioned, black phone on the window sill going off, startling the quiet of the room with its shrill insistence, in faraway Sultanpur.

For the first time in his life, Salim is afraid.

TEN

The Dog of Small Things

Shantanu Roy never calls meetings. He merely walks upstairs to the boiling-hot canteen on the roof with Mrs Kulkarni by his side fluttering the menu-list in the air like a much coveted invitation for all to join. The informality of the meeting is a sign of Roy's power.

'What's left for us to do, apart from the routine coverage?' Roy asks the anxious group of reporters.

'Let's do a graphic,' John Lobo says with a nervous cough. 'You know, a blow-by-blow account.' What else? His reporting team had been emasculated despite his muted protestations. A year or two ago, it might have been different, when the paper had on its roll experienced and well-networked senior correspondents who had access to exclusive information. Most of them had left as the new policy was to hire freshmen out of college. They were cheaper and more enthusiastic. Also, Roy and Mrs Kulkarni found them easier to control.

'We could always do that,' Roy says, not quite convinced. 'Have we got good pictures?'

'The photographers are still out. We can take a call as soon as they get back.'

'Rotate the photographers, will you? Don't want the field

left vacant for even a moment. An exclusive picture is as good as a scoop.'

'Why not a graphic novel on the front page, based on the attack? Frank Miller kind of stuff?' says a trainee reporter.

'In 1993, when the first-ever serial bomb blasts ripped through this city, I was at my desk in the corner of the hall,' John says, pointing his finger in a rough, northerly direction. 'This paper was in its previous avatar: a broadsheet. When the bombs went off, killing over two hundred, the floor trembled under my feet. I can tell you, no one suggested a graphic novel then.'

'The 1993 blasts! John, the times have changed,' Arun says with a double-edged smile. Arun is the news editor with two wives, six kids and a taste for loud T-shirts. 'What's the bet no one here except you, me and the big boss has even heard of the serial blasts?' Arun deliberately leaves out Mrs Kulkarni's name from the august list of people with memory and experience. Let her seethe. 'This paper now caters to the young. So a graphic novel is not a bad idea at all. You need to be careful where you place it, though.'

'What's happening in Bandra?' Roy asks, aware that the suburb is not getting as much attention in the media as the Taj.

'Well, this boy seems to have taken hostages in a building called Zircon,' John says.

'The place is inaccessible owing to a Cow Sena procession. But we still managed to get some special stuff on the tenant of the flat, Lakshmi Menon,' Arun says.

'It's a company flat,' says John. 'She stays alone and works for an online porn firm. She is rumoured to be rather close to the proprietor.' John taps his crotch: he is making an important point.

'Her personal relationship with her boss is not material

to our discussion, I'd think. For all we know, he might be exploiting her,' Mrs Kulkarni says.

'I wasn't casting aspersions,' John says in his neutral voice.

'Yes, yes, of course,' says Roy, looking approvingly at Mrs Kulkarni, whose principled gender stand reinforces his belief that she is a cut above the rest, a woman who has thought out her stance on key issues. Unfortunately, business is business. 'I understand Mrs Kulkarni's concerns. Still, there are possibilities in the Lakshmi situation: Terror pays a visit to porn writer. Let's play that up. And is an eyewitness account of the Breeze incident possible? There's a girl survivor. What's Lakshmi Menon's site called?'

'kavitadidi.com. Kavita is a blind girl who is apparently insatiable,' an excited young reporter says. 'She loses her sight in an accident. Kavita could get her vision back if she went in for an operation, but she chooses to put it off indefinitely as she finds the experiences in the dark more titillating. Isn't that something?'

Interesting, Roy thinks. 'Let's get a clip or two from the site,' he says, glancing in Mrs Kulkarni's direction. Would she agree with him?

'Just ensure they are good to reproduce, and not totally lurid,' Mrs Kulkarni says. That seems to her an appropriate thing to say. She's keen to be seen as striking a fine balance between her professional commitment and personal politics of gender and development issues.

'What about Placid Hari Odannur? He has been taken hostage as well,' John says.

'Well, that is a bit of a windfall, too,' Roy says. He doesn't care much for Placid Hari Odannur and his writing. He's all right in his own way, but you can't allow someone like him too much space in an upbeat paper like *Bombay Express*.

But the fact that a writer with his newspaper is a hostage has changed everything. Roy hopes Placid will not get killed. But if he does, Roy will not be shattered. In fact, it would turn out to be good for the paper. 'BOMBAY EXPRESS COLUMNIST TAKEN HOSTAGE, SHOT'. That would put the paper right in the middle of the action, and give an edge to the edition that rivals would find hard to match. 'Do we have any pieces by Placid on hold?' Roy asks Arun.

'A couple,' Arun says. 'All colour and angst.' He smiles in carefully constrained deprecation. 'Not the kind of stuff Mrs Kulkarni or you would like.'

Arun has no intention of being seen as holding views different from his editor's. He hopes he is doing the right thing running down Placid Hari's writing. There are so many ways of defending the freedom of the press, and, of late, Arun's chosen method has been to go along with whatever his editor said. He's certain that Roy and Mrs Kulkarni are conspiring against him. She must be holding his hand and feeding him all sorts of things. 'You want to carry them?' Arun says tentatively; he is not sure which way Roy is going to swing yet.

'What are they about?' Roy asks.

'One is on a photographer who specializes in dogs and who feels one with his subject. The other is on retirement homes for senior citizens. There are a couple more, really old ones, somewhere in the computer. Placid has always been a little disappointed with us that we never find much use for his talent.'

'It'd be smart to put Placid on the front page. He's in the news now, and we gain by playing him up. You know what I mean?'

'Sure. And in case he is shot, we are made. Only, how do we connect the dog piece to what is happening to Placid or to the city?'

'You don't need any direct connection, Arun. We just need Placid's name for a bit of cross-branding. The intro to the copy is the thing.'

Roy smiles with his false teeth and lapses into some intricate thought which no one else in the room can fathom, if only because he is the editor. His power begins where the knowledge of others ends.

Roy tightens his jaw in concentration, sucks in his cheeks and blows out, all in a matter of seconds, and, click, the denture comes out in his hands. He gazes at it without expression and releases it into a bowl of water, where it drowns to the bottom, laughing hysterically.

The gesture means others are free to talk and argue. The journalists are adept at the game. They voice their opinions with passion. How could the terrorists who were on Indian waters for so long go undetected? How? How? Why were the security forces so slow in responding to the attack? There are theories, explanations and strategies.

Roy sits well back in his chair, hands on the armrests, legs crossed at the ankles on the pitted floor littered with cigarette stubs, matches, wrappers and empty cans. His face is florid and sweating; his eyes are bloodshot from alcohol; a cigarette hangs loose from his lips. He listens to the rabble for an hour or so, and then stretches his hand towards the bowl. 'Right, let's use whatever piece we have by Placid and factor it into the general package. Arun could work out an intro that talks about the paper's close relationship with Placid, and that we are publishing it as a token of appreciation. Just show Placid's copy to me or Mrs Kulkarni before you quark it on to the page.'

A snub, Arun thinks. Arun is senior to Mrs Kulkarni and is not bound to report to her. But Mrs Kulkarni thinks that is a liberty he shouldn't be taking, considering her sway in the grand scheme of things. She knows that for all Arun's unctuousness, he is an arrogant bastard. She is certain Arun thinks her his intellectual inferior and a journalistic lightweight. Mrs Kulkarni bares her teeth to Arun, a kind of unsheathing of the dagger.

'Done,' Arun says, thinking, as if I have an option; I've got six children.

The journalists get up to go, Arun carefully avoiding John Lobo's eyes. Although both of them have been working under Roy for long, they still dare not be seen talking together, because Roy is likely to think they are conspiring. Or, equally dangerously, Mrs Kulkarni might see in the shared corner-whispers the hush of a rebellion, a scheme to subvert her authority. She would pass her intimations to Roy in one of their million private moments; a communication that would consolidate their confidence in each other, reinforce their belief that they are in it together, in this life journey that they have come to undertake against all odds.

'Meet me 4 chai dn,' Arun sms-es John.

'K,' John replies, feeling like a truant schoolboy, and makes his way carefully downstairs to the seedy back alley of the office, the narrow sides of which are covered in blue and black tarpaulin awnings of makeshift food stalls.

'The old man is mad,' Arun says, sipping his tea from a crumbling plastic cup, paper thin from repeated recycling.

'Hey, what was that about a graphic novel?'

'Just playing the role of the loyalist, John. You know me by now, for god's sake. I've got families to take care of.'

'Sure. Just do whatever he wants,' John says, jogging his groin with stubby fingertips. 'The days of hard reporting are over, my friend, and we are now into the marketing of news.

Roy thinks he has a take on it, so be it. Graphic novel, comic strip, short story, skit, give him whatever he wants.'

'Look, John, this piece on dogs has nothing to do with terror. It has no connection with what is happening to the city. People will think it absurd if you put it on the front page.'

'Don't be too sure about people. They are a strange lot. They like to feel they are good and sentimental and for all you know, they may shed tears over the last piece written by a columnist who may fall to a terrorist bullet even as they read his words. They love to place candles and flowers on graves of people like Placid. And, listen, I have gone through the dog piece and it's not half bad. It's just that it seems as if he is reporting from another world.'

'Still, the fact is, it has nothing to do with what's happening.'

'True, but why should it? Placid never knew this city was going to be taken over by a bunch of boys with guns.'

'Well, in any case, I have no alternative but to go along with what he says.'

'Have you read Placid's copy?'

'I don't know if I want to waste my time on some soft, maudlin stuff when the city is going up in flames.'

'Just run an eye over it and pass it to the desk. Then go home for a drink.'

'It won't be that easy today, but I will certainly try.' Arun listens to a police van racing down the main road.

'And listen, don't suck up too much. They will make out if you lay it on too thick.'

'I'll certainly try,' Arun says. 'I'm going in from the front. You come in a while later from the back. And pay for my tea, will you?'

THE DOG OF SMALL THINGS

Dear Reader, Mr Placid Hari Odannur, a regular contributor to this paper, has been taken hostage by a ruthless terrorist from Pakistan.

Even as he is at the mercy of the jihadis, we publish below, with a prayer on our lips and hope in our hearts, a recent piece by him.

This gesture is a token of our regard for him. Who knows, tomorrow, upon reading this reflective piece, the terrorist, experiencing a change of heart, might even release him. In which happy event, we promise you Mr Odannur's reportage of the events leading to his captivity and freedom.

At the basement of the National Gallery of Modern Art, Bombay, the Delhi-based Udit Rai is holding an exhibition of his photographs on street dogs. Maybe it is the afternoon heat, but the hall is deserted. It is so quiet, you can hear ants walk. Rai sits near the door, contemplating the table on which is kept the register for visitor's comments. 'Not too many people coming,' he says in cautious English. 'The heat, maybe.'

Or maybe the dogs. These are not feel-good dog portraits, not cuddly dogs that look like naughty children, which is a bit of a sin in a country where even tigers are made to look like calendar beauties with long-suffering souls. The cuteness is totally missing. So is the assured air of the pedigreed dog that takes its owner for a walk. Rai's dogs don't look like they talk English either.

These are aimless dogs, who bark in Hindi. Dogs that sit or stand, hang around men who sit or stand. Or sleep—next to men who sleep. Or just wait. Dogs that didn't have much of a childhood. Dogs that don't look like they are going to have a comfortable old age either: drop-out dogs, misfits. Just like millions of ordinary Indians. Just like Udit Rai.

Rai passed his bachelor's in Hindi and then took a master's in Buddhist studies, neither of which was a sunrise subject in a country that worships money. Then, inexplicably, he switched to photography, from which he does not make enough to make a living.

'My wife is employed,' he says, reaching for a flask of coffee brought from home. Rai's wife is a teacher and that partly explains his freedom to be marginal. Your liberty is almost always someone else's slavery.

Rai is 47. He wears his hair long, his kurta longer. He looks like an unpaid ad for the poor man's Fab India. His smile is without focus, and is flavoured with a kind of tedium; the tedium of knowing the inescapable limitations of the rooted, dogged ordinariness of his talent. 'It's not dogs,' Rai says, 'that I shoot. It's street life. Normal Indian life.'

He pauses. Rai is a slow talker. And after a while, you too tend to talk slow. The pauses in our conversation get longer, as if there has been an unspoken, mutual pact. The world perceptibly decelerates.

To shoot the pictures, Rai travelled to a lot of places in India. He clearly believes travel is a way of living. And he is modestly proud that he has been up and about. His biodata says, 'Places in bold have been visited more than once.' It is as if travel in itself is a kind of achievement, a Zen-like specialization he has attained a certain proficiency in.

'Isn't it expensive to get around?'

'I travel second class. Stay third class.' He smiles. The smile is all Buddha. It means acceptance. A man who knows his place to be the corner-stool in a hall of thrones.

'What's this exhibition doing for you?'

'I don't know,' he says. 'I was not too keen. The Indian Institute of Culture asked and I said yes. They footed the bill for everything.'

Though the portraits are not great studies in grunge or grit, they come across as snapshots of an India we tend to consider as not really relevant to our scheme of things. Yet they say something. Perhaps a muted statement of sympathy for a less demanding, less hierarchical culture.

There is, for instance, a photograph of a tiny waiting hall for women at a wayside railway station, occupied by a clutch of listless men who sit, sleep, or read a newspaper. In the foreground lies a dog. The activity they share—sleeping or waiting—blurs the spiritual distinction between man and dog. Evolution grinds to a halt at the waiting hall: man and dog are reduced to the same level, united by the alarming purposelessness of their existence.

This is what you read into the picture. Rai himself is not willing to be overly articulate about his work. His camera just senses a philosophical similitude between man and his best friend.

Does he have plans for the future?

'No. No plans. Best to take it as it comes.' He sits back. After a longish while, he reaches for the coffee again. 'Want some coffee?'

'Sure, thanks,' I say. I sit back in the chair too, watching coffee being poured into a white cup in front of me. It is quiet in the hall, where two men are about to drink coffee while the dogs look on. Just another moment. Perhaps that's all there is to it. The future seems extravagant, unnecessary.

'Let me tell you something. If this guy wasn't in terrorist custody, this piece would still be sitting in the trash bin.' Roy smiles.

'Well, as you said, it helps to milk the situation,' Arun says.

'Don't make it sound so crass. After all, you make a living working for this paper. And what's good for us is good for you, don't you think?'

'Absolutely.'

'Let's go with it, then.'

'I'll give you the front-page line-up over the phone later.'

'All right.'

Roy hesitates for a moment and half turns—a secret signal—in the narrow aisle in the direction of Mrs Kulkarni's cubicle, then makes his way to the door. Arun locks his eyes to the ground as Mrs Kulkarni gets up from her chair and passes him, the tail of her sari trailing in the air, leaving behind a whiff of some herbal perfume. Soon, the two will be in the leather-bound privacy of Roy's car, taking stock of the day's proceedings, assessing signs of stray revolt, but always grateful for the reassuring miracle of each other.

Arun stares at the computer screen. Did he overplay his hand with the graphic novel? He is aware that they have been interviewing young candidates for senior news management positions. They had never called him to sit for any of the meetings.

One of those candidates, Arun knows only too well, could be his replacement. He had, of course, sent word out into the market that he was available. But it was not easy to break into another establishment at his level.

Arun punches his password. The computer stacks up the menu. Of late, Arun has been finding the glare of the screen too much to bear. His eyes constantly blink. The ocular muscles are so tired, he finds it hard to keep his eyes open. The doctor had said his tear ducts were drying up. Nothing serious, but he would do well to keep them lubricated at all times. The doctor had smiled at him in reassurance. He had seen so many such cases; no one had yet lost his vision because he couldn't cry. But Arun should try not to stare at the screen for too long—'the human eye is not made for the computer, Arun sir,' the doctor had said with a laugh—and, of course, there was the factor of age.

Ah, age, Arun thinks, and two wives. A middle-aged bigamist with an eye problem. Arun opens the front-page folder to look at the edited articles. He would probably place Placid's piece as a narrow anchor and take the turn on page two. A lot depended on the other stories. He feels bad for the dead. The terrorist strike has been so fast and deadly, it has been unreal. But deep in his heart, he knows he is more concerned about his career than the day drowning in blood.

Arun closes his eyes. They grate. The glare seems extra virulent today, as if a white-hot sun is reaching out through the screen and radiating plasma all over the room, erasing every object to a sandy white ache. Arun shakes his head, reaches into his pocket for GenTeal eye cream. He squeezes the tube tight and lines his eyes with the cool gel in an effort to keep them open in a world turning slowly blind.

ELEVEN

Any Instructions, Master? I'm Dying

On the first floor of the Taj, Colaba, in room 141, Shafi is lying on his stomach on the floor of the bathroom, gun in one hand, mobile in the other, warily watching a damaged TV set that roars into life once in a while, showing x-ray images of the action outside.

Shafi has been shot in the leg and is waiting for the showdown. He knows he and his boys have done a good job. A very good job. The kind of job a whole army couldn't do. They have killed hundreds, scared the pants off an enemy nation, proved that a battle is won in the heart before it is won on the ground. Six of them had shown India her place. And, no, the enemy did not come across as a superpower.

Shafi wipes the sweat off his forehead with his tattered shirt sleeve. The AC ducts had ceased functioning long ago. Shafi had got shot outside the room in the long dark corridor, but had managed to dive into a room. He had closed the door before dragging himself on his elbows into the bathroom from where he can see the main door with relative advantage of perspective.

Shafi shifts, rests his weight on his left elbow. He presses the keys of the cellphone. He will talk to Maulana Abul Razak now. Shafi wants instructions. He hopes the Maulana will have something to say, a secret wisdom, a command that will make his last passage lighter, a password to be uttered in Allah's presence.

But the Maulana's number is busy. When he finally gets through to Abul Razak, all Shafi can bring himself to mention is his immediate partner's death. 'Abdul Rehman bhaiyya Allah ko pyaare ho gaye'—Allah has taken a liking to Brother Abdul Rehman.

Abul Razak listens to his disciple from across the sea and looks around for help. It would be best for him to hand the phone over to one of his assistants as he is not well at all, but none seems at hand. He is alone as ever. 'May Allah embrace him,' Abul Razak says with feeling, at one with the heroism of the jihadis. 'Deaths are to be expected, and a hero's death is dear to Allah. When the time comes, He will hold you close to His heart. But you have to be patient. Have courage and carry on fighting.'

Tears spring to Shafi's eyes. How well the boys had held on to their faith! How trivial they considered their lives! How they fought to their last bullet! Shafi takes stock of his ammunition. There isn't much left. 'I am trapped in the bathroom. Not much ammunition left either.'

Abul Razak looks at his watch. The dial seems to show the wrong time. Has he strapped it upside down? In any case, it seems to Abul Razak, he is getting late for something, an important event whose nature is hazy, but is heavy with promise. 'My brave Shafanullah, you have to come out and fight. Try to escape to another position by lobbing the hand grenades.'

Shafi can make out on the TV that soldiers from the National Security Guard are taking position in the stairwell. Any time now they would burst through the door. There will be no escape or another position to fire from. 'Grenade phek di hain dono'—I have already thrown the two grenades that I had with me.

Abul Razak forces himself to remember that there is a war on and his soldiers have run out of ammunition. Surely, they should have taken a bigger arsenal with them? 'How many AK-47 magazines do you have?' Abul Razak asks, shaking his head furiously to stay focussed.

'Just two.'

'That isn't much. My brave Shafanullah, take care not to be caught alive. They might burst open the door and throw smoke bombs into the room. If you fall unconscious and they arrest you, it will be a great loss. Use a wet towel and hold it against your nose. Keep firing till the last bullet and try to force your way out. That way, they will have no option but to shoot you down,' Abul Razak dictates to Shafi like a recorded message.

'Yes, that's the way to go,' Shafi says. No secret wisdom, then, Shafi thinks; no messages from the Maulana to Allah, either. Just basic lessons in dying.

'Did you get the master?' asks the Maulana suddenly.

'Who?' says Shafi.

'The English teacher. Did you get him?'

'Who?' Shafi is puzzled. The Maulana's voice has become distracted and faint. Shafi thinks he has heard right, but there really is no time to solve this mystery, not when he is about to die. A moment later, he hears Abul Razak speak again and to Shafi's relief, his words are firm even if not revelatory.

'Allah awaits you. And my brave man, keep your mobile switched on in your pocket so I can hear what's going on. Khuda hafiz.'

'Khuda hafiz,' says Shafi, as the door of the hall comes down in a burst of gunfire and the TV blows out.

TWELVE

Mere Anarchy Is Loosed upon the World

Hoofed and horned, confusion runs amok in the Cow Sena procession. Hundreds of thousands of people scatter in panic, spilling all over the road, bringing traffic to a halt.

The rank and file of the procession have come to know that the made-up cow, with beads around its neck and gold plate on its forehead, has gone missing. It is not clear how this happened or when. The beast was leading the movement from the front, blessing seekers and devotees and accepting gifts and grass since morning when the procession began, ominously enough, from Mahim Mosque, to the apprehension of the bearded tribe of beefeaters collected there.

Till the rally wound its way to Anderson Road, all was well. The slogans rang out loud and clear, the human chain of volunteers was doing a good job of keeping the procession confined to one part of the straight and narrow path, occupying only half of the road.

True, quite a few had got drunk and begun dancing to Bollywood music. But the revelry was confined to pockets. In a five-kilometre-long procession, such aberrations hardly mattered. On the whole, the Cow Sena leaders would have been right in thinking that they were about to pull off a great show of strength.

Then, suddenly, a little before Zircon, a small blue pickup van with 'Karachiwala' written in red on the side barrelled in from left to right through a delusionary window in the traffic to the procession side of the road, instantly creating a logjam. In the back of the van were three cows. The driver of the van desperately tried to find a way out of the snarl, but each turn of the wheel and shift of gear drove him deeper into trouble.

The cows in the back were tied to each other with barely any standing space. They stood like statues and looked out, their heads to the procession, their tails to the driver's cabin. Their horns were painted red, which meant that they were marked for the slaughter house.

At the sight of the cows, the procession broke up. Their worst fears had come true: the holy animal of Vedic fame had no future in its homeland. The Sainiks had always known it, of course. But here was incontrovertible proof: a Muslim driver with a cargo of the holy animals deliberately disrupting a Sena procession whose stated theme was to protect the cow!

The sheer effrontery of it! Immediate action was required. Once and for all, who did the country belong to? The Muslim minority—compulsive cow consumers—or the Hindu majority, its worshippers? Which way lay true democracy? Whither Vedic India? Cow Cola or Coca Cola? The time had come to answer these questions. The moment of truth for the country was here—on Anderson Road.

With the Cow Sena leaders delegating this important task to themselves, they extricate themselves from the entangled procession and begin discussing the development.

'Flatten the tyres and free the holy animals,' says one of them.

'Give it to the driver, son of a bitch. Let him go tell his sisterfucking Pakistani boss. Karachiwala!'

'Here, I've got a knife,' says another. 'Just the thing for a Muslim tyre.'

'I have a sword,' says another, his hand reaching under his collar for the weapon strapped to his back. A third draws out a country-made revolver from his pocket.

The leaders and their followers approach the three cows, weapons drawn. The cows look at their potential assassins and roll their eyes. Will they be slain in full public view? If Hindus too are turning hostile, the future looks bleak.

The leader with the gun fires into the air as the Cow Sainiks come close to the van. Raghuram, the driver, and his assistant take one look at the armed and advancing Sainiks and, killing the engine, bolt.

This is the second time a misfortune of this sort has happened to Raghuram. The first was when his father, an untouchable Hindu, thought he was being clever opening a sweetmeat shop in the far-flung suburb of Bhiwandi in Bombay and deciding to call it 'Karachiwala' after the famous sweet makers from Karachi, Pakistan.

In a riot that killed over a dozen a few years ago, aggrieved Hindus set fire to the shop. It was much later that they realized their mistake. They did apologize, but their hearts were not in it, and there was certainly no compensation. If Hindus christened their enterprises with Muslim names, it was a risk they took. Raghuram's father moved to another part of Bombay and, not learning his lesson, named his next business—the dung-dotted transport of cattle—also Karachiwala.

The leaders look at the fleeing driver and his assistant. Here now before them is the solution to India's Muslim problem.

Clearly, the only way to deal with them is confrontation. Instead, what does the Indian government do? Treats them with kid gloves, gives them concessions at the expense of Hindus, just to get the votes of the 160 million Muslims in the country. Secularism is just a trade-off! It is religious appeasement. And it has been going on since the 1947 partition.

But it need not be so any more. The Cow Sena leaders have just shown how to deal with the Karachiwalas and put errant Muslims to flight. Confrontation, surely, is the name of the game.

The procession splinters into groups. Thousands spill all over the road. The traffic is a mess. Scores of saffron shirts shout lustily and pursue the pickup driver and his assistant, both of whom seem to be flying in the air over the bonnets and tops of a million stranded cars, from which arise into the air, like birds out of beaten bush, startled cries of shock and indignation.

But there is no sign of the bedecked lead cow, that gem of an animal. 'That plate was pure gold,' someone shouts, 'pure twenty-four-carat. Purest.'

To be fair, though, the gold takes nothing away from the cow. This one is a special animal even by the Cow Sena's exacting standards. For one, it is really huge. It has a presence few ruminants can aspire to. For another, it is white, a great asset in a country which cherishes fairness as a moral virtue. For a third, it has a growth on its back, shaped like the holy letter ॐ. For a less visible fourth, this cow has been trained to climb steps to reach platforms and stand in benign grandeur while Sena leaders make speeches on its behalf. Clearly, a cow among cows. And now it has vanished into the clamouring air without a sisterfucking trace.

'The man who got that cow is going to be very rich,' a Cow Sainik with a material mind says.

'That gold plate belongs to the Cow Sena. The treasurer is going to throw a fit,' another says.

'But where can it have disappeared?'

'There was no need to fix that gold plate on the cow. Tell me, what was the need?'

'The gold looked good on the cow. Cow is the same as our mother.'

'Maybe your mother.'

'Hey, watch your tongue.'

'All right, I am sorry. But you shouldn't be sending a cow about the city with gold all over it. It's asking for trouble.'

'But who would have thought someone would stoop so low as to kidnap a cow? The cow is like a mother.'

Has the cow been kidnapped? By vengeful Muslims? There are rumours that terrorists have entered the city. Did they infiltrate the procession and make off with the cow? If that is the case, some people will dine well tonight. The thought is unspeakable. The Sainik leader with the gun fires into the air again.

THIRTEEN

The Lasting Fragrance of Tata Hair Oil (Jasmine Flavour)

If he ever gets out of this alive, he would stop writing for newspapers, Placid promises himself. He is through with the fame game. He has had enough of the rumour rags and their petty office politics.

But extricating himself from this mess seems nearly impossible. In an irony he might have laughed at had it been less immediate, he and his custom-built femme fatale responsible for his premature end are on the same boat starting out across the Styx. They have come together for the last hand-in-hand ride over the dark waters.

'What is all this about? Is this one more of your games?' Placid asks Lakshmi, who is sitting next to him, bound like the others to the four-poster in the room.

Lakshmi glances at Beverly and remains silent.

'It's about what you did to Lakshmi years ago,' Beverly says.

'What I did to Lakshmi years ago? I am talking about what she did to me last night and how that's going to kill me today.'

'I think you deserve what's coming to you.'

He wants to say, what's coming to me is also what's coming to you, you self-righteous bitch. 'For god's sake, what did I do to her?'

'Why don't you ask her?'

'What did I do to you that I am with you today, waiting for my death?' Placid asks Lakshmi.

'Appa, this ees a praivate mattar and wee should not be heering eet,' Githaa says.

'Oh, give me a break, Githaa,' Rajgopal says. Private matter, he thinks, some private matter. We are about to be killed and these people are settling old scores. And he, Rajgopal, who has nothing to do with it, is right in the middle of the crossfire when—had Lord Ganesha willed it—he could have been happy watching that Latino babe at work. 'You like to listen to this sort of thing, Githaa. I know you.'

'Wot naansense,' Githaa says. 'At least ai yyam not watching dirrty pictures.' As if, Githaa thinks, I don't know what he is doing behind those closed doors. Insurance work with a towel!

'Quiet,' Rajgopal says, as if he hasn't heard his wife. 'Please allow Lakshmi to speak. This is a serious matter.' Under the circumstances, he thinks it best to pitch himself as an elder statesman. He is surprised that Githaa knows what he was up to, but he would be damned if he admitted it.

'You remember a night some sixteen years ago?' Lakshmi asks Placid.

'What night?'

'A night on a Churchgate–Virar train when it rained and the lights went out?'

'No, I don't.'

'He just won't admit it,' Lakshmi says, turning to Beverly.

'How do I proceed with someone who, after all these years, is still in a state of denial?'

'You forced yourself on Lakshmi that night and you don't remember?' Beverly is outraged. 'You should be turned over to the police. Unfortunately, we have landed here and you got lucky.'

Some luck, Placid thinks. 'I forced myself on Lakshmi on a train sixteen years ago? And so I was trussed up while you two thought up a retribution plan?'

'That's about it,' Beverly says. 'More or less. Glad you finally figured out what it's all about.'

'Well, all I can say is, I am sorry, but that wasn't me on the train.'

'What did I tell you?' Lakshmi looks at Beverly who is shaking her head.

What I need is a cigarette, Beverly thinks. And maybe a whip. A whip would do very well. I could teach this son of a bitch a thing or two. 'Men,' Beverly says, shaking her head. 'The least you can do is to admit and apologize. Lakshmi might even forgive you, though if I was in her shoes, I'd be looking for something hard and sharp.'

'You two are crazy, aren't you? I am *not* the man Lakshmi is looking for! I was not on that train. Hell, I was not even in Bombay sixteen years ago. And I don't rape—on principle. Why don't you go ahead and accuse me of murder as well? There are so many taking place in this city.'

'Principle,' Lakshmi says, 'as if people commit rape or murder on principle.'

'That is not what I meant.'

'I know what you meant. You needn't bother to explain. It's all quite clear.'

'Give me proof. A shred of proof.'

'What proof?'

'You damn me with a vile charge and you keep repeating it as if everything has been proved. Give me some evidence.'

'I am the evidence.'

'That is hardly evidence!'

'You smelled of alcohol, Tata hair oil, sea.'

'I don't know if that's true, because I can't remember.'

'Is your forgetfulness supposed to be a clinching argument in favour of your case?'

'It's as good or bad as saying a remembered body odour is proof.'

'Did you or did you not use Tata hair oil?'

'Jasmine scent? That was the most popular hair oil fragrance then. I may have used it along with a million others.'

'Did you or did you not?' Beverly comes to Lakshmi's defence.

'Look, I don't know who you are. And I don't think I like that tone of yours.'

'Rapist,' Beverly says.

'Fuck you.'

'Plees,' Githaa says, 'plees, we are going to die soon, and thees ees not the language we should use just before avar death.'

'I may have used the oil. I used to share a room with somebody who liked Tata hair oil, but I certainly don't know if I used it on days that I went raping women.'

'Let's not talk about that day, then,' Lakshmi says.

But even in this state, Placid finds her attractive. He feels a vague fondness for her, a few faint stirrings of sympathy. Lakshmi has gone to great lengths to have him—if indeed he is the man she is looking for—at her mercy. And when she finally got him where she wanted, she was not sure what to do with him. That was why she had gone out, leaving him in the bathtub. She couldn't decide. But Placid cannot get over the bizarre story: rape in a moving train in the dark.

He finds Lakshmi attractive, all right. If the situation were different, he might even want to see more of her. Is it possible, though, that she suffers from delusional fits? He doesn't know. Maybe she was raped, after all. It is possible, of course. Everything is possible. There are fifteen million people in Bombay. They do at least fifteen million things at any given time. A rape on a train is perhaps a configurable eventuality, given the odds that the city constantly gambles with. Or murder.

Or pretty much anything.

FOURTEEN

A Monsoon Offering

When the call comes, Fatima is in her favourite rocking chair in the darkened drawing room. She spends her afternoons there. It is very quiet in the hall, except for the occasional screech of a parrot from the mango orchards which surround the house. The heavy curtains keep the heat and light of the day out. Actually, it is quite pleasant just now, after the rains. The ceiling fan, a brown Orient with bronze inlay and a lamp at the hub of it, slowly threshes the air.

'Hello,' she says.

'Ammi, it's me.'

'Salim! Finally you found time to call,' Fatima says.

'Are you all right?'

'Am I all right? What am I supposed to say? That my son will get shot any moment now and that I feel good?'

'Ammi, I am sorry. I am not allowed to call you.'

'What *are* you allowed to do?'

'Something has happened. Will you be honest, please?'

'You have no right to expect anything from me, Salim.'

'I said I am sorry. I am doing this for a cause.' It's so difficult to explain these things, Salim thinks.

'Islam doesn't demand death.'

'Let's not get into that now. This is not the time, Ammi. The reason why I called is, I have run into your other son.'

'What? Are you all right?' Fatima asks, disconcerted.

'Yes, your other son. And I am not mad, if that's what you mean.'

'My other son!' Fatima says as a forgotten ache grips her heart. The only other son she had died at birth long ago. She had gone to the hospital in the middle of the night, fully expecting to be a mother by morning. She had borne the pain joyfully, in anticipation of her baby. And when it finally arrived, assisted by surgery, it was lifeless. 'Which son? How do you know he is my other son? Some stranger tells you I am his mother and you believe it?'

'No, he doesn't know you,' Salim says. Hesitation creeps into his voice. 'He didn't know you existed till he ran into me a little while ago.'

'Where are you?'

'I can't tell you that, Ammi.'

'Another top secret that only I don't know.'

'It's just that I am following orders.'

'You have already broken one.'

'I asked you a question.'

'I thought you were accusing me of something.'

'Just answer me.'

'What are you trying to say, Salim? That I have a son from a secret relationship?'

'He is my twin, Ammi.'

Fatima places the receiver like a baby in her lap and keeps utterly still for a moment. She watches the shadows on the floor play in the breeze, listens to the chiming of the bells in the portico.

'Ammi?' Salim says, sitting against the door in Lakshmi's apartment.

Salim should be *here*, not wherever that he was. Fatima feels sick. Where is everybody gone? Her father, her mother, her missing husband, her dead son, Salim. She picks up the receiver and says gently: 'Yes, Salim? I am here.'

'He is my twin, Ammi. His name is Nirmal. Can you hear me? My twin brother happens to be Hindu. You know what that makes me? A Hindu jihadi. Isn't that funny?' Salim lowers his voice to a whisper. 'Did you have two sons?'

'No. Not two sons.'

'Am I your son?'

'Yes, of course, you are my son.' If he wasn't her son, whose son was he? If he was anybody's son, he was hers. Surely, that much was beyond doubt. There was not a moment in their relationship when he could have thought he was not wanted. She couldn't think of a life without him, though that too had happened in the last year or two, thanks to the Maulana. The unthinkable, Fatima now knows, always happened. Who would have thought that Salim, so good at his studies, would become a jihadi!

'Ammi, how do you explain my twin? How do you explain his being Hindu? My being Hindu?'

'He is your twin? And he says he is Hindu? Why should you believe him more than me? How does he know he is Hindu?'

'Do you want to talk to him, Ammi? To your other son?'

'No.'

'Please tell me, am I your son or not?'

'I refuse to be questioned like this,' Fatima says.

'Are you my mother or not?' Salim's voice has become louder. It comes across cold and clear.

'I am not going to be bullied by you even if this is our last conversation.'

'Please answer me.'

'All right,' Fatima says slowly, as if reciting lines from a lesson learnt long ago. 'You are my adopted son. I got you from Bombay.'

Fatima listens to the silence.

'I am your adopted son,' Salim says. 'An Indian by birth.'

'Salim? But that has made no difference to me and you know it.'

For a long moment, Salim says nothing. His heart races under his shirt. His gun feels heavy in his hand. He leans his head against the wall. He is exhausted. For the first time since the mission began, he feels inadequate. He is aware that Nirmal is watching him. It is very odd, he tells himself, to have someone who looks exactly like you stationed outside your body. 'Oh, I see,' Salim says. 'That makes sense, really.'

He glances at Nirmal and is filled with affection for him. So we are the two guys, he thinks, we've got just ourselves. That I was rejected at birth by my own mother is not good news, though. But I could have done worse. Look at Nirmal. He really must have had a tough time of it, a street for a bed, a stone for a pillow. I at least had Ammi, who loved me. But now, in any case, it does not matter. Now that I am about to get killed. But I do wish to know who my mother is. That is only natural.

'Now that you know,' Fatima says into the mouthpiece, 'does it make any difference to you?'

'No, not really,' Salim says. Does it really make no difference? He is not sure. It is odd to learn in another country that you had a few very basic things wrong.

Now that Salim knows, does it make any difference to Fatima? Yes, it does. The fact that Salim knows that she has not given birth to him is painful to her.

Fatima never lied to Salim. But she had kept that vital piece of information to herself. He didn't have to know. Now that he does, it feels as though something has been taken away from her, a certain authority that has no basis in fact.

The fact was a night in Bombay years ago. A night in June, when the city was going under the rains. Her father had sent her on a tour so she could travel her way out of her depression following her abortive pregnancy. She was on her last lap home.

Fatima had got stuck on her way to Bombay's Sahar International Airport near a traffic island shimmering red and green in the rain. Around her taxi, the water kept rising; with it, all kinds of objects. A red bucket, a yellow helmet, a tricycle, a single sandal, a dead dog. An hour more of this rain, and her taxi would lose its moorings and float.

It had rained the whole evening, each drop sharp as a nail, heavy as lead. The windshield of the taxi she sat in misted over so fast that the driver had to stop the car every now and then to wipe it with a dirty piece of cloth, which he also used to mop his neck and face.

As the wipers struggled, thick worms of water ran up the windshield and down to the sides. The lights of the city broke into pixels in the rain, hung and glimmered in the glass of the window, wet, crying splotches of colour. The road had become an open drain through which the rainwater flooded out. Fatima hoped she would be in time for her flight. The traffic moved, stopped, and moved. If she was lucky, the flight too would be delayed. It was hard to imagine a big plane taking off in this stormy weather.

She was somewhere in Andheri, an empty-looking junction from where the road sharply turned towards the airport. It seemed to her that she had been in the cab and in the rain for a very long time. It never rained so hard in Sultanpur. She closed her eyes. It would be good to get home. She was used to the solitude. Her father was mostly away on business, and her mother had stayed away from Sultanpur since Fatima was six years old.

Fatima's mother was a former college beauty queen from Islamabad. Cold, distant, surgical. One day, in Sultanpur, she had gone out for her morning walk, cut it short because of a sprained ankle, and returned home to find her husband in bed with the servant. 'I am sorry, but this is not the first time, is it?' she said. Her expression hadn't changed. The same morning, though, she had packed her bags and moved.

Before she left, she came up to Fatima and asked in a matter-of-fact tone—as if she was running a temperature—whether she wanted to come with her. Fatima had thought for a moment, weighed the consequences, and said with the clarity only children have: 'No. I'll take care of the house.' And she had.

Fatima loved her father. He treated her as a grown-up, gave her the freedom to be herself. Still, in the beginning, it was hard to grow up with a single parent, to gradually wrest control of the house from maids who were willing to sleep with her father for a little more power and money. By the time her father passed away, she had grown too independent to seek the emotional support of her mother.

Fatima must have dozed off for a few moments, because when she opened her eyes, a young woman was standing outside in the rain, an umbrella held over her head. She was knocking on the window. With the water streaming down the window, she couldn't make out her face. The woman seemed too well-turned-out for a beggar. Fatima lowered the glass and the rain reached right into the taxi.

'What is it?' Fatima asked the woman.

'You shouldn't have opened the window,' the driver said to Fatima in the rear-view mirror. He was experienced in the ways of Bombay's streets.

'You want a child?' the woman said.

'What's that again?' Fatima said.

'You want a baby?' the woman asked again.

'Please, roll the window up, madam,' the driver said. 'The rain is coming in.'

'Just a minute,' Fatima said to the driver. She couldn't help noticing how good-looking the woman was. 'Do I want a baby?' she said to the stranger in the rain.

'A good baby. Healthy and beautiful.'

'No,' Fatima said. 'I don't want a baby.'

'I have two,' the woman said. 'Two babies. The gods have been kind.'

'No, thank you. If the gods have been kind, why don't you keep them?' Fatima couldn't help asking.

The woman said nothing.

'I recently lost mine,' Fatima said. But the woman didn't seem to have heard.

'They are new. Just three days old.'

'Please go away.' Fatima raised the window glass.

The taxi inched forward through the rain. The wipers struggled like broken hands warding off blows.

'She is mad,' the elderly driver said. 'Full pagal.'

The car picked up speed momentarily but the woman ran by the side of the car, knocking on the window.

'Stop the car,' Fatima said, distressed.

'There are so many of them out there. You can't stop the car for all of them,' the driver said. He knew where all of it was leading to: business.

'Stop the car.'

'You will miss the flight.'

'Stop the damn car!' Fatima shouted.

'It's your flight,' the driver said, stopping the car and wiping the windshield vigorously with the cloth. But it was of no use, as it misted over again in no time. He folded the cloth and returned it to his shoulder.

The woman had been left behind. She now ran up to the car. The umbrella bobbed over her head clumsily.

Fatima lowered the window. 'Show me the baby.'

'Two, I will show you both.'

'You'd better get in the car,' Fatima said, opening the door.

The woman fumbled with her umbrella, which was oversized. The wind pulled the cloth back, reversing the top completely, turning it into a crown with spokes. She turned around, her back to the wind, and closed the umbrella. Over her shoulders hung two bags made of thick khadi cloth. She climbed into the car, leaned the umbrella in a corner, its handle down. A pool of water collected at the spot almost immediately. 'The babies are in the bags. You want to take a look at them?' She made them sound like pups.

'Why are you doing this?' Fatima asked, half in dread and half in fascination.

'Doing what?' The woman looked up. She seemed drained, as if she was at the end of a long act.

'Selling the babies.'

'I am not selling my babies,' she said sharply. 'I am giving them away. It is difficult for another person to understand. Very difficult.'

With great care, the woman brought one of the bags forward to Fatima's lap. 'I am giving them away free, you understand. This has nothing to do with money. It's charity,' she added brightly. 'You have a cigarette on you?'

'No, I don't smoke. We are not encouraged to smoke in Pakistan, where I come from.' I am getting late for my flight, Fatima thought. 'Does it rain like this every year?'

'Nearly every year.' But this year, the woman explained, the rains had been exceptionally heavy. 'You want one baby or two?'

'How did you get to have two babies?'

'They are twins. Twins happen, don't you know? Take both, please.'

'Are they really yours?'

The woman stared at Fatima. For a moment, Fatima thought she would slap her. Then she said, 'Yes. Both are my babies. My own babies.'

'I'll take one,' Fatima said.

'Take both if you can. You look rich. It's just that they will be together. Twins like to be together.'

'Ah, but they don't know they are twins.'

'All right, then. Take one,' the woman said.

She took a swaddled baby out from the cloth bag and handed it over to Fatima. Her hand was long and smooth, her fingers round and tapering. 'It's a boy. He is just three days old. He has a black mole shaped like the map of India behind his right ear. Just like the other one.'

'I don't know if I am doing the right thing.'

'God will bless you. All the gods. We Hindus have thirty-three million gods. They will all bless you.'

'What about the other child? Is it a boy too?'

'Yes, a boy. I don't know what I can do for him. I am praying for him.'

'I could give you some money and you needn't part with your babies.'

'I can't live here with these babies.' She looked out at the city shrouded in the rain.

'What will you do with the other child? The brother?' Fatima asked. I wish I could take both, she thought. But it would prove to be too much. 'What will the other boy do?'

'I'll look around for someone like you.'

So this is how people behaved when they lost everything, Fatima thought. They smiled, spoke words people normally used when they were relatively intact, brushed the hair back from their eyes. Every pore of their body bled, and they still acted as if they could still taste the coffee in their mouth so that strangers around them did not get upset and think they were not normal or capable of reasonable reactions.

When Fatima lost her baby, a nurse had come along a few hours later and asked with a kind smile: 'Are you all right?' And Fatima had turned to the wall, the white cliff that she had fallen off, and said, 'I'm fine.'

She was not fine at all. Everything inside her felt twisted and broken. Her mind was a rag that fluttered with each breath she took. Yet, that is what she said. That she was fine. People tried to act normal even if it broke their hearts. They said words without meaning them. It was a way of conducting the business of life. A transaction that did not stand up to close scrutiny, but was functional. It kept things going. In the absence of the compulsion to be normal, everything broke down. Appearance was at the heart of sustainability.

'Are you sure this is what you want to do?' Fatima asked the woman.

'Yes. You will take care of him, won't you?'

'Yes, I'm from Pakistan.' She repeated the information, as if the mention of Pakistan was a kind of assurance. 'Don't you want to know my name and address?'

'No. Pakistan is fine. It's as good as India, I'm sure,' the woman said, wiping the mist on the window and staring through the glass. The landmarks appeared to her out of context. As if she had just woken up in a car that was travelling backwards. 'I'll get down here, if that's all right with you,' said the woman, glancing at the deserted road.

'I could drop you some place where there are people. A restaurant, maybe?'

'No, this is just fine. I am sure there is a bus stand around the corner. I will take a bus back to the city. The service in Bombay is good.'

'Here, take this money,' Fatima said, taking a wad of notes from her bag.

'No, that's fine. I just want money for a night's meal.'

'No, take it all.'

'All right, thank you. I'll accept this as a gift, but please don't think the money is for the baby.'

'I won't. It's just a gift. Don't worry about the baby.'

'I know he is in good hands,' the woman said, stepping out of the car. 'I got lucky. My baby got lucky.' She opened the umbrella and asked Fatima, one hand on the door handle: 'You are sure you don't want the brother? They will be good for each other.'

'No, I am sorry.'

'Not much I can do, then.' She seemed relieved. Perhaps because she could hold on to her other baby for some more time. 'Bye.'

Fatima held the baby close to her chest. He was sleeping. In the dim light of the car, she could see his face, shrivelled like an ancient's. A tiny old man—sleeping through his first monsoon—who had closed his eyes in one country and would open them in another, under the aegis of an alien god.

Fatima looked back. The woman was cradling her bag in one hand. With the other, she held on to the umbrella. Her hand seemed to strain against it. It had become another burden. Any moment now, it would be pulled inside out all over again. The rain beat down with renewed vigour; and the water running down the rear window and the milk of the vapours curdled Fatima's view.

She rocked the baby. She would take him home. There would be no trouble about that. She did not think anyone would question her at the airport. If someone did, she could always say that she had just given birth to it. No official would be mean enough to question her about a three-day-old baby. Besides she looked like she was from a well-to-do family. No, there would be no problem about taking the baby home. Her father would understand. That was the best thing about him. He knew that the world was big enough for the unexpected. And there was no one else to whom she cared to explain herself.

The driver shook his head and shifted gear. His conscience was free. He had warned her. He had been a taxi driver for thirty years. He had seen a lot. He had known right away where this was going to end up. Now there was nothing he could do. He was only a driver. He just had to drop his passenger at the airport and look for a return fare.

Fatima looked back again. She couldn't see the woman any more. There were just headlamps of the cars at the back splintering through the water in the dark, the air a sodden, yellow haze. There was no mother, no baby. Ya Allah! God was great. Fatima held a kerchief to her face and wept at both the justice and injustice of it all. But mostly she cried for the other baby, the one out in the rain, separated from his brother, looking for a taker in his sleep.

'You are all right, Salim,' Fatima says into the receiver. 'Nothing happened to you. I got you from Bombay. I took you home. I loved you and took care of you. We had a good time for many years.'

'I'm not complaining,' Salim says. 'I just wanted to know.' All the same, he was disappointed. It was not fair.

'Now you do. I'd like to speak to your brother.'

'All right. He just finished acting in a movie. Ammi, your other son is a star. Here, speak to him.'

'I am an adopted child. So now you know that she is not your mother either.' Salim hands Nirmal the cellphone, without looking up.

'Hello,' Nirmal says into the phone.

'Hello,' Fatima says, a catch in her breath. 'I should have taken you in as well. I had the chance. Your mother offered you too.'

'Why worry about it now? I've come good,' says Nirmal. She might have been his mother but for a sleight of hand. He notes that, for long, he has been in a position where anybody could become his mother.

'Your mother tried her best to keep you both together, but I couldn't have gone back home with two kids. She tried very hard. I was scared. I thought it would be too much for me to handle, or to explain twins.' Our fears guide us, she thinks, not our courage. 'I am sorry.'

'I guess I just missed the bus,' Nirmal says lightly. Really, that was quite a big bus, actually a plane, which he had missed back there. But if he had got on to it, he wouldn't have landed in Davis's movie.

'You are an actor?'

'Yes. Just finished a movie. I want to be a Bollywood star.'

'Your voice sounds exactly like Salim's.'

'We look the same. *Totally*.'

'I know. That's what your mother said on that rainy night in Bombay years ago.'

'My mother. What did she look like?'

'She was very good-looking. A perfectly round face with two big, dark eyes in it.'

'Didn't she give her name or address?' Nirmal asks, drunk for a moment with hope.

'No. She didn't want my name or address either. I think she wanted to get the past out of her way even if it hurt a lot, and get on with her life. As for me, I thought, grab one of the babies and be gone. Once I was out of India, I would be ok. But memories don't fade so fast, do they? There has been no day I haven't thought about that night.'

'Where in Bombay did you meet her?'

'Somewhere in Andheri, I think … before the road turned in towards the airport. It was raining heavily.'

'I know the place. A flyover has come up there now.'

'It was dark inside the taxi, but when a car at the back came very close, it would light up your mother's face and I kept thinking how pretty she was.'

'A round face with big, dark eyes. That's not much to go on, but I'll be on the lookout,' Nirmal says. He feels empty.

'I am so glad I am talking to you.'

'Me too. It will all turn out well.'

'You think so? Not with Salim taking to guns, surely?' She can never bring herself to say he is a terrorist.

'Let's see what we can do about that. Now that I have run into him, I have to take care of him. You don't lose your brother in a hurry.'

'I have never seen you. Not even that night.'

'Didn't Salim get lucky? That's all over now, though.'

'I know, but I just want to tell you that I still feel bad I left you out in the rain with your mother.' What was I expecting? That he would comfort me? He is my victim, and I expect him to absolve me, she thinks.

'Probably why I don't catch cold easily.'

'I am really sorry,' Fatima says again. She would have hugged Nirmal if he was within reach.

'Don't think about it. Here I am with my terrorist brother. Who would have guessed! That counts for something. We need to save him now.'

'I'm not sure …'

'Let's see. You are my mother, too … as much as Salim's,' Nirmal says, holding on to the phone as if it is a lifeline. Will she ask him to come over, no matter what happens to Salim? He is afraid of her answer. 'You want to speak to Salim?'

'No, I don't want to speak to him. What's left to say to a son who has decided to die when his mother is still alive? Has he already killed?'

'I think so.'

Fatima greets the news with silence. 'Khuda hafiz,' she says. 'Take my number from Salim. Call me when it is all over. Do well.'

'I am Hindu,' Nirmal says. 'Is Salim Hindu or Muslim?'

'I don't know. I just don't know.'

Hindu. Muslim. She doesn't care.

Everybody's god is an accident, she thinks. Some people recover from it. Some people don't. Salim is one of those who didn't. There is nothing she can do about it now. It is too late. It always was too late.

A stone lifts from her heart and rises to her throat. Please don't, she says to Allah. Please, let him come back. Let him lie on the divan here while I listen to my ghazals from another world, a world of roses and moonlight and impossible loves. Let him not do what is irrevocable, let those he killed come back to life, let them rise from the ground, dust themselves and go about their business.

She prays quickly and without break, so she will not have to think of anything else. Let him come back. Let him come back. Let him come back. Ya Allah, Ya Allah, Ya Allah. But it doesn't work. She can think of nothing but Salim and his death in the far city of his birth, his running into his brother moments before he takes leave of this earth. There is a kind of justice in it, she thinks, twisted enough to be labelled poetic.

Fatima takes a deep breath and opens her eyes, hoping the nightmare will fade. That the world will be made whole again. She sits absolutely still as bullets fly, cities burn, and children sit up and cry amidst running feet and rising clouds of dust.

Outside, a breeze shakes itself off the blossoming mango trees and ventures in. Fatima hears the bells outside tinkle faintly through the wreckage of her life.

FIFTEEN

A Trite Tragedy and the Triumph of Rome

Placid was not speaking the truth when he said he was not in Bombay in the year of the rape. That much he would grant on second thoughts.

That was the year he had fallen out with Susan in his home town. And, no, he was not going to forget it in a long while yet. He was never good at dealing with his present; it came across to him as unreal, fraying threads in the winds out of which he could weave no cloth, discern no pattern. But when the moment had gone, he could see the significance of it with clarity. He was good at leading a posthumous life; he was the Keats of Kerala, Professor, Posthumous Studies, as Susan well knew.

'I don't want to see you any more,' Susan said, looking away—as was usual with her when she thought she was furiously right—towards the narrow alley leading to her house, on either side of which were old, tiled houses whose roofs and walls were covered with red-and-white bougainvillea flowers. 'It's not working out for me,' she said.

Oh, it was her birthday, Placid remembered guiltily, and

he hadn't wished her. Placid had just got back from a little travelling—a bit of trekking to find the source of a dried-up river—and hadn't seen Susan for a fortnight.

'You are self-obsessed, and I don't think you are capable of caring for anyone.' Susan almost stammered with rage at her inability to relate to a man who was at all times tense, fraught with the anxiety of making it big as a writer, who was unable to see the value of togetherness in a shared joke, the romance of going out for a walk together, who considered birthdays a chore. He hadn't even bothered to tell her he was off on a two-week trip. Her relationship with Placid fluctuated like a heart patient's ECG.

'No, don't be foolish,' Placid said. 'You wait right here. I am going to get your flowers. It is just that I forgot to pick them up from the florist,' he lied. He had completely forgotten about her birthday. He had never attached any importance to birthdays. Neither his birthday, nor others'.

But he knew that was wrong. People considered their birthdays important. A birthday was a clear indication that they had been born, that they existed. Placid himself dreaded his birthday, because each passing year added to the burden of proving himself a writer.

Placid realized he had committed a grave mistake in neglecting to wish Susan. A bunch of flowers was the least he could have done in belated compensation. Red buds. 'Wait right here,' he said, 'unless you prefer to come along.'

'Flowers on second thought!' Susan said.

Ah, I have been found out, Placid thought.

'Please don't,' Susan said. 'If you do, I will throw up. You don't believe in any of it and I don't like people pretending.' She was sick of this relationship. It was all understanding on her part and convenience on his.

'No, I am serious. Just wait here or at the library, and I'll be right back with the flowers.'

'Library on a birthday! Not a movie, not a drink, but books? For god's sake, Placid, do you ever *care*?' Susan said. She took a deep breath and said in a low, measured voice as if she had realized that anger was of no use, and that it was time to reach a decision: 'You bring those fake flowers and I will throw them in the gutter.' Susan's face was red with rage and the last of the sun.

Placid glanced at the open sewer in a sudden fit of apprehension. Had she rejected the roses even before he bought them? Of course she had. The roses lay there, glimmering redly in the dark of the drainage, like rubies rotting, their fragrance smothered by the stink. His gift. A gift he did not believe in perhaps, but had taken pains to procure. And she had flung them down. Such scant regard for a lovely thought.

'All right then, no flowers, if that's the way you want it,' Placid said. He was furious that so much was being made of so little. Just an act of forgetfulness, really. 'No flowers, no nothing.'

Clearly, Susan didn't understand him. Nobody understood him. He was alone, and he was constantly explaining himself to people of limited intelligence. He was fed up of relationships.

'Thank you.' Susan bowed to him. 'It has been a great pleasure making your acquaintance. But I just want to tell you that I am no longer in a position to suffer that pleasure. Please thrust that pleasure on someone else, some meek woman. One who wears a bindi on her forehead and welcomes you home with a lit lamp.'

'Right,' Placid said. 'Right. I will find someone. Someone with a bindi and a lamp. Someone, in fact, who doesn't mind my tracing a river to its source and won't throw a tantrum if I happen to forget a birthday or two. And while we are at it, I would like to tell you that though I am not totally sure of the bindi and the lamp and the river, I will find someone who is not as vain as you are. And I suggest you refrain from using four-letter words like *care*.'

'I said you don't care. For sure, you have shown no sign of it these last two years. Get the context right. And get it right now, not tomorrow. Idiot.'

'As if *you* care for me. As if you care for *anyone*. You are so vain. Vain, you understand? If you were a little less good-looking, you wouldn't be so vain. Or even if you were a little less fair, you wouldn't be so vain. Fair may be a big deal in this country, but not for me, all right? Take your good looks and your fairness and go. Give them to a suit and a tie. And don't forget the briefcase and bank balance and bad breath. I am so glad it's over between us. I can't tell you just how glad. I feel light. *Free!* I could *fly*. Imagine floating above vanity.' Placid spread his hands in a clumsy imitation of taking to wings.

Their voices had risen, and passers-by turned their heads to look at a man and woman falling out of love.

'It's been awful with you,' Susan said. 'Just awful. You are an awful man. Awful and frightened. And the really bad news is that you are frightened of yourself. You don't know how to get out of yourself. You don't know how to live. You know only to die. You have been dying for a long time. Maybe you are dead already, and much before your time. Maybe you are just pretending to be alive. People do that all the time, you know. People like you have a talent for death, not life. And as for vanity, it is slightly better than wallowing in self-pity.'

'That was a very long speech.'

'There should have been a longer one, long ago. Before you started writing those letters to me.'

'Oh, yes, the letters. I want them back. You don't deserve them. They are literary pieces. You won't understand their value. You are more into suits and briefcases.'

'Ah, the great letter writer! I'll have them mailed to you,' Susan said. 'Frame them and hang a garland around them. And don't forget to light the joss sticks.'

Placid suddenly felt sick, and deeply disappointed with both Susan and himself. They had been going out for over two years. And she was a stabilizing factor in his life. She merited better treatment.

I am sorry, Placid wanted to say. I am like this. Please don't go. And keep those letters. Why on earth would I want them back now? Think, please.

But he couldn't make himself say it. She wouldn't understand. Understanding was so difficult. Specially understanding *him*. He was a complex man.

The shadows running up the street leaped over Susan. She stared at him for a long moment, hesitating, then turned and walked, angry and sad, unable to articulate the wrongs in their relationship, the fated incompletion of it. What a birthday, she thought, what a lovely birthday I am having.

'Go then,' he muttered. He knew that unlike the earlier quarrels that they'd had, this one had crossed the limits; it had shown them to each other in the worst light. No, it was over. Placid picked his way to the nearest bar.

The break-up with Susan tipped Placid over. He took to alcohol as if the incident was precisely the license he had been waiting for. At home, his mother turned hysterical, resorted to the high theatre of maternal lamentation, self-flagellation, stupendous suicide attempts, martyrdom. Placid needed to escape. The place was too much. Too much its green. Too much its familiarity. Too much too were the people. Bombay! A big city would be different. It should have been New York or London, but he didn't have that kind of money. Bombay would have to do for the moment. He just needed a place to forget an old love, begin a new life.

On that first trip to Bombay one late evening, Placid had eaten chocolate laced with locally processed bhang—charas balls—from Babulnath temple, Chowpatty. The bus ride that he took from Girgaum to Gateway of India was the longest ride ever in his life. People elongated like lamp posts. Colours exploded behind his eyes. Speech turned to slush. Words slowed down, and between letters, whole seas flowed.

When the bus stopped near the National Gallery of Modern Art, Placid got off carefully, a soldier negotiating a terrain under enemy observation, and crossed the road towards the Gateway of India, skirting Regal Cinema, on whose wide, curving steps sat heavily made-up whores in pink saris and sleeveless blouses.

He sat on the parapet near the Gateway looking out at the dark sea. Below him, skiffs and boats eddied, chafing against each other. In the middle distance, a ship had weighed anchor, dark and spectral, like a mansion unlit. He could barely make out its dim presence against the horizon. Placid stared at the ship for a long time, considered swimming towards it, stepped down the stones and stood waist deep in water, the sea tugging at him.

He stood there a long time, lost.

When Placid finally turned, he found himself rising from the water. His muscles were lax, as if someone had massaged him for long. He dragged himself up over the parapet and walked heavily towards Gokul, picking his way through the narrow back road behind the Taj, right next to the Gateway of India. He paused for a moment in front of Baghdadi restaurant and wondered if he should eat Iranian rotis with mutton do pyaza and then decided in favour of a drink at Gokul, which was diagonally across the street. All the time, he was aware of the warm sea breeze rushing about him like a furry animal.

An elderly waiter at Gokul, Simon De Costa, and he had become chummy over the last few days. The waiter knew that Placid was having disappointing days with the newspaper offices. Simon welcomed him and sat next to him, his arm around Placid's shoulders. 'Writers lead tough lives,' he said to Placid. 'That's the way it is.'

'Yes,' Placid said.

'You know Dom Moraes?' Simon said, pushing the glasses and empty bottles of soda back towards the centre of the table, away from harm's edge. When you drank, Simon knew from experience, you grew many hands.

'Met him at his home, once; through a crack in the door, late one night. His wife, Leela, blocked the door. Dom looked over her shoulder and said, hello, can we meet in the morning. I said yes, and apologized for my midnight call. I was drunk. He was drunk and so, I think, was his wife.'

'You went back in the morning?'

'No. Mornings are always different. The things you do in the morning are different from the things you do at night.' Placid raised his glass. 'Dom,' he toasted. 'Great poet.'

'His home is at Allana Marg, right next door. 13 Sergeant House. A three-storey, red brick house. The lift never works.'

'I know. It's right here. A stone's throw away.'

'If he has money, he drinks at the Sea Lounge, Taj. If he is not flush, he comes here. And I always take care of him myself. Both of us are from Goa, you see.'

'Well, I am no Dom Moraes. Nor was meant to be,' Placid said.

'No, not now, but you could be.'

'You think Dom's happy?'

'No. Why would a man drink like that if he was happy? But writers can't be happy, can they? Or writers' wives.'

'At least, Dom writes well,' Placid whined. 'Everybody knows him. If you are very famous, you can take a lot of shit.'

'Don't know about that. But you have just started out.'

'I know. Such a long way to go.'

'You will be all right. Have one for the road. Sleep it off.' Simon said, standing up, patting Placid's back. 'Your clothes are wet.'

Placid was silent. He noticed that the restaurant was nearly empty. Simon made his way to the bar between tables, on which the waiters were stacking the chairs upside down. At one end of the hall, a boy was pouring soap water over the floor from a bucket. His work had just begun.

Simon brought Placid the drink. He swallowed it down. Simon accompanied him out onto the pavement. Across the street, Bade Miyan, a restaurant famous for its paranthas and minced mutton, was closing down, as was Baghdadi. In any case, Placid no longer felt like eating.

Placid was drunk. He hugged Simon, overcome with intimations of parting and the laden significance of the night, and made his way along the deserted road from Colaba to Flora Fountain and then took the turn towards Churchgate. He was just in time for the last train bound for Virar.

Had Placid swum to that ship after all? Yes. He had climbed the rope ladder that fell to the sea over its side, hauled himself up in the brilliant, kaleidoscopic high of the bhang, on to the deck, where he was welcomed in hushed voices by a bunch of men and women in the dark. A rave party, he thought. A girl in a toga had held him by the hand and led him to a deckchair, offered him a glass of, was it ... *wine*?

'The night is blue,' she said, 'and Rome is ours.'

Later, he sensed, as if in a dream, the pressure of swelling breasts, hips and smooth legs against his body as the ship moved under him with the sea. And he had pressed on, till an equal assurance was yielded, a rising satisfaction exacted against the pliancy of another body, warm, fragrant.

When he finally left, a man wearing a crown and a cloak had escorted him to the rope ladder. 'I am the Holy Roman Emperor,' he said. 'Come again, when the grapes are ripe. We will be here. This is what it is all about.'

He must have swum to the ship, after all, because he could recall even now that the water had been deep and warm, the heavy, sensuous sea supporting his body as he first stroked and then floated on his back towards the ship. He had watched the stars come out in crazy bursts like some fireworks gone wrong and crowding the sky. But, later, on the way back, he saw that they were few and faded, and that the crescent moon was pale. Within the space of a night, Placid had swum from one constellation to another, from ship to shore.

SIXTEEN

The Burden of Love

If something did happen later that night, the night when he hugged Simon as if he were a soldier taking leave to fight a distant war, Placid would still guarantee you one thing: it was, whether ship or train, not rape. There was no force. Please, he was not that kind of guy, drunk or sober. He was the weak, sentimental type, who couldn't stand the sight of a child begging. He was soft. Rape was hard. It was just not his style. He wouldn't commit rape. Sorry. Not him. Never. Nyet.

'Suppose I did it,' Placid says, 'and I am not for a moment saying I did it, but *suppose* I did, what would you want me to do at this moment?'

'I don't believe this,' says Beverly. 'So you did it? Just admit it and let's take it from there.'

'Take what from where? I am saying this is the end of the world for us. We are locked up in this room, and, outside, there is a boy with a machine gun and murder on his mind. We are as good as dead. So now tell me, if I really did to you what you think I did, what would you want me to do?'

'He is right,' Rajgopal says. 'We are here. Not on that train. I don't think I care about that incident now. You shouldn't either, Lakshmi. That was in the past. But if we don't do something now, none of us will have a future.'

'It *happened*. And it is *important* to me!' Lakshmi says.

'What difference does it make to you now?' Rajgopal asks.

'Lakshmee, ai yyam von yuvar saide. But wottu do now?' Githaa says.

'This kind of thing happens in Bombay,' Shinde says, considering his reflection in the mirror. 'Yahan sab kuch hota hai,' he adds, not without a certain pride in his city, the biggest in India, the most populous, the largest-slummed, the most sky-scrapered, the most number of raped. It is number one in everything. First City.

'It happens?' Beverly turns on Shinde. 'Well, it shouldn't have. You wouldn't like it if you got buggered by some pervert and someone else said, "It happens".'

'But was it rape?' Rajgopal asks Beverly.

'What kind of question is that?' Beverly shouts. 'She just said it was.'

'Of course,' Rajgopal says. Since he is the elder statesman, he is not sure how to question Beverly without offending her. But the argument appears specious to him.

Placid says, 'If this happened, if I believe it happened … you know?'

'If you believed it happened?' Lakshmi asks.

'I don't know,' Placid says. 'I am being asked to accept too much too fast.'

'You've had sixteen years,' Beverly says. 'That's a long time.'

'I know, and I know you know,' Lakshmi tells Placid. 'That night is vivid to us both.'

'Not to me, and I swear to god I am speaking the truth,'

Placid says. 'But I was in Bombay around that time, I can now recall.'

'Of course you were,' Lakshmi says. 'And it was the fifteenth of August.'

'Was it? The lights in Bombay kept going and coming through the evening and night.'

'So there,' Lakshmi says.

'Tell me what happened to you afterwards?'

'Why do I have to explain myself all the time? You first tell me whether you are ready to take the responsibility for that night.'

'Look, I really don't know. There was a night of shadows once. There was water in it, a whole body of water, drugs and alcohol, and I was young and spaced out. There was a ship in the middle of it, and maybe a train at the end of it. I really can't remember. It's like one of those nights when you stumble about in a haze – catching the wrong train, sleeping through the trip – and wake up in a huge railway yard, with the sodium vapour lamps high above and iron sleepers stacked all around you. You feel for your wallet in panic and it's not there, and for a moment you have no idea who you are and what you did in the night that got you there. So that's what I mean by saying I don't know.'

'Well, it happened. I am telling you what happened.'

'It's your word against mine.'

'But you didn't get to be pregnant. I delivered nine months later at a hospital run by the Sisters of Charity.' Choose the wrong words and I will break down, Lakshmi thinks. 'I had to run away from my parents because I was scared and pregnant. I should have aborted. But I did not. I waited. I thought I would run into you sooner or later and you would be proud because I was going to be the mother of your children.'

'It can't have been rape.'

'I don't know if that's the point any more,' Beverly says.

'I was selling trinkets on Goan beaches till I was too heavy,' Lakshmi says quietly. 'I came back to Bombay when it was time. Got myself admitted to a hospital. When I finally delivered the twins, the first thing I thought was that I have to give them away like the junk I used to sell.'

'Voh mhai god,' says Githaa.

'Try giving something precious to a person who doesn't know its value; it's like offering yourself to an ape,' Lakshmi says to Placid. 'Your children are the dearest treasure in your possession, and you roam the city's streets doing all you can to get rid of them. "Please, do you want a baby? Two babies. I've got them here. They are twins. Take both, please,"' Lakshmi mimics herself.

'Twins?' Shinde asks.

'And then you give them away. Just like that. You hand them over, and turn and walk away before the people who have agreed to take them can change their mind, praying to God that everything will turn out well. You walk, and all you really want to do is to run back and grab your babies. But you keep walking. You are aware you are lighter, the weight you carried about you for nearly a year is gone. You want to feel in your hands that weight again. The burden of love. But it is gone. Gone clean out of your life. Desperate, you cheat yourself into believing your babies will be all right. Someone will take care of them. People are good. They won't starve little children. They won't be raped, they will go to school. But, deep down, you know all of it could happen because that is the way the world is, the way people are, and you feel like ripping your heart out and tossing it to the dogs.'

The room is silent.

Placid doesn't look up. Maybe I *am* guilty after all, he

thinks. If not for this, then for something else; guilt is my ruling passion.

'I am really not blaming you,' Lakshmi says. 'I just want you to share the responsibility. It is too late for anything else. I died with my severance. For what I did to my two children.'

'I am sorry,' Placid says.

'Give me my children back,' Lakshmi says, tears welling up in her eyes. 'Give me my babies. I can look after them now.'

Placid is drained. He closes his eyes. He is turned inside out. He wishes to be absent from the proceedings. Please, will you excuse me, he wants to say.

'Easy, Lakshmi,' Beverly says.

'And on the third day after delivery, I went around the city on a rainy night and actually gave them away. One to a lady in a taxi on her way to the airport. She was on her way to Pakistan. The other I left at a temple exactly the way they do in the movies, next to a Krishna playing the flute, leaning against a white cow. The Krishna was painted deep blue. I waited behind a pillar for a while to see who might come around and take my baby away. It was late night. No one turned up. Nobody would come, I thought, not on a night like this. I went out to have a cup of tea without a thought in my head. I bought the tea with the money that the woman in the car had given me for my other baby. I felt light in the head. I wanted to laugh, be normal. I had forgotten what it was to be normal. I hadn't laughed in such a long while. I hummed a song. I had the tea in a white cup with a broken ear. I told the man behind the counter to keep the change. And when I came back, not humming any more, my baby was gone. I ran out of the temple and threw up the tea that I had just drunk. I was breathless. I walked in a daze to a hostel I had seen in Santa Cruz. It was first light, and I was vaguely aware that the rain had eased. I saw a train go past me, very close to my face, across my eyes. Everything was over. The umbrella was gone. The babies were gone. There was a moist breeze blowing, and the road was clean, washed out by the rain. A clean, blue road. When I reached the hostel, I did not go in. I couldn't understand the meaning of a room. I sat down on the road. What to do, I thought, what to do? I lay on the road and, close to my face, the water ran, curling. I saw my world clearly.'

'I didn't know,' Placid says.

'Now you do,' Beverly responds. But Placid realizes that the edge has gone out of her voice.

'Look, if this happened, it's between me and Lakshmi. We'll settle it between ourselves.'

'Faargiv and faarget, Lakshmee,' Githaa says.

'I said if ...' Placid says.

'If what?' Beverly says.

'If it happened, I really can't tell.'

'Don't backtrack now, because this is the place and time.'

'I just don't know, is all I am trying to say.'

'You have a moral responsibility,' Shinde says. 'If you are the father of the kids that she gave away, you have a moral responsibility.'

'I don't see why I should be talked to by so many people on what's really a personal issue, even if it's a misunderstanding.'

'This is India,' Rajgopal says. 'Everything has to be done before two-four people. We are a family.'

'Oh, fuck off,' Placid says.

'A misunderstanding?' Lakshmi says.

'I hate India,' Placid says.

'A great country,' Rajgopal says. 'A country that could think up the Vedas when others were still making primitive noises.'

'A fuck-all country. Close to four hundred million people

live on less than a dollar a day. You know what that means, don't you?'

'Tell us about it,' Rajgopal says patiently. He has resolved not to be provoked by a man who by all accounts—or at least one—was adept at rape.

'It means you live on next to nothing. Try living on forty rupees a day. See what that gets you.'

'So?'

'Whose responsibility are these people? Superpower! World's largest democracy! The whole country is a tissue of lies, starting with the Constitution, which says everybody is equal when they're not. I spit on your great country, do you mind?'

'You are part of that fraud, Placid,' Lakshmi says, resting her face on her knees. She is finding her position on the floor with her hands tied to the four-poster uncomfortable. 'Look what you did to your children.'

'I am not part of any fraud. I am not part of anything. And I certainly don't know if they are my children. And, excuse me, I was not the one who threw them away.'

'You are responsible. Don't shirk it. Not that it makes any difference now. We'll soon be dead.'

'Lakshmi?' Placid says, tired of everything, but most of all, tired of himself.

'Yes?'

'I am truly sorry.'

'I have wasted my entire life.'

'You are still young. But if it's my fault ...'

'If it's your fault?'

'No, what I mean to say is, I am with you. I am accepting the responsibility for my act. If we survive this, let's work on tracing the kids,' Placid says, not sure of himself, but groping for a way. He is aware that he is in the dread-pit of life. He had tried his best to avoid it, thinking he was above and around it. But no, he was at the very bottom. He had been digging himself deep into it all along, and now that he realized it, he had no option but to clamber out of it, or at least try. Try, he tells himself, please try.

SEVENTEEN

Objects in the Mirror Are Closer than They Appear

Shinde watches Placid and Lakshmi from his corner in the mirror on the wall. There are twelve of us here in this mixed-up nightmare, he thinks. Six here in the room, and six in the mirror. Split images. Exactly alike, yet different. Shinde finds mirrors fascinating; they are screens that divide a twin world.

Shinde has been listening to the conversations in the mirror, watching the crazed actors play out their bits as in a movie. He has not seen so many lonely people crowded into one room. When he gets out of this terrorist nonsense, he is going to ask his father to look for a girl for him. Enough of stag parties and Good Luck country liquor bars. The stage has come in his life for a wife and children. Something to live for. A home of his own to come back to after a hard day's work.

The unhappy people in the room are proof to Shinde that the key to life is a wife. An uncomplaining woman who takes care of him and raises his kids while he goes out in the sun and brings in the moolah. He can imagine his two—two would be just right—kids playing around the rickshaw, acting as driver and passenger.

Shinde likes children. But he is not sure if his should be both boys or one a boy and the other a girl. His friends and relatives prefer boys to girls, because girls have to be married off and their dowry paid. Girls do not make for a sound investment, not in this country.

Boys are different. They grow up, they take up a job and go on to become men and Shiv Sainiks who can take care of themselves and vote for the Thackerays. There will, Shinde knows, always be a Thackeray to vote for. Thackerays are immortal. When father Thackeray's time is over, there will be a son Thackeray, or a nephew Thackeray. But there *will* be a Thackeray. Of this he has no doubt. That is the thing about boys. You can pass your legacy to them.

Besides, there is no danger of boys getting impregnated like Lakshmi. When she got into his rickshaw, he could have never suspected her of having gone through so shocking and vagrant a past.

No, boys are best. Two boys who look like their parents and resemble each other. Children are strange. They both appear like recognizable versions of their parents and yet they are different.

He wonders what kind of parents the killer boy outside has. Or Nirmal. The boy must have been disowned at a pretty young age and thrown into the streets. There is something uncanny about both boys. They are of the same height and colour. In fact, they even look the same: mouth, nose and forehead. Except that the terrorist has longer hair and a stubble. Shinde turns towards Lakshmi and says, 'The two outside are twins.'

EIGHTEEN

The Many Uses of the Map of India

Lakshmi feels as if someone has landed a blow in the pit of her stomach with a crowbar. She leans weakly against the frame of the cot, her body drenched in cold sweat. I'm running a temperature, she thinks. She is exhausted. Are they her children, the babies she lost in that far-off rain? How they have grown! 'I want to see them,' she says softly. 'I'll die if I don't.' But, apart from the overwhelming need of wanting to see them, she cannot think clearly. 'Can you ask them to open the door, please?' she asks Shinde. 'Now?'

'Yes, of course,' Shinde says, swelling with pride. He had seen while others had only gazed. 'Open the door, please,' he shouts. 'Life and death matter.'

The others join Shinde in the demand. When the din climaxes, Salim unlocks the door and comes in; Nirmal follows him. Nirmal is no longer wearing his goggles. In the light of Shinde's revelation, their resemblance to each other seems all too obvious to the crowd in the room.

'You are my children,' Lakshmi nearly retches. 'Both of you.' She strains against the ropes.

'Cut the crap,' Salim says. He has had enough. I should just shoot them all and be done with it, he thinks. But he is aware of Nirmal's restraining hand on his shoulder. He takes a deep breath. 'My mother is in Pakistan …' he says as if he is about to begin, all over again, a long story whose end keeps changing even as he narrates it.

'Show me your ears,' Lakshmi says with uncharacteristic authority. 'Just show me your ears. The right one, please, both of you.' Her breath comes in gasps.

This is a ridiculous situation for a jihadi to be in, Salim thinks. 'You're out of your mind.'

'There is a mole shaped like the map of India behind your ear,' Lakshmi says

'Let me see,' Nirmal says.

Salim shakes his head in extreme irritation.

'Ah! Salim, you've got a mole behind your ear, no question,' Nirmal says, feeling the spot with his thumb. 'Can't tell if it's India for sure, because it's smudged. You are her son, all right.' Nirmal nods. He feels as if he has scored a goal. 'Check mine, will you?' he says, letting go of Salim's ear.

Good god, Salim thinks. All his past, all the things that constituted the person that he knows himself to be, are being shaken, rattled to their last breath; the confident Salim of yore now stands cowering in a dim corner far away, in another country, an alien Pakistan, the place he cannot go back to. And he wants nothing do with India, the country where he was born and where he would die. He is a cartographic catastrophe. 'All right,' he says, turning Nirmal around with a sense of unmitigated defeat. He knows that he will find the mole. There will be no escape. India is his fate. 'It's there!' Salim says.

'Now, you reelize? Lakshmi ees yuvar mathar, you knowh?' Githaa says. 'And Placid hear ees yuvar faathar.'

'Eh, what? Who said?' Salim snarls, raising his gun desperately in Placid's direction.

'Don't shoot your father,' Rajgopal says. 'No crime is bigger than that. And don't kill anyone while your mother looks on.' He has himself topmost in mind. 'Please listen, we've just got to know everything here. Everything. Don't worry, we'll take care of it, we are a family.'

'Ammi and Abba,' Salim mutters. The words sound strange to his ears, as if they were the names of eccentric foreigners. 'You two and Shinde come out. Nirmal will free you.'

Salim walks to the kitchen. He drinks water from the tap, then puts his head under it and rubs the back of his right ear as if to wash the stain of India away, but no, it will not come off.

Salim returns to the hall and takes a deep breath. He makes his brand-new family sit on the sofa and begins asking Lakshmi questions. A while ago, he had cross-examined Fatima. It seems to him that he has been asking the same set of questions the whole day; like an interrogator who has lost his way.

When Lakshmi stops talking, Salim puts his hand around Nirmal's shoulders, if only due to a need to be anchored to some physical truth. He stares at the sea spread outside the window; sees his past with all its certainties drifting over the water like an island into the mist. I am really too young for all this, he thinks, I should be with Ammi in the drawing room, sleeping on the divan.

But the lost jihad has won him a brother, too, and he can't deny himself that trophy. A lightness sweeps over Salim, a joyous wave of camaraderie. He has his brother right here; he can touch him. He is not alone, after all, in this new world of uncertainties that he has discovered at the end of his voyage.

He feels no pity for his real mother. She is his real mother; of that he has no doubt now. She had sacrificed her children for social respectability. If she had had a deeper sense of honour, she would have kept them, brought them up, made them proud of her. But she had acted as if she was in some second-rate Bollywood movie, willed tragedy upon herself, and on a rainy night shrugged her burden off into the lap of a stranger who chanced to pass by. It was just Salim's luck that the stranger happened to be Fatima. It could have been a pervert, or a serial killer, and Salim wouldn't have been here.

Nirmal's case was worse. Lakshmi didn't even know who took him away. Her desire to get rid of her babies at such cost baffles Salim. How on earth can you leave a three-day-old baby in a temple, thinking he will be taken care of? From where does such trust in the efficacy of chance come? She had deserted her kids in the hour of their direst need, when they were the most helpless. The compassion that she expected from total strangers was lacking in her. Who knew what Nirmal had gone through all alone as a child?

As for the man she said was his father, Placid, Salim thinks, he has about him the distinct air of a rake. If Salim goes by his mother's version, he is responsible for her suffering. And if he buys it wholesale, Placid is, in addition to being a rake, also a rapist. What kind of father is that? It is an impossible situation.

'What to do?' Salim turns to Nirmal.

'What do you want to do?'

'I don't know.'

'Are you still looking to reach jannat by nightfall?'

'No.'

'What about the people inside?' Lakshmi asks Salim.

'Let them go, I guess.' Salim feels like stepping into a room and closing the door on the world.

'Good.' Lakshmi sighs in relief.

'Cut your hair, shave your beard, drop your gun and walk out free,' Nirmal says.

'But they must already know I am in this apartment.'

'But they don't know we are twins. Or that I am here. I will take your place.'

'No,' Lakshmi says. 'You're not going to suffer any more.'

'I won't suffer. Eventually, they will let me go because they can't prove that I am Salim.'

'It won't work,' Salim says. 'Besides, I started this.'

NINETEEN

An Unexpected Guest

There is a noise right outside the main door of the hall. A noise not quite human, as if something ponderous and clumsy had more or less hopped and half dragged itself up the staircase, determined to scale heights it is destined not to grace. Salim freezes for a moment, then covers Shinde with his gun and, holding him as a shield, moves towards the door. Nirmal, Lakshmi and Placid look on in apprehension.

Shinde applies one eye to the peephole and starts. He clutches at his scarf. There is a cow staring at him from the other side. Shinde turns pale. Has the cow been trailing him? Has he no fate separate from the beast? Not a moment of respite from this relentless persecution?

'What is it?' Salim asks.

'Cow. There is a big cow outside.'

'A cow? Up here?'

'Take a look yourself.'

Salim takes a peek. No question, there is a cow outside, large as life.

'Open the door and let it in,' Nirmal says. 'You'd better do it before it draws someone's attention.' He is sitting between his mother and the man who his mother says is his father. In the morning he was an orphan. By evening, he has around him a whole family. His riches are yet to sink in. The family is still names and faces, not yet a dependable feeling.

'I have seen this one before,' Shinde says by way of warning.

'A right-wing cow,' Placid says after taking a look at the cow through the peephole. He completely ignores Salim and his gun. He is not sure if he is the man Lakshmi takes him for. But if he is, then Salim is his son, and there is no question of a son shooting his father. 'Consider the cloak and the saffron powder on its face.'

'Open the door and let it in,' Salim says to Shinde.

Shinde opens the door. The cow enters the room. The vermillion cloak still covers its back, and the garlands of hibiscus round the dewlapped neck are intact. But the gold plate on its forehead is gone, and so are the beads. It is panting heavily and there is saliva hanging from its mouth in long threads. The steps must have been a strenuous exercise, despite its political training. The cow fills the room with its presence, challenging them to make sense of its appearance.

TWENTY

A Ride into the Sunset

'The cow is lifting her tail,' Shinde says. His eye has been fixed on the beast since its arrival on the scene. 'It's going to pass urine.' He has become a compulsive running commentator on the bovine proceedings.

The cow is raising its tail indeed. The implication is not lost on anyone. It is going to urinate and, from the way its posterior muscles are going into spasms, the autistic animal is going to pass motion as well.

'Dung is quite useful,' Shinde says, recalling his essay on the cow, a watershed in his English studies. 'Many are the attractions of the dung, such as floor waxing purposes. Cleansing is a specialty of this rare waste,' he had written.

The cow having relieved itself in steaming, voluminous quantities, stares fixedly at Shinde and proceeds to walk in his direction.

Shinde moves aside, thinking he is in the way of the beast. He doesn't want to be provoking anybody, not terrorist, not cow. The day had got off to a wrong start and it had steadily worsened.

But, no matter how inconspicuous Shinde tries to make himself, the cow seems to be after him. It is as if it has eyes only for Shinde. He is beginning to sense danger, given his lifelong, uneasy engagement with the beast, and takes a few indecisive steps back from the advancing enemy.

His eyes lock with those of the cow. Oh, my god, he thinks, this is the same cow that I had run into when I had just bought my auto-rickshaw. Fear pecks at his heart.

The cow must sense its advantage. It comes after Shinde, the glint of a new determination keening its large, black eyes, around which the mascara has spread. The beast is beginning to look like the inmate of a brothel after a night of wild abandon. It should apply some lipstick to complete the picture, Shinde dares to entertain an unholy thought.

The cow picks up speed. Although it has been trained to climb stairs, racing on smooth, marble floors is not one of its strengths. Acceleration, it is discovering, is best done in a graded fashion.

Shinde walks backward faster, like a junior circus artiste doing minor stunts before the main item.

'Take off that scarf,' Nirmal says from the sofa. It could be the scarf, Nirmal thinks, but he wouldn't bet on it. The cow does seem vindictive. As if it has something on its mind, perhaps an old score to settle. 'Best if Salim shoots it,' he says.

Shinde doesn't say anything. He is short of breath. But he waves his hands in wild negation; no, never, don't kill the cow.

Shinde is now running round the large hall with the cow clattering after him, horns shaking. 'The cow, his horns have forward motions only,' Shinde had written in his composition. How innocent he was! He can see now that the horns of this cow can move sideways as well; three hundred and sixty degrees, in fact.

'Take that scarf off from around your neck and throw it away,' Nirmal says again.

'I can't,' Shinde says, struggling with the orange cloth around his neck, a sartorial sign of his political loyalties. He tries to pull it from one end, but that serves only to tighten it. His face is red with exertion and a constricted windpipe. And he is making a strange noise at regular intervals, like a dog systematically trying to vomit a bad meal.

'Shall I shoot?' Salim asks.

'Don't,' Shinde rasps.

'No, not you, the cow.'

'Aagh,' Shinde manages to say. 'No. No.'

The cow is after Shinde with visible tenacity of purpose. There is no longer any room for doubt. Perhaps the animal has recalled the accident that knocked out two of its teeth? Its hooves come hard on the white floor. The urine it passed is flowing in all directions. The heaps of dung no longer steam. The cow is stepping in and out of the dung. The white floor is splattered with it. 'The cow, he gives plenty dung,' as Shinde had phrased it back in school; plenty grief, too, he would now like to add, plenty, plenty grief.

On one side, the hall opens out to the sky through a French window. The fourth time Shinde approaches it, he catches a glimpse of the sun about to set, the sky a carnage of reds. I can't keep this up any more, Shinde thinks. Right behind him, half a tail away, he can hear the mountainous beast breathing hard, its abnormally long horns pointing at his rear. Who knew Death is vegetarian?

Outside the window, vistas of space extend, tempting Shinde with the promise of freedom. Freedom of movement. Freedom from the cow. Freedom from his complicated passengers. He has to break free. He must reach his low, asbestos-roofed tenement, his tacky room done in blue, the comfort of the familiar, noisy TV. He wants to get out of this absurd situation far removed from his understanding and logic. Go, Shinde tells himself, go, get out of this crack house. Just step out of this universe of chaos. Make up your mind. Step over, step out. Get back into your world. Go. Go. Go.

Shinde crashes through the window glass into the blood-red evening air, one hand still struggling with the scarf, the other reaching out as though for something to hold. Suddenly, the scarf comes away in his hand. Shinde gulps in air as if it is water. He is free! He turns his head back for a moment in triumph, and his eyes widen to find that his nemesis is right behind him. The cow has ferociously followed him, its shawl flying in the wind, its tail up in the air, its horns in the classic charging position. Super Cow. Still in mid air, Shinde finds himself astride his enemy. He is exhilarated. Has he tamed the wild beast at last? Have the gods relented? He can't tell. All he knows is that he is riding the cow into the sunset.

A moment later, the man and the beast tumble through the air, now Shinde on top, now cow, in an intimate tussle, indistinguishable in their embrace of death. They crash through telephone wires, cutting short a million conversations, down through treetops, and land in the middle of the road.

The sound on impact with the hard earth is like a load of carpets fallen from a great height. Splintered glass, broken branches, an orange scarf and a shower of leaves follow in Shinde's wake. Down below, the road is jammed. A cow has clogged the city's traffic again.

BOOK III

ONE

Never Say Die

GIVING SALIM A CHANCE

Is the dreaded terrorist Salim best kept alive, a monument to his own tragedy? Or should he be given the death sentence? Placid Hari Odannur argues, a week prior to the trial, in favour of commuting the punishment.

The case against the accused terrorist Salim rests on the assumption that he is twenty-one years old. Which means that he is an adult capable of independent thought and action. But, if the prosecution is unable to prove he is an adult, and the death sentence is carried out, it will be little better than child murder.

My interest in this case is personal. My partner, with whom I now share a warm relationship, believes Salim was born of a tryst I had with her seventeen years ago. But, for obvious reasons, the Indian government does not want to pursue this line of inquiry.

Salim is not just a common criminal, he is a terrorist. A jihadi who thought he was doing what his unreasonable God demanded of him. In short, he is a priceless curio from the museum of Islamic fundamentalism.

And Islamic fundamentalism is a question we will have to figure out sooner or later. There are over 160 million Muslims in this country, most of them at the bottom of a generally backward society, and our future depends on how we answer the minority question and how well we understand why fundamentalism finds the soil fertile in the subcontinent. Salim is a study. Why would an upper-middle-class, industrious student like him gravitate towards guns and bombs?

As with any rare thing, the thing to do with Salim is to preserve him, not destroy him. Hand him down from generation to generation; watch him grow from boy to man. Read in his time-worn body and face the slowly evolving map of a story gone wrong from the start.

I don't for a moment devalue the pain of the victims of the terrorist attacks. But pain, physical and mental, is the price war exacts, and we are at war with the terrorists.

At the same time, we must not be blind to the ironies at play. Had Salim completed his mission and returned to Pakistan, he would have been treated like a hero there, at least among his peers. That's how history works. One people's hero is another's villain. Depending on which side you are on in a war, everyone is right.

The ultimate victory over Salim would be to forgive him, whether he is seventeen or twenty-one. Forgive, whether he is a Pakistani national or not. Forgive him, whether he was—as police officials claimed in the first shaken days after the siege—under the effect of drugs, or not. Forgive him whether he was misled or not. Forgive him for the failure of his imagination that led him eventually to a room with walls but no doors.

Most of us are just not good enough for this. But if the father of this nation, Mahatma Gandhi, were alive and well, we can hazard a guess that Salim would have been forgiven.

Gandhi himself fell to bullets fired by Nathuram Godse, a fundamentalist of Hindu right-wing persuasion. We don't normally call Godse a terrorist, perhaps because he was a Hindu. Some even call him a patriot. Gandhi expected to be killed. In a prayer meeting on 16 June 1947, he said, 'I shall consider myself brave if I am killed and if I still pray to God for my assassin.' Gandhi famously did that on 30 January 1948.

We are lesser mortals. Forgiving others must come hard for us, especially since we are poor at forgiving ourselves. And we are, in turn, so hard on ourselves because we believe others will not forgive us. Our unkindness comes from fear. But, surely, our test as a people is to try and live with Salim's great failure, his failure to find his better self; to understand the nature of a way of life that constantly claims divine sanction for its violent validations; to comprehend, if possible, the great question of why the authority of God is at the heart of great evils.

Yet, the bare truth is, only in life will Salim discover his humanity, not in death. The test of our civilization is to try and give him a chance to redeem himself. Who knows, when Salim is ninety, he may turn into a saint and sing to the birds. We may not live to see that change. But our children will. And they will wonder why a man like this would kill when he was a boy.

TWO

Lost, Found, Lost

Visiting hours at Arthur Road Jail are between 9 a.m. and 12 a.m. Undertrials are allowed one visit a week from friends and relatives. The duration of the meeting is ten minutes. For prisoners, it is once a month. For a high-profile terrorist like Salim, there are no fixed rules. As ever, it helps if you know someone up there. If not, you go very early and stand to the side of the massive blue gates and wait.

But there is another way, as Lakshmi learns right on the first visit. Instead of going straight to the gates and testing your luck, you cross the road to the other side, to the old woman sitting on an armchair with a writing board across her lap. She is ugly as death and her clothes smell of the dirt in dingy places, where neither a speck of sunlight nor a flake of soap has fallen in years.

Lakshmi goes up to her and hands her a twenty-rupee note. The woman takes out a form and asks for her personal details. She gets Lakshmi's name wrong. All the other details are equally fictive, because she is half deaf. But it doesn't matter. The system works, somehow. Perhaps there is a secret code to it.

Out of the money the old woman gets, half goes to the guard

outside the gate, who passes fifty per cent of his share to the officer on duty. The place works on supplementary incomes.

Much later, a small panel opens in the gate and a man frames his face in the square. He calls out Lakshmi's name like a curse and she goes in to see Salim.

Immediately as she enters is the administrative block. In the foyer, behind a table, sits a corpulent man whose thighs, Lakshmi dreads, would burst through his khaki pants. He shouts 'Time up, time up' every two minutes or so, though, of course, time is not up. But his constant warnings mean that the visitors are always under pressure to end the meeting.

Behind him is a narrow door, which leads to a hall divided by a series of barred windows. The inmates listed for the interview throng around on the other side in striped shorts and bare torsos.

The jail was built in 1926 to house a thousand people. But at any given time, there are close to 5,000 prisoners. Inside the interview room, Lakshmi finds it hard to make herself heard in the clamour.

The kind, reassuring things she wants to say to her son drain themselves of all dignity and the dearest word turns crass in its haste to make itself heard. She can't tell her son: I love you, it will be all right, and has to scream terms of endearment like abuse.

People jostle for space, shove against one another as in a packed local train. They swear at each other and refer to the private parts of their sisters and mothers. It is as if their grief is of no consequence. Pressures of time and space seem to have conspired to nullify their individual worth. They, like their wards behind bars, have become just a function of the Least Common Indian Denomination. Zero.

Soon after Lakshmi's first visit, for security reasons, Salim is transferred to a special, solitary cell next to the administrative block. Here, with special permission, Lakshmi can go right in and meet him in private.

The next two sessions are tense. Pauses stretch between their sentences, vast and heaving, and Lakshmi is in constant agitation in her son's presence. He is detached, depressed. Their spare words drift like flotsam on stormy seas of silence.

At the end of the third visit, as she is about to leave, Salim says, 'I know I am hurting you. But, please, don't come again. I find these sessions very taxing.'

'Oh, I am sorry,' Lakshmi says, as if it is of no consequence. 'You should have told me earlier. I'd have understood.'

All I want is to hug you, Lakshmi thinks. To hug him, hold his hand as the world shakes its mane and bares its fangs at him, reassure him with a look that she is with him. That though he might have killed people and all of India calls him a mad dog and a terrorist, he is her son. She had lost him once, and found him, and she isn't going to let him go—if only he'd let her.

'I just find it upsetting. I can't get used to the idea of you being my mother. I am sorry,' Salim says.

'That's fine. I'll come only if you send word,' Lakshmi replies. 'You should have told me, really.' She affects cheer, as if he has asked her to bring a particular kind of cake.

The first time Lakshmi had visited him in jail, three months after they met in Bandra, she had been shocked. Salim had shrunk. All his bones had risen in fearful prominence. His prison clothes hung on him, loose and flapping. He looked hunted and haunted. What have I done to him, she thought. She had brought this fate upon him.

In her nightmares, she sees herself leading Salim to the gallows, tying his hands behind his back, slipping the noose around his neck, asking him if it is ok now, and whether he is comfortable. She wakes up with his decapitated body in her arms.

What amends can she make now, besides her love for him, which he does not want? Every time she takes a step towards him, he shrinks back to the stone walls that hem him in. He prefers their cold, confining touch to her maternal overtures. How he must hate me, she thinks. 'We don't get to meet again, then, I guess.'

'No. I am sorry.'

'I know you deserve better,' she says. She means better than what life has doled out to her.

'It's not that. I am just not used to this part of my life.'

'You mustn't think I am here to steal your affection for Fatima.'

'I am going to hang. I don't want a total stranger introduced to me as my mother at this late stage. I want to keep things simple.'

'If you don't want me to come, of course I won't,' Lakshmi says. 'You will let me know if you want anything?'

'Yes.' But what could I possibly want apart from the life that all of you have taken away from me? he thinks. He feels pity for himself, and strangely enough, seeing her quiet acceptance of his harsh words, pity for her. 'It's not your fault. It's nobody's fault.'

'Nobody's fault.' Lakshmi tries to smile.

That's not entirely true, she thinks, it's my fault. The inexorability of her fate swamps her. She staggers, thinks she will stumble and fall, as Salim and the superintendent look on. 'I am feeling a little giddy,' she tells the superintendent weakly.

'Sit in my room under the fan for a while,' the superintendent says. 'There is a sofa as well, in case you feel like lying down.'

He knows Lakshmi and Salim's story. The papers are full of it. And he reads all the three mainstream English newspapers, whose standards of language, in his opinion, are falling by the day. It must be hell for the mother and son, the superintendent thinks. He always compares his life—steady job, doting wife, three children—to the life at his workplace and draws relief from the difference. God is great. 'Come this way,' he tells Lakshmi, but refrains from holding her elbow in support, since a man is not supposed to touch a woman unless they are married.

THREE

Freedoms of the Press

'How did this crap get carried?' Shantanu Roy asks Arun, tapping the page on which Arun has carried Placid's piece. Roy is agitated. His cheek muscles jump about his face as if attached to springs, his hands tremble, and there is alcohol on his breath.

'Tell me how the fuck this happened!' He takes his black-framed spectacles off in a gesture of nervous confusion and places them over the page.

That morning, Roy had got a call from his proprietor, M.N. Nanda, a textile tycoon who prided himself on being a patriot. Nanda bankrolled right-wing Hindu parties because he genuinely believed India belonged to the Hindus. The others could stay if they behaved, but under Hindu Raj. Nanda was shocked that Placid's defence of Salim, clearly a Pakistani terrorist, had been carried in his paper.

'Roy, I thought you knew what you were doing and where the interests of this paper lie.' Nanda's voice was thick with anger. 'I am not a fanatic, but this man is a mass killer and you have let his father use the paper to plead, on his behalf, for mercy! This is serious business and I am getting worried calls from my political friends. The reason why I hired you is that

I thought you knew my mind, what I stand for. Editors are a dime a dozen. You owe me an explanation.'

Roy couldn't have told the angry man that he had been on one of his binges the day before. As a matter of fact, he had come in early, before the others, taken his wallet, which he had misplaced in the toilet cupboard, and made his way to the bar round the corner.

He had ordered three large vodkas, on the rocks, with lemon on the side. He liked to see his resources in full, so he didn't have to worry about waiting for his next drink. He couldn't bear the pause between drinks, just as the idea of food between them put him off. He felt secure with three vodkas standing tall on the table like guards on duty. Roy had watched the ice melt in the glasses, lose their size and shape, and wondered how people got by without alcohol. Alcohol made life bearable and, on a good day in his case, it actually quickened his interest in the world he inhabited.

He had finished his three vodkas and ordered one for the road. He watched the waiter nod in grudging respect, or maybe it was the vodka sloshing in his head. When he got to his feet, he had to hold on to the arms of the chair to steady himself. He was high. There was, he had thought, no point going to office in this state. Work bored him anyway. It was all so predictable. Besides, Mrs Kulkarni knew what needed to be done in his absence. He felt relieved that he had in Mrs Kulkarni an able deputy who wouldn't curry favour with the proprietor and bide her time to oust him from his chair. He was so lucky to have her by his side. Lucky Roy, he had smiled to himself.

When he reached home, he had switched on the TV and listened to familiar faces talking past each other about the vexed India–Pakistan relations. Indian TV was made up of fifty faces, he thought. They kept shouting among themselves, and that audible excitement passed for meaningful debate in the electronic media. Indo–Pak relations! So long as Kashmir was at the centre of it, there wouldn't be a relationship, he knew. The thing to do was to send nuclear missiles to Pakistan from end to end and wipe the wayward tribe out. After that, we can talk, Roy had grimaced, of India–Pakistan relations.

In fact, that could be his next column, he had thought. Maybe he would write it just then. He certainly felt like writing. The Muse was close to his ears, whispering. He was a good writer. Mrs Kulkarni, of course, liked his writing and she was a demanding reader. You must write more, a book maybe, she would tell him. Sooner or later, he would, of course. Right then, he had decided that he could write his column, no problem. The vodkas were inspirational.

Roy had risen from the sofa. Words rushed at him from all sides like a litter of hyperactive pups. He wanted to tell the wide world, especially the garrulous group on TV, that he was around, that he had a few definitive things to say. He could out-argue every single one of them hogging the limelight on the screen. He had felt ready to go on air. It was time he presented his insights before the camera. *His* take on the world.

But for the moment, he had to be satisfied with the printed word. He regretted that he could not be present simultaneously at both a TV studio and his office. A crass human limitation, he thought. He had looked around for his laptop. He couldn't see it. Nothing was ever at hand. That was the story of his life. He got up. The room, with all its objects, swayed before him as if suspended by a rope in a windy place. It was too much. Then he had decided that it would be better to put off the writing till evening. He had sat down heavily, leaned into a corner of the sofa, and passed out.

In the evening, when he awoke, he had more drinks. There had been no choice. He had then watched *Miami Vice* for a couple of hours on the DVD player. The Americans made superior serials to the British, he thought. All their successful serials were formulaic, but they delivered. They knew their stuff. They were thorough with the structure of their work. When to tweak your heart, when to tease your brains, when to pump up the adrenaline levels in your blood. It was precise as mathematics. They knew what it took. It was their universities and the education, of course. They had the best institutions anywhere. Maybe, he thought, he would send his daughter to the US for her master's.

Maybe. He didn't know what she wanted. The thought of his daughter and her sullen silence had made him want to drink more. He wished they were friends. He filled his glass again. And again. He couldn't remember when he stopped or how he reached the bedroom, which seemed a long way off. But he had made it. He was going to sleep in his own bed. That much he was sure of. It was a question of character. He had fallen on his bed, the shoes still on his feet, the denture still in his mouth, and the spectacles still on his face, but at an angle across his forehead.

In the morning, Mr Nanda's call had blared next to his head like a siren before a blitzkrieg, and a minute later, his day lay before him in smoking ruins.

'Roy? Are you there?' Mr Nanda asked. There was a snap in his voice.

Roy stammered. He sweated. He hadn't read the edition. He stuttered apologies. Fear cut through his brain like a scalpel: would he lose his job? Mr Nanda had never spoken to him in this fashion. If he lost his job, it would mean Mrs Kulkarni's job was at risk too. Roy had to get someone to take the rap. Exemplary punishment had to be seen to be meted out. Arun, he thought, Arun was to blame.

'Mr Nanda, I had given specific instructions not to carry the piece. Let me find out who is responsible. I'll get to the bottom of this and call you back by evening.'

'I'll be waiting,' Mr Nanda had said, and disconnected.

Roy called up Mrs Kulkarni, who was immediately receptive to the urgency of the situation. They were on the same page. 'Sack him,' Mrs Kulkarni said. 'He is the news editor. He is responsible. In any case, we need to replace him with someone younger who can see, you know what I mean? Arun is blind as a bat.'

'I have got to be hard on this guy to save the institution,' Roy had said.

'No question,' Mrs Kulkarni had replied, 'the institution is bigger than the individual.'

Roy then had had a couple of drinks to set himself up for the day. Then he telephoned Arun. 'I want you to come to office by ten,' he said in a voice that underlined his rank and insinuated Arun's incompetence.

When Arun reached office, Roy was waiting.

'You need to give me an explanation,' Roy says. The paper lies between them like a crime.

'You said we should carry,' Arun says in surprise, 'whatever Placid wrote. Boss, you said it in front of everybody just a few weeks ago.'

'That was ages ago, for god's sake. In any case, this piece is sedition. Arun, you are senior enough to know what is publishable and what is not.'

'What sedition? Placid is not arguing that Salim be allowed

to walk free. He is saying, commute his death sentence because killing him doesn't achieve anything. He is saying, put Salim behind bars for life. That is a perfectly valid line to take for a columnist.'

'Not in my paper,' Roy says. It then dawns on him that *Bombay Express* belongs a little more to Mr Nanda than to him. In fact, a lot more, if Mr Nanda's tone this morning was any indication. He is just another employee. But he can't afford to show Arun his sudden estrangement with the product since the call from Mr Nanda. That would amount to undermining his authority.

'Besides, it was marked to you. You could have told me not to carry it if you didn't like it.'

'You marked the copy to me?' Oh, hell, this was a new one, Roy thinks. How am I going to get out of this now?

'You can check your email.'

'I don't believe you sent it to me.' What he would do is delete the mail from his inbox, Roy thinks. That is what he would do as soon as Arun got out of his cabin. Delete the mail from his inbox and trash bin. 'Did you mark it to Mrs Kulkarni?'

'No.'

'There,' Roy says, as if he has proved something. 'Look, I don't want to have a long conversation over this. I want you to take responsibility for this act of negligence and put in your papers. This may be a market-driven paper, but not one that is treasonous.' He pauses. 'Besides, I love my country.' He hopes his voice modulation makes it clear that Arun is not a patriot, certainly not in Roy's league.

'You want me to quit over *this*?' Sedition. Treason. Crime. Arun can't believe his ears. This is what they call a set-up, he thinks. What am I going to do? There isn't anything in his bank account, what with so many outgoings. It takes a lot to keep two families going. Everybody he knows has one set of expenses; he has two. Oh, to hell with it, Arun thinks, something will work out. Someone will eventually give me a job. I may have to take a salary cut, but I will get by.

'You are out of your mind, Roy,' Arun finds himself saying. 'That copy was marked to you and you know it. You are dragging me to the chopping block because, for all I know, Nanda must have called you and you need a fall guy.'

Roy tries to say something, words that would be cutting and grave and fully reflecting his onerous position as the editor of a leading paper, but he can only open and shut his mouth several times. He tries to prise a cigarette from the pack. It turns out to be a difficult operation as his fingers shake too much. He places the pack of Wills on the table and leans back in his chair. He eyes it hungrily. He grips the arms of his chair for support. He should have asked Mrs Kulkarni to be present at the meeting. Her aggression would have been handy. He spits his denture into his hand and says something cutting. But it isn't clear. He puts the denture back in his mouth where it clicks obediently into position. 'Dereliction of duty,' he says. 'You are fired.'

'No, I am quitting,' Arun says. 'And I will serve the three-month notice period.' He gets up, and adds: 'Asshole.'

Arun goes to his cubicle, past Mrs Kulkarni's desk, as she makes a show of subbing a particularly tough copy. She must have listened to every word, Arun guesses. He feels like giving a hard tap on the back of her head, but refrains. You tap a woman on her head, and she could turn right round and say you are molesting her. He knows women.

Arun surveys his desk. It is a mess, not unlike his life, he thinks, littered with papers and clippings and issues of magazines he had thought he would refer to later. But, of course, the later never came to pass. Let it be, he thinks.

Arun opens his drawers: more old papers, clippings, bills, and travel vouchers which he never filled in. Trash. There is nothing of him here after all these years, nothing to take home. He stares at the notice he had stuck on the wall a decade ago, in 72 point size, in black, YOU WILL NOT FIND IT, and feels vindicated in a perverse way. He hadn't found it, whatever it was that he had been looking for all these years.

He collects his tube of GenTeal gel lying next to the computer and puts it in his pocket. He realizes with a little sadness that there is no one he wants to say goodbye to, except John, whom he figures they would ease out soon enough. He would talk to him later. So much, he thinks, for making the most of my workplace.

He goes down the staircase, out onto the tree-lined footpath and watches a red double-decker block his view and, a moment later, speed past him. He stares after the bus, struck. It has been so long since he travelled on a double-decker. He might do it today. He has time. Overhead, the branches and leaves shift in the breeze and when he looks up, the sun falls on his face, hard as a slap.

FOUR

My Brother the Terrorist

Nirmal meets Salim the day before he is to hang.

Salim's cell is lit by a single rectangular window high in the wall. He spends hours looking out through it. There is nothing quite as free as the sky, he feels.

Through the window, he can see the odd plane high in the air, like a floating cross. And if he stares hard enough, he can see Ammi in the rocking chair in their house; the green expanse of the mango orchards and the parrots flitting through, sharp as flung knives, from tree to tree, singing. 'That's really a cinema up there,' Salim says to Nirmal, pointing to the window.

'I guess,' Nirmal says. He sits next to Salim on the cot, which is just a raised platform in cement. 'This is for you,' he says, handing him his harmonica. Placid had to call up a few people before they let Nirmal bring it in.

'Oh. It's beautiful, thank you. But I don't know how to play it.'

'Just keep it with you.'

'I can't take it anywhere, Nirmal. You keep it for me.'

'It's yours.'

'All right, then.' Salim holds the harmonica tight in his hand.

Salim's face, now shaven, looks much thinner. His nose seems large in proportion to his emaciated features. He wears a white skull cap over his shaven head. He looks different, different from Nirmal as well. No one is likely to say they are twins any more. Nirmal steals a glance at him, guilty of being free and of surviving him. Guilty of life. He can understand what Lakshmi must be going through.

Salim gets up from where he was sitting and the chains around his feet slither after him like a pet snake. 'They were having problems getting an executioner.'

'I read about it. I wish they had never found one.'

'Oh, obviously, they did. One old Kallu Singh from Meerut. He had retired from the profession a decade or so ago. Said he didn't want to kill any more. Went back to his house in the village, where he had some land. They brought him in from the cold. Must have told him he was doing a service to the country, and promised him some money. Apparently, he is one of the best.'

'What does that mean?'

'Well, he slips the rope around your neck snug like silk. And he is very good at calculating the slack of the rope and the distance of the fall. You get that wrong and the head comes off. Death at his hands is supposed to be nearly painless.'

'An artiste,' Nirmal says.

'Very few Indians specializing in the great rope trick now.'

'The death of a tradition.'

They laugh and then fall silent.

'What's happening to your movie career?'

'They are releasing *Wind Surfer* next month. I should get some offers after that.' The truth is that he is not up to pursuing his career, with Salim in the shadow of the noose.

'I thought I was not afraid of death. That's not true. I am,' Salim says.

'Everybody is afraid of death.'

'I wasn't always like this.' Salim recalls the day he had landed in Bombay, anxious to kill and die, so he would be with Allah by nightfall. 'Nirmal,' he says, 'you believe in God?'

'I don't know. I hope he is around, though I see little evidence of it.' Nirmal thinks about the streets he has lived off.

'I almost saw Him once.'

'Almost?'

'At Breeze, the day I got off the boat.' Salim looks at his hands. I miss my gun, he thinks with a sense of shock. 'Ajmal was going off in all directions. Everything was exploding, catching fire, falling apart. I think I had begun shooting too. I felt protected, I was aware of a massive white presence, swaddled and turbaned, standing close to me. It was Allah, of course.'

'Really?'

'I wasn't afraid to die then.'

'You still have your God. And, in addition, you have a whole family.'

'I don't know about that. Not sure of that at all.'

'But you *do*. You have a mother, father, brother. In fact, you have two mothers.'

'One would have been enough.'

'You mean Ammi?'

'I am not meant for complications, Nirmal.'

'Lakshmi doesn't mind that you prefer Ammi to her,' Nirmal lies.

'I am sure she does. But I can't help it. I can't switch my affections because of an accidental discovery.'

'She is all right with it.'

'But I know that I have changed too.' Salim stares at the rough concrete floor between his feet. 'This trial has taken a lot out of me. I am no longer a jihadi. Just a criminal. I am not even a Muslim.'

'But you were once, and that's what brought you here. If you were not a jihadi, none of us would have met. I wouldn't have run into you for sure.'

'But was it worth it? I don't know if I care for anyone in the family except for you. I am awfully glad I found you.'

Nirmal doesn't say anything for a while. Was it worth it? Whatever Nirmal says would tend to be a wish that can't be fulfilled or regret over a word that shouldn't have been uttered or a deed that shouldn't have happened. Either would be unkind to Salim. 'But we did meet. We now know.'

'Yes, yes, of course. Allah is great.'

'I asked the superintendent if I could stay here for the night.'

'And?' Salim says. 'And?'

'He took his time, but finally refused.'

'Ah, of course. I don't think you are in touch with Ammi, are you?'

'Not really, but I know that she wanted to come here for a visit. The Pakistan government wouldn't let her travel.'

'How stupid.' Stupid and sad, Salim thinks.

'Yes.'

'Something strange happened yesterday.'

Nirmal looks at him.

'You see the grille of that window?'

'Yes?'

'A length of twine blew in and got hooked around it, and a pigeon kept pecking at it for hours. It would peck and try to take it away and the wind would blow it right back. People think pigeons are dumb. They are just obsessed. After a while, I lost interest. How long can you watch a pigeon play with a piece of thread? A little later, I heard a wild fluttering of wings. I looked up and saw the bird hanging from the thread, thrashing about. I watched it choke and die, its small, pink legs outstretched like hands.'

'That's awful. To have wings and die like that.'

'Nirmal, I am scared.'

Nirmal takes Salim's hands in his. They are warm. 'You want me to pull and crack your fingers?'

'Sure, go ahead.' Salim smiles.

Nirmal cracks all his fingers except the thumbs, which he finds resistant.

'I feel better,' Salim says.

Nirmal thinks about the pigeon hanging by the thread from the window.

'It was an accident,' Salim says, looking up at the window across which dark clouds slowly sail.

'The rains are early this year,' Nirmal says. He doesn't want to think about the pigeon.

'My last monsoon,' Salim says.

Nirmal realizes, not for the first time, how difficult it is to talk to a dead man. The space between them widens with each breath they take. 'Some day we will all be dead,' he says, not quite liking his own words.

'But not tomorrow, or the day after. I only regret the faith I lost.'

'You are still a devout Muslim. You haven't lost that, surely?'

'I am still a Muslim, but not as sure as I used to be. And if you are only half sure, what kind of Muslim are you?'

'Does it matter any more, Salim?'

'It hurts that it may not matter. I can't ignore the fact that I was born a Hindu. In the end, what have I got?'

Nothing, really. Nirmal can tell him that he got to find his real mother, a man who might be his father, a brother. Put together, all of it might have even amounted to something—if Salim's clock was not running out. Most things make little sense in the dark, pervasive presence of death. Meanings get depleted in the absence of a future. 'Is there peace in little things?' Nirmal asks.

'Little things. What little things?'

Nirmal doesn't know. He could say breeze playing with water. But Salim is in a solitary cell.

'Do you mean the Koran?'

'Yes, that's what I meant,' Nirmal says.

'I pray all the time. I pray for you and Ammi as well.'

Nirmal turns his face away from Salim. A burst of blind rage riots through him. He takes a deep breath. There is nothing he can do.

'I should have got killed that day. Fought the cops and got killed. The bastards killed my spirit, Nirmal. Took my God out of me.' Salim's voice breaks. 'They turned me into a mass murderer; into nothing.'

'They were doing their job. But it makes no difference to me that you killed, Salim. You are my brother. I am a new man because of you. You have given me a lot.'

Nirmal puts his arm around his brother. Salim leans his head like a sick man on Nirmal's shoulder and cries without making a sound. Nirmal knows that kind of crying. It is the crying you do with your whole face, not just your eyes, the whole of your face crumbling in the grief that can't be put into words.

After a while, Salim calms down, lies on the cot and sleeps for a few minutes. When he wakes up, he says, 'Tomorrow morning five is the hanging.' He makes it sound as if it is someone else they will be coming for.

'I'll be right outside the walls,' Nirmal says.

'You'll be my last thought. You and Ammi.'

'You will be in our thoughts, too.'

'Tell Amma, I am sorry.'

This is the first time Salim has referred to Lakshmi as Amma. 'Don't worry about that. She understands.'

'I always thought of her as Lakshmi,' Salim says.

'You've known her only for a year or so.'

'I know. It's my limitation really, not her fault.'

'I'll tell her.'

'And tell Placid, I have no intention of being his son.' Salim smiles. 'You think he is really our father?'

Salim looks good when he smiles, Nirmal thinks. 'Amma wouldn't allow him to take a DNA test.'

'She must be scared. If the test is negative, she will be proved wrong.'

'Besides, they are very fond of each other and a negative test might take Amma on a tangent all over again.'

'I don't think Placid is our father. I am pretty sure about that.'

'I don't know if I care, really,' Nirmal says. And he doesn't. He has a mother now for sure and a man who doesn't mind playing the role of dad. He is happy to accept these gifts at their face value. For a guy like me, he thinks, everything is a bonus, except tomorrow's hanging.

'Live happily, Nirmal,' Salim says.

'I would be much happier if you were there.'

'Allah wills not,' Salim says.

'What are you going to do now? The rest of the evening?'

'Pray, I guess.'

'I want to tell you, you will not be alone when you go. I will be here with you the whole night. In the morning, when they come for you, I'll be holding your hand and walking with you all the way. You understand? You are not alone.' But Nirmal knows that men who are about to die are alone. You cannot share death.

'You shouldn't worry about me. Once I start praying, I'll be quite all right.'

The superintendent comes in, runs his baton along the bars.

'Time up,' he says.

Nirmal gets up. Salim holds his hand. Nirmal sits down again. 'I've got to go,' he says, hugging Salim.

'Take care. Grow up to become a big star,' Salim says.

'Yes.'

'Will you be outside the walls?'

'Yes.'

'It might rain, though.'

'Keep praying and go in peace. Hold on to my hand even when I am not there.'

'So long, Nirmal. Khuda hafiz.'

'Khuda hafiz.'

Nirmal walks the long, empty corridor leading from Salim's cell to the main door. The superintendent opens the door. Nirmal turns around. Salim raises his hand slowly, as if a weight is attached to it. Nirmal waves to him once, and then steps out of his sight for the last time.

EPILOGUE

Surviving Salim

It rained through the night. Nirmal tried to take shelter under a tree and was offended by his own pettiness. He quit hiding from the rain. At first, the rain was slight. By about midnight, it was pouring.

The media had turned out in strength. Nirmal kept away from them. They knew him by sight. The rain helped too; it held them back from wreaking total havoc. As soon as Nirmal saw the first TV van rolling in, he moved away from the main gate to a far corner, away from the crowd and the lights. He sat on a stone next to the wall and waited.

Around two in the night, the man who ran a mobile tea stall across the road came up and asked, 'Tea?' He was a dark, stocky man, with large white teeth and an oily face.

'Yes,' Nirmal said.

'Tea or coffee?'

'Tea.'

The man poured tea into a steel glass from a steaming kettle whose handle had a padded grip. 'Who is it?' he asked, handing Nirmal the tea, his head to his side so that the umbrella was wedged between his shoulder and cheek, leaving his hands free.

'My brother,' Nirmal said.

'The terrorist?'

Nirmal sipped the tea, a hand on top of the glass, so the rain did not drop into it.

'When is the hanging?'

'Five in the morning.'

'They like to do it early.'

'It hurts a lot?'

'Takes just a second if the knot is right,' he said as if out of experience. 'Kallu Singh is good. Was your brother a terrorist? I mean, he still believes in it?'

'I don't know.'

'That's the tough part. We never get to know till the very last.'

'Sometimes, not even then. Is your shop open the whole night?'

'Till morning. Got to make a living.'

When the man left, Nirmal went back to sitting on the stone, his back to the wall. Later still, a constable came along and asked him to go away.

'It's my brother Salim,' Nirmal said. 'He's going to hang in the morning and I'd like to be close to him.'

The cop held a torch to his face, stared at him for a long moment. Finally, he shook his head. 'Don't try anything funny.'

'No,' Nirmal said.

At five to five, Nirmal got up and prayed for Salim. 'Please, let him go easy,' he said, not sure of the name of the God he was appealing to.

When it was time, Nirmal looked up at the dark wall. It seemed to have grown in height. He leaned his forehead on the stones, soft with moss, till he thought it was over.

He made his way to the tea stall. It was lucent like a painting, with the greenish-white light from the petromax.

'You are wet. Tea or coffee?' the man asked.

'Tea.'

Nirmal sipped the tea, thinking of the corridor down which Salim had to journey—its bare cement floor worn smooth by the footfalls of people walking to their death—before he reached the rope. The slowest and longest walk in the world, he thought. Nirmal tried paying for the tea, but the man wouldn't have it. 'It's over. Go home and sleep. You got people at home?'

'Yes,' Nirmal said. 'Can I get a taxi somewhere near?'

'Straight down and first turn right.'

Nirmal walked to the corner and found a taxi parked: an old-black-and-yellow Fiat, with its glasses up.

Nirmal peered in through the glass that was running with water. The driver was sleeping inside, with his legs over the back of the seat. On the dashboard was a black-and-white framed picture of Jesus on whom flakes of blood fell from a tiny red bulb. Nirmal knocked on the windshield. The driver stirred himself awake. 'Where to?' he said, opening the door at the back.

'Andheri,' Nirmal said, getting in.

'You are soaking wet,' the driver said.

'Yes.'

'I've got a towel here, if you want to dry your hair. It's quite clean.'

The black sky was fracturing in the east, exposing a thin bone of light. But the rain hadn't eased. How frail Salim had become, Nirmal thought.

'No, I am all right, thank you.'

'I always keep a towel handy during the monsoon.'

What's with the rain? Nirmal thought. He leaned back in the seat. He was going to work hard the rest of the year. Maybe he would join an acting course. The clothes clung to his body. He sat up again. He was cold.

'Here, take the towel, you are making my car all wet.' The driver smiled, reaching for a plastic bag in the dashboard and handing the towel to Nirmal. 'You will feel better.'

It was a white towel with a green border, and it smelled of engine oil and carbolic soap. Nirmal held it in his hands like a curtain, looking out at the rain which fell thick and heavy across the early, blue morning, fencing it in. Anytime now, Nirmal expected a girl to materialize by the side of the car and knock on the window, saying, 'You want a child? A baby? I've got two here.'

Nirmal folded the towel carefully and kept it to one side. He didn't want to dry his hair. The taxi had stopped at a signal. When the lights changed, he pressed his knuckles hard against his eyes.

But the tears kept coming.

Acknowledgements

Lost and Found has had many drafts. Almost as many as the friends who read them. I believe the novel greatly benefited for their comments and criticism. Suhit Kelkar. Madhavankutti Pillai. B. Ramachandran. Mita Kapur. V.K. Karthika. And my late father, Pavanan, a writer himself, who helped me in spirit, especially in the months when I was out of a job, when I still managed to finish a substantial portion of the book despite the worries. His calm was mine for an exacting while. My warm thanks to all of them, and fond remembrance of their support and friendship.